THE DEMON, THE HERO, AND THE CITY OF SEVEN

A. E. KINCAID

THIRD AND DRAGON, LLC

First printing, 2021

Print ISBN: 979-8-9851622-1-9

Ebook ISBN: 979-8-9851622-0-2

Cover Design by Sara Oliver

*To my family who
believed in the dream and
helped make it happen.*

CHAPTER 1
THE DEMON AND THE HERO

In my 550 years of existence, I'm not sure I've ever met anyone who exasperates me more than Sir Reginald P. Asstradle, the ersatz Hero of Widdershins. When he speaks, I imagine drop-kicking him off a cliff. When he snores, I fantasize tossing him into a fiery volcano.

Don't get me wrong—he's a good lad. For a human, anyway. But when you are magically entangled with another being in such a way that putting just ten yards' distance between the two of you triggers the spell to physically smash you back together? That can wear on anyone's nerves. Like my nerves, for example. Right now.

Zing!

"Ow!"

"Oof!"

We crashed together, then toppled onto the dirt path— Reginald on his knees and me on my ass. I gazed up through the arch of tree branches above us, willing patience into my bones. It didn't work.

"Dammit, Reg! Stop falling behind!"

Reginald struggled to his feet, wiping dust from his knees.

"Can't you just magic us there, Mal?"

"There," in this case, was not our ultimate destination where we hoped to find and ask a wizard to disentangle us. "There" was a tavern. For lunch.

"I cannot," I said. "That's really not how demon magic works. And even if I could, I would 'magic' us straight to a wizard. Not to some beer hall for their world-famous goose droppings—"

"Duck wings."

"Whatever. We don't have that kind of time." I pulled the collar of my ebony morning coat up around my neck. There was a chill in the air that foretold the coming of winter. Not surprising as it was only a week away. It was the absolute worst possible fucking time to be traveling—especially as we were trying to make good time. Well, *I* was trying to make good time. And we'd already wasted two full days just learning how to coexist in close, spell-induced proximity. We were both bruised, battered, and bothered by our lack of privacy.

Reginald shrugged.

"I don't know. It seems to me we have plenty of time. The dryad queen said that when we broke the stone, we got magically attached for eternity. Eternity is a long time, Mal."

I clenched my fists and resisted the urge to scream.

"It *is* a long time, Reg. That's exactly the problem. I don't want to be attached to you for eternity. And you shouldn't want to be attached to me that long either. I barely kept from drowning you when you threw up in the swamp on the way to the dryads. I would like to get to Seven as quickly as possible, get the wizards to unbind us, and go home. *Alone.*"

"To . . . what was it? 'The Underworld Suburb of Atlas-on-Leaf'?"

"*Artif*ice-on-*Lethe.*"

"Oh yeah. Right."

"So let's just get the damn food and get on our way."

Reginald sighed.

"You know, Mal—they say life's a journey, not a—"

"Reginald," I cut across him. "If you're about to say, 'Life's a journey, not a destination,' then *this* journey is going to continue with a sock stuffed in your mouth." Reginald grumbled something under his breath, but the only word I caught was *mean*. I ignored him. "So how far is this place, anyway? We've made almost no progress for two days and today we've been walking for hours out of our way."

"Not far now," he said. "Probably about three or four stone's throws?"

I placed a hand on his arm to hold him up. His previously white, muslin shirt had gone grayish-brown since our first meeting. I gingerly removed my hand and asked, "The King's stone's throw? Or the Giant's stone's throw?"

"Actually," he said, "I'm talking about the Beadledonian stone's throw, which is 1.8 King's stone's throws."

"Ah," I said and let go. I let him walk ahead of me for a while, both because he knew where we were going and also because I didn't want him to see the confusion in my goldenrod eyes as I tried to do maths.

We were in a small wood; tall oaks and maple trees lined our path. It was a sunny day, and the shadows of the branches traced whirling patterns on the ground as we walked along. My mind wandered as we went—back through the journey so far. Hearing the Summoning Bell in the Underworld, rising through the firmament to meet my hero. The crushing disappointment when I discovered mine was a lanky, red-headed man-child named Reginald. Then learning that the whole thing had been a mistake.

You see, long ago in the "Glorious Land of Widdershins," as its citizens like to call their "humble" home (A rather narcissistic title if you ask me, but who am I to judge), there lived gallant heroes who did great deeds and carried cumbersome swords. The more popular the heroes became, the more popular heroing became as well. To disrupt an oversaturated market, one hero by the name of Quill Valor summoned a demon to help ensure that his quests would go to plan. This set a new standard for the heroes, and demon summoning became a popular fix for tricky missions. The problem with making a deal with a demon, however, is that if you succeed in your good deed—the demon gets to do something evil at equal or lesser impact as payment.

The actual *people* of Widdershins resented being cast into eternal darkness and having their rivers run dry all for the glory of a handful of celebrity thrill seekers. So they put together a committee and drafted some Hero paperwork. Turns out it was enough bureaucratic nonsense to put off all but the most studious, subservient, painstakingly virtuous Hero applicants. *Diabolical.* I was a young demon trying to prove myself and live up to my familial expectations. I snuck in to Beadledom City Hall just before they officially signed this document into existence and added a loophole to keep demons in the game. It said that if the box on the bottom of page ninety-four remained unchecked, then a demon would automatically be summoned to aid the hero. But the committee just reminded people to check it, and for five hundred years, no one's paperwork got approved without that checked box.

Until Reginald.

Boots scuffed on fallen leaves, and the sound of a lively crowd broke me from my reverie.

"Here we are!" exclaimed Reginald proudly as he thrust his arms out toward the tavern. "The Cock o' the North!"

From the outside, it was a modest, log-constructed building whose yellow-oak wood had darkened with age. Flying high above on a flagpole where I'd expected a weather vane to be flew the flag of Widdershins—the outline of the continent with a slightly askew white triangle within, all set on an azure field.

"We're not in the north, though, are we? We're . . ." I cast my gaze skyward and shaded my eyes from a shaft of sunlight, "west."

"Oh," said Reginald, squinting in the direction I was looking. "I'd never thought about that before." He shrugged. "Still, the wings are amazing."

"So you've said. But that will not help me much unless—"

"I know, I know. Unless they prepared the food in anger or sorrow."

"Exactly."

"Well, we won't know until we go in, will we?" asked Reginald, inching toward the entrance. I sighed and let my shoulders slump.

"I guess we won't. Let's go, then."

I extended my arm toward the door and let him lead me inside the Cock o' the North.

———

WE PUSHED through the swinging half door into the tavern. It was larger on the inside than it appeared from outside. Thick wooden rafters striped the towering ceiling, and long tables bookended on either side by benches sat in orderly rows across the floor. A polished oak bar lined the back of the building, where two barmen and three barmaids were pouring ale at a pace that suggested it was on the house. Unlike most taverns, which smelled like piss, old beer, and body odor, this one smelled . . . well, better than that. I detected hops and roasting meat and well-oiled wood amid the expected but fainter smell of animal excrement creeping in through the mostly open doorway.

The tables were filled with patrons. Many were digging their fists into woven baskets lined with waxed cloth. These were clearly full of the duck wings Reginald had alluded to: the faces and fingers of these individuals were smeared with a honey-brown sauce, and the piles of bones discarded on their plates were a dead giveaway. Others were sloshing their beers and singing bawdy songs in a variety of keys and volumes. The resulting cacophony was ear-splitting, and I nearly turned to leave when I caught sight of a diminutive older woman standing atop of one of the long tables. She appeared to be the one leading the sing-along as she danced up and down her makeshift stage, beer in hand.

The girl was quiet as a sheep
And here he laid, so fast asleep
Now what did he get for all he'd dooooone?
She'd taken his pants
And gone off at a run!

The woman had her broad, slightly hunched back to us until the last line, when she turned and scampered down the table. Leaping high, she tossed her drink up in the air, landed deftly on her feet, then caught her glass just before the beer splashed back into it. Applause and laughter exploded around the room—but it wasn't loud enough to drown out Reginald's strangled cry.

"Gran?!"

The conversation and merriment continued as before, but Gran's head spun toward us. She cocked an eyebrow and shuffled over.

"Well, if it isn't Sir Morals and Lord Turpitude. You two are still together? I *told* you this wouldn't go your way, demon." Then she looked at Reginald's scandalized face and sighed. "Come on over and tell your gran all about it." She led us away from the main part of the tavern to a quieter corner opposite the bar. I slipped the bag off my shoulder and placed it on the ground as she signaled something complicated to the bartender. Within moments, we each had a steaming mug of tea laced with brandy placed in front of us.

"Here, demon," she said, reaching into her pocket. She

pulled out a handful of small packets no longer than my littlest finger.

"How do you have those?" I asked, selecting one, opening it, then pouring it into the tea. The liquid fizzed and hissed for a handful of seconds. Then it let out a brief shriek before quieting back down. I took a sip. It was perfect.

"What are those? And what were you just doing up there?" Reginald's pained expression was a pathetic mix of horror and confusion as he thrust his hand out toward the table where his grandmother had been performing her acrobatics.

"These," she said, picking up and gently shaking the packets, "are a solute called 'demon dust' that makes any food or drink palatable to demons. They also have a hallucinogenic effect on humans. More specifically, they are made from the salt tears of jilted lovers. That," she said, gesturing behind her toward the table, "was just a bit of fun."

"But . . . but Gran! You're, like . . . a hundred! What about propriety?"

"Psh," said Gran. "I'm not a hundred, boy, but I am old enough to know that propriety's not all it's cracked up to be." Reginald blinked at her and didn't respond, so she turned to me. "Now—out with it, demon. When you left me four days ago, you'd tricked Reginald into a blood oath so he'd let you help him return the Stone of Eno to the dryads. But here you are now. What happened?"

"First of all—I didn't trick him. He summoned me, remember?"

"By accident!" she shouted.

"And yet I was still summoned. The blood oath was the only option to get us through the quest, extract my payment, and return to the Underworld."

"So you say," said Reginald's gran. "But it clearly didn't go to plan—so what's the story?"

I tried to think of a way to tell the tale that made it seem as if our failure was entirely Reginald's fault. "We ran into an old friend of mine while we passed by the Marais, and he invited us to visit. So that was the first detour."

Reginald took this moment to break out of his trance.

"His 'friend' is an ogre named Ob. Ob used to be his lover, but Mal broke up with him, and now Ob says we can never return to his swamp."

Reginald's gran raised both eyebrows at me.

"The situation is a bit more nuanced than Reginald is letting on, but in essence, yes. That happened."

"I see," she said. "And what happened next?"

Keen to take up the next part of the story, Reginald barreled in.

"Next, I told him I wouldn't return the stone and complete the quest. A demon's payment for helping us do good is to do some evil in return, yeah? And the Stone of Eno is a bigger deal than I realized when we started out. So I stood my ground and refused."

Reginald's gran looked surprised and pleased as she sipped her tea, and Reginald's cheeks flushed pink. She crossed her arms over her chest and looked back and forth between us.

"Well, you're still together and you've still got that sack, so something must have gone wrong. Spit it out."

"After Reginald's noble but misguided stand," I continued, "I followed him—"

"Chased me—"

"Yes, fine! Whatever! I chased you into the Forest of Arden. Where Reginald tripped and fell. Then we wrestled for the bag and smashed the Stone of Eno on the ground."

Reginald's gran ran a hand over her face as Reginald continued our tale.

"We tried to fix it. But it was oozing all this magical dust and goo. We couldn't get it back together. And that's when the dryads showed up."

"Yes," I said. "It perturbed them that the stone was stolen from them, then lost, then returned broken. Which doesn't seem fair at all since the first two items on that list of grievances had nothing to do with us!"

"But when the dryad queen discovered that we'd broken the stone and seen the magic and put our hands to it—she thought that was pretty funny."

"Well, she was laughing, Reg, but it was at our misfortune." I turned to Reginald's gran. "Apparently the magic flowed out of the Stone of Eno—a connection stone, as you know—and bonded with the next strongest connection in the vicinity."

"Let me guess," she said. "A blood bond between a human and a demon."

I winced.

"Yes. That."

"So they chased us out of the forest and told us not to come back until we figured out how to fix the stone, and now we're stuck together for eternity," finished Reginald. "Can we order some wings? I'm starving."

Reginald's gran reached across the table and clunked our heads together.

"You idiots!"

"Ow!" I yelped and massaged my skull. "For your information, we only *might* be stuck together for eternity. We're traveling to the City of Seven. We're going to request the help of the wizards to magically unstick us."

Reginald's gran smirked.

"Asking the wizards for help? Good luck with that."

"Why?" I asked.

"Have you ever heard the term 'a quarrel of wizards'?"

"No."

She patted me on the hand.

"You'll understand when you get there."

Seconds after she made another complicated gesture with

her hand, I watched as a barmaid stopped pouring ale and made her way over to us with a basket of wings.

"You come here a lot, it seems."

Gran lifted one shoulder.

"You could say that."

I waited for a more lengthy explanation, but she selected a wing from the basket and started eating.

"Aren't you going to have some?" asked Reginald, his mouth stuffed with duck.

I sighed and reached for another packet. How long would it be until we ate a proper meal again? I chose a wing, sprinkled it with demon dust, and got to eating.

THE BASKET empty and my stomach satisfactorily sated, I pushed away from the table.

"Well, that was a pleasant interlude, Reginald's gran, but we really must be on our way."

"Hold up!" she cried. "What do you mean 'on our way'? What's your route? Do you have a map? Do you have food, supplies? . . . *money*? Do you know how long it takes to get to Seven? If everything goes perfectly and according to plan— which, with you at the helm, I doubt—it will take three weeks. You'll be lucky to get there in time for Yulesticetide!"

These were all completely reasonable questions, which irked me.

"I love Yulesticetide!" said Reginald. "Do they have it in the Underworld?"

"No," I said.

"Oh, it's neat. It celebrates this old forest king. Every year he drives away the witch who makes winter by giving gifts to good children and boiling the bad ones in oil. We celebrate it with lights and food and music. It's my favorite. But I stay away from the fried foods. You know. Just in case."

Reginald's gran cocked an eyebrow at him.

"Did I tell you that? I may have exaggerated what they do to bad children."

"Anyway," I interjected. "It won't take that long. We'll be there in seven days, tops. From here we'll head to the Empty Plains, across the Giant's Fingers, and then into Seven."

Reginald's gran narrowed her eyes at me.

"That . . . is the stupidest idea I've ever heard, demon. The Empty Plains are a desolate wasteland offering no shelter and no food—and more than likely there will be a Centennial Storm at this time of year. And the Giant's Fingers—well, you know what dwells in the Giant's Fingers."

"Spiders?" piped up Reginald.

"She means giants, Reg. But she also means *dwelt*. Past tense. There aren't any giants. None living, anyway."

She scowled at me.

"Says you."

"Yes. Says me. Who is 550 years old. In this, at least, I think we can agree I am correct."

"We shall see," she said. "But whichever way you go—you need supplies. So come along." She stood up and led us to a table full of cheerful, brawny men in too-tight shirts enjoying a post work pint.

"Stuff. On the table. All of you," she commanded, snapping her fingers and pointing at the tabletop. The entire table fell silent, and immediately the men started emptying their pockets and tossing their rucksacks onto the wooden surface. Reginald's gran circled the table, picking up and inspecting the occasional item. She grabbed a faded green oil-cloth bag and a worn leather satchel and started filling them with canteens, tart apples, knives, rope, and assorted other necessities from the pile before her. When she was satisfied, she motioned for the fellows to resume their activities, which they did without question. The entire scene was masterfully dictatorial, and if I wasn't careful, I was going to develop a crush on Reginald's gran.

"You're stealing their stuff?" The words sounded wrenched from Reginald's throat. "Who even are you? I'm a Hero of Widdershins, Gran—what will people think?"

"Don't worry about them. It's my job to take care of you."

She held the sacks out to us. I took the one closest to me—the leather satchel—and added the bag with the broken pieces of the Stone of Eno to it.

"I slipped some extra dust in there for you, demon."

"Thank you, Reginald's gran." I dipped my head in her direction. She snorted, then turned toward Reg.

"Now, Reg. You're in a pretty pickle here, being attached to a no-good, egoistic megalomaniac—"

"You're saying that like it's a bad thing," I interrupted. Reginald's gran growled in my direction.

"An-y-way—I know that you're magically attached to him and he's going to try to make you do things his way. But he's attached to you, too. Don't forget that. You're a bit of a pushover most of the time, but you're a good lad with strong morals, and I believe in you." I rolled my eyes. "Now, what am I forgetting?" She patted around her hips, then shoved a hand down into a pocket. When it came out again, she was clutching an eggplant-colored velvet purse. "It's not much—maybe 12 rounds and change? But it should get you food and some proper bedrolls when you have time to buy them."

As the self-appointed leader of this expedition, I reached for the bag, but she swatted my hand away and gave it to Reginald.

"Now give your gran a kiss and get out of my sight."

Reginald leaned in and landed a peck on her proffered cheek. I knew better than to try.

"Thanks for everything, Gran," called Reginald as she shooed us out the door. We turned around once to wave good-bye, but she was already perched on a tabletop, smoking a cigar, surrounded by a rapt audience.

"When this is all over," I said to Reginald, "I'm coming back here to buy that woman a drink."

WE WERE ABOUT to walk off down the path in search of additional supplies when I overheard the word "demon." Two men in dusty work pants were standing on either side of a horse, conversing over its back as the one on the left brushed the animal.

"That's ridiculous. There hasn't been a demon in Widder-shins for five hundred years," said the one on the right. "Not since Beadledom came up with that there Hero application. I mean—gosh—after that, there were barely any more heroes either!"

"Fine. Don't believe me. But I'm telling ya. They say a portal keeps flickering in and out by the Forest of Arden and that this morning they saw the image of a demon in it before it closed!"

"Psh!" said the first man, waving a hand in dismissal. I grabbed Reginald by the arm and pulled him in their direction.

"Excuse me, *sirs*." I interjected as much sarcasm as I could into the "sirs," but I don't think anyone noticed. "But I believe the rumor mill has churned out some incorrect information. I am the demon in question. I was summoned four days ago in Beadledom, not the Forest of Arden, by this fellow." I waved Reginald's arm for him. "He forgot to check the box to forgo automatically summoning a demon to aid him."

"See?" said the first man, thrusting a hand toward Reginald and me. "There you go. He's the . . . wait. You are a demon? Where's your tail and horns?"

I narrowed my eyes at him.

"They are vacationing in a little town called None of Your Damn Business."

"Wait, wait, wait," said the second man, who paused his horse grooming to look at me. "You're not the demon I'm talking about. The one I heard about was tall like you, but broad." He paused and cocked his head to the side. "You got demon style, though. That's a nice coat, that. Not too frilly." He gestured to my ebony morning coat, and I puffed out my chest while tugging at the lapels.

"It's made from . . ." I started, but he interrupted.

"But, nah. The demon in the portal had the horns and tail and all. *And* he's got a scar running from his forehead across his eye to his ear."

I felt as if the air had been wrung from my lungs. I knew a demon with that very scar. Shaking my head to recover myself, I said, "From whom did you hear this?"

The man drew himself up as if I'd just challenged him and looked me straight in the eye.

"Folk."

I smirked, relieved. Whenever people answer the question "Where'd you hear that?" with the word "folk," you can be sure that they had an unreliable narrator. "Folk" probably heard the rumor from their next-door neighbor's cousin's sister's cat. The man's description was unnervingly specific, which bothered me, but "folk" were not to be trusted.

"I see. Well, rest assured, humans. I am almost certain that I am the demon, and you need not worry about me. I have a much bigger problem to deal with than bothering with the likes of you."

The two men looked me over again, then shrugged and turned back to the horse. I led Reginald back toward the path away from the tavern, and he immediately launched into a line of questioning that I didn't want to discuss.

"Do you think it's true?"

"Do I think what's true, Reg?"

"About the portal? Do you think the other demon got out?"

"How could it be? Did someone else fuck up their paper-work as you did? And, no. Even if it's true, they said the portal closed before he stepped through. No harm done."

"But the flickering portal. What if . . . what if this is our fault? What if the Stone of Eno has something to do with it?"

The timing and location *was* suspicious. I thought about regaling him with my concern regarding the identity of the described demon but thought better of it. It was just a rumor gone wrong. There were no other demons topside. There couldn't be. Because if breaking the stone had somehow weakened the connection between Widdershins and the Under-world—then it wasn't just our lives that were at stake.

Everyone's life was.

CHAPTER 2
FOLLOW THE MUSHROOMS

The Cock o' the North, it transpired, was only a Beadledonian stone's throw from a quaint village on the Inner Sea where we could purchase the aforementioned bedrolls. We also bought a map, a block of hard cheese, and half-a-dozen flatbreads each. By the end of our shopping spree, we still had three rounds plus seven half-rounds. I wanted to spend the lot on drinks and *companions*, but Reginald was a miserly purse-keeper and said we should be "reasonable" and "ration our spending."

"We don't know what's going to happen, Mal. Maybe we'll need it later and say, 'Oh why did we spend that so early in our journey—we could have used it now.'"

I adjusted my pack so it wasn't rubbing against my shoulders as I walked.

"Or we could fall off a mountain later in our journey and on the way down think, 'Oh why didn't we spend those rounds when we had the chance!'"

We wandered onto the front stoop of a shop that advertised travel planning. It was closed, but there was a case full of pamphlets boasting about the virtues of a variety of enticing destinations. I rummaged through the wooden box. There was a bulletin for the Hidden Isle, one for a spa town on the eastern side of the Inner Sea, another about the Ruins of Thret, and half-a-dozen others. I picked out a colorful pamphlet about the City of Seven and another about the Academy of Wizards. Then I sat down on the wide stone steps under the eaves of the building to peruse them.

"Look at this," I said to Reginald, who was looking over a single-page ad for Slopecastle—a gloomy but enchanting castle-town on the ocean side of Widdershins. "It says that the headmaster of the academy's name is Steadly and that he is the most famous and powerful wizard alive."

Reginald's eyes lit up.

"That sounds promising."

I nodded.

"And there's more. There's a testimonial here that says, 'When I accidentally trod on an old magical land mine, I lost the ability to walk in a straight line. With the help of some friends, I traveled to the City of Seven and met with the head-master—and within minutes I could walk straight again! You do not know what a luxury that is until it's gone.'"

Reginald clapped his hands together, stood, and practically bounced into the street in his excitement.

"Well, that's it, then! We need to go see Headmaster Steadly! He seems like a helpful fellow from that description."

"For once, I completely agree," I said, following him. "Let's figure out where we are so we can see where to go next."

I surveyed the area. Horse trough; wide dusty road; small timbered houses and shops. I led us around the corner to the side of the last house on the road. Taking the map out of my satchel, I unrolled the parchment onto the side of the building. Reginald scanned the map, then pointed to a spot just west of the Inner Sea.

"There. That's where we are right now."

"Far out of the way of where we should be," I muttered.

I touched the spot with the tip of my finger. Then I ran it straight north across an unnamed forest, to the Empty Plains and the Giant's Fingers, until it hit a star with two towers marked next to it.

"And there's the City of Seven."

Reginald tilted his head to the side.

"If we took the long route along the coast of the Inner Sea, we wouldn't have to cross the mountains at all. There are plenty of villages along the way. Places to stay, food to eat. It would be a more comfortable journey."

"And let you dillydally at every inn and tavern along the way? This is not a walkabout, Reg! Who knows what this connection magic will do to us? Maybe it will turn you evil. Maybe it will make me good. Maybe, if one of us dies, the other one dies. Maybe it will make me," I gulped, "*mortal.*" I shuddered at the thought. "We are taking the shortcut!"

"But if we don't get there at all because we starved on the Empty Plains or got caught in a storm or fell off a cliff, how will that be better?"

"It wouldn't be better, but we're just going to avoid doing those things." (Spoiler: We did not avoid doing those things.) Reginald looked uncertain but I stood my ground. "If you get to be the banker on this journey, then I get to be the navigator. We're going the short way. We can be at the Empty Plains by tomorrow night."

Reginald smushed the sides of his face together with his hands for so long, I thought perhaps he was going to leave them that way for the day. Then he let his arms drop with a long breath out.

"Okay, Mal. But if I throw up, it's going to be your fault."

A chestnut-colored horse came galloping down the major thoroughfare, rider high in the stirrups. It came to a halt outside the bakery where we'd purchased our flatbreads. It was hard to tell from this distance, but from the look of the ears and the flawless beauty of the rider's face—I'd say it was one of the amaranthine. She dismounted in one fluid motion, then rummaged in a saddlebag until she came out with a long, clear crystal.

"What's that about?" I asked, as she disappeared into the bakery.

"Amaranthine messenger. Folks can record messages on the crystals, and the messenger will deliver them. Costs about forty rounds, though. Too dear for most people."

The messenger exited the building and was at her horse in three long strides. Then she was on its back and galloping away, and when I blinked—she was gone.

THE INITIAL JOURNEY that got us into this mess took us from a park on the outskirts of Beadledom to the Forest of Arden to the village. As we set off toward the Empty Plains, we were reaching the end of our fifth full day together, and I felt deep in my bones that it was five days too many.

"What did you say your whole name was, again? I keep forgetting."

"Malgon Belroth Kirranith, Fifteenth of His Name, Lord of the Underworld Suburb of Artifice-on-Lethe, Giver of Papercuts, Collapser of Soufflés, Inventor of the Humblebrag."

"I didn't realize that the Underworld had suburbs."

"Now you know."

"And how did you get those distinctions?"

"I gave a paper cut, collapsed a soufflé, and invented the humblebrag."

"Isn't that kind of a humblebrag? Casually mentioning that you invented the humblebrag?"

"I guess so."

"How old are you?"

"550 years old."

"Wow. So is that like, young for a demon? How old would you be if you were human?"

"There's not really an equivalency. I'm immortal."

"But if you had to guess."

"I don't know. Maybe about . . . thirty?"

"I'm twenty-two! That's not a big age difference."

"If you say so," I said. "Look—is it possible to walk in silence for five minutes?"

"Yeah. Of course."

We'd gone five paces when Reginald spoke again.

"Want to hear a story?"

"No."

"It's about my dog, Bitsy Wigglebottom. She is just the most adorable, fluffy little creature. She's probably confused that I've been gone so long. Anyway—this one time we were out for a walk, and . . ."

Reginald continued to drone on. At first it made my blood pressure rise, and I nearly blew my top at him. But after a while the sound of his voice was like a distant hum—soothing in its own way—though I vaguely wondered how he could talk for so long without drawing breath.

"I think we should stop for the night, Mal. It's getting pretty dark."

I blinked and looked around. Sure enough, the sun, which had been just past its zenith when he started his story, was dipping below the horizon. All that was left of the day was the pale pinkish light reflecting off low clouds. As if to make Reginald's point, a gust of wind blew, catching my cravat and blowing it up in my face.

"Very well. Let's get off the road."

We were still in the wood, so we picked our way through the underbrush until we found a spot clear of both trees and detritus. Green grass covered spongy earth—the perfect place for a fire and bed. Reginald had been picking up small dry sticks as we went along, and he dumped them on the ground, saying, "Hand me the stones. I'll start a fire."

"What stones?"

"The broken ones."

I blinked at him.

"You want to use the broken pieces of the Stone of Eno to start a fire? The stone to which we hope the magic within us will return? Is that what you're saying? Don't you think we ought to be a bit more careful with them?"

Reginald considered this.

"Yeah, okay. But then what are we going to do? Does rubbing two sticks together really work?"

"Leave it to me, Reg."

I tossed my bag down on the ground, then picked up the wood Reginald had collected. I walked to the center of the clearing and dropped the wood at my feet. Kneeling, I placed my hand on the ground, and when I lifted it, a small flame sat flickering amongst the branches in the dying light.

"How did you do that?"

Furrowing my brow, I said, "Magic. Obviously."

"Yes, but *how*?"

I shrugged.

"I don't know. That's like me asking you how you breathe. It's just something that happens. I can't do everything by magic. But the things I can do I do by instinct."

Reginald's face took on an expression of puppylike eagerness.

"Can you make food?"

"Nope. Can't make food."

His face fell.

"That's disappointing."

We sat in silence, listening to the crackle of the small flame. There were other sounds too: the hoot of an owl in search of a meal, the skitter of mice across the undergrowth trying to cheat fate.

"So if you can do whatever magic you can whenever you want—why do you have to wait until we fix the stone to do some big evil thing? Why not just do it?"

"First—because we have a contract that says I cannot. Second—because in order to do 'some big evil thing,' I have to sort of—borrow power from Lucifer."

Reginald's brow furrowed.

"I guess that's good for us humans and stuff. But why not just let you all loose with as much power as you'd like?"

I stretched my arms up over my head and felt the bones in my upper back crack.

"If your goal is to remain the most powerful demon in history, then you do not go about spawning minions who can challenge you. You keep your power to yourself and dole it out when necessary."

"Oh. Right. Smart."

I shot him a grim smile.

"That's why he's the Archfiend."

"But you can obviously still be uh . . . mean."

I smirked.

"Yes, Reginald. Thankfully you don't need magic to be an asshole. I'm sure I'll prank a human or two along the way for amusement. Anyway—enough about all that—what happened to the King's measurements? And while we're at it—the Giant's measurements?"

"It just got too confusing. A King's yard was less than half of a Giant's yard, but no one could ever decide exactly how much less than a half it was—the construction industry was a mess."

I nodded. Made sense.

"So it may not surprise you to hear that the mayor of Beadledom decreed that a committee be formed to make a new standardized form of measurement. The Beadledonian measurements."

"So how long is a King's foot in the Beadledonian measurements?"

"They kept it the same. Luckily, the mayor's foot was the same size as that old king's."

"And a league?"

". . . They're still working on that one. Right now, the interim measurement is 'shouting distance.'"

"How precise," I said, tone flat.

"Well, it takes a long time to come to decisions by committee."

How true.

"And how long have they been working on this project?"

"Thirty-nine years."

"Ah."

Wind hissed through the leaves on the trees and sent a shiver down my spine. Reginald noticed and started rummaging in his pack. He pulled out a blue woolen blanket and tossed it to me.

"Thanks," I said, catching it in both hands. "It's warmer in the Underworld."

"Eating will help keep you warm too."

Settling the blanket around my shoulders, I pulled my satchel over and grabbed some cheese and a piece of flatbread. I tossed the cheese to Reginald, who broke off a chunk, then sent it back my way. We ate the bread and dehydrated milk curd —and it pleased me to discover that it didn't need any demon dust at all. The person who had prepared these items had been mad as fuck about something.

After dinner—such as it was—we pulled out our bedrolls and settled down for the night. Reginald was asleep as soon as he lay down, as evidenced by his incessant snoring. I had a harder time getting to sleep. The music of the night forest was more percussive than its melodic daytime counterpart. Sticks crunched, birds flapped, and wind howled at odd, unpredictable intervals.

But eventually, even I succumbed to slumber. Though if I'd known what we'd wake up to in the morning, I would have held my eyelids open all night.

———

"By the Triplets, Mal! What's happened to our stuff?"

At the invocation of the Triplets, I itched all over.

"Please don't mention them in my presence," I said, scratching at my forearm.

"By the Triplets" is a common Widdershinian saying referencing Threeism—the worship of the Triplet Gods. Each point of the triangle on the flag of Widdershins is supposed to represent one of them, but those gods have never made themselves known to the people as the demons have. In fact, I'd completely dismiss the truth of their existence altogether if it weren't for the fact that every time someone mentioned them I started to itch.

"Sorry. Is it true that talking about them will make you burst into flames?"

I stopped itching and stared at him.

"Ob-vi-ous-ly not."

He screwed up his face in embarrassment.

"Right."

"Poor phrasing aside—you're not wrong. Where *has* our stuff gone?"

I rubbed my eyes as I stood, turning in a circle as I rose. It was then that I saw what I'd missed in the dark the night before.

"Hellfire and fucking damnation! We slept in a fucking fairy ring, Reginald!"

"So?"

"So? So according to their quixotic rule book—our stuff is their stuff until we've done them three favors."

"That is inconvenient."

"Yes. Quite."

I ran my hand through my hair, thinking.

"I heard of a dwarf once who traded the three small favors for one big favor. Maybe we could try that."

Reginald shrugged.

"I'm fine with that, but how are we going to find them?"

"That's easy," I said, pointing to a spot just outside the circle where a trail of colorful domes covered the forest floor. "We're going to follow the mushrooms."

WE TREAD the toadstool path carefully. Who knew what the fairies would demand if we dragged our boots through it and destroyed them? But soon enough we arrived at a copse of hawthorn trees surrounded in twinkling, silvery light. Set into the bark of each tree were a thousand tiny homes with acorn-shell roofs and bound-twig walls. Peering inside, we saw maple-leaf rugs, moss comforters, and mushroom tables and chairs.

On the center-most tree was a fairy castle. Birch bark covered this larger structure, giving it a lighter, more composed air. And on the parapet stood a portly fairy wearing an amber tunic and a silver crown. He coughed.

"Oh, hello, little fellow!" crooned Reginald, bending over at the waist to smile at the monarch. This earned him a barrage of acorns shot from unseen fairies within the branches. "Ow! Oof! Okay, okay!"

"Sorry about him," I said, pointing my thumb at Reginald. "He's new to this."

"Ah, a demon!" cried the fairy king, casting an appraising

look from my black boots to my goldenrod eyes. "But not the one everyone's talking about. Interesting. And what brings you to Widdershins?"

I felt my skin prickle at this second mention of another demon. But when I turned my head to gauge Reginald's reaction, he was cowering with his arms in front of his face.

"He brings me to Widdershins. Long story. Anyway—we're on a quest of sorts and we're short on time. While I know it's customary to do you three favors to get our stuff back—we were wondering if we could, perhaps, just do one big one for you this time?"

The fairy tilted his head, holding his chin in his hand as if considering the proposal. Slowly, he said, "It's unorthodox, but I suppose we could come to an arrangement."

"Fantastic."

"If you slay the monster who has been trampling our toadstool forest and bring us one of its teeth as proof, we will return your belongings to you, and you will be free to go."

I'd originally been thinking the request would be something like "Fill this rain barrel with water from a crystal stream" or "Capture starlight in three silver bottles." Those were more in line with the usual fairy requests. I hadn't expected to become a monster hunter.

"And there's nothing else that we could do? You know, instead of that?"

One thing to know about demons: our self-preservation instincts are well-honed.

The fairy frowned.

"No monster. No belongings."

I looked at Reginald.

"What do you think?"

"I don't think I can kill a monster, Mal."

I turned back to the fairy.

"Fine. We'll do it."

"What?!" cried Reginald. "I just said no!"

"Too late now," I said. "Where is this toadstool forest?"

The fairy adjusted its crown, then pointed farther into the trees.

"Not far, for your kind. About a hundred Beadledonian yards away."

Who knew that so many races would be into a standardized system of measurement?

"Great. And what kind of beast is this?"

The fairy shuddered.

"It is most fearsome! It has two heads and eight limbs but still slithers and rolls about the forest. It writhes amongst the toadstool, grunting and moaning and screaming. It comes almost every midday, then slinks away again. We believe that it might have come through the portal from the Underworld with the other demon."

Lucifer's giddy aunt.

"I'm at least seventy percent certain that this Forest of Arden portal rumor has no substance. I am the demon who was summoned. Just me. But all the same, this monster sounds terrifying."

"Thanks a lot, Mal," grumbled Reginald.

"If there's nothing else we need to know, we'll be off."

The fairy jumped up and beat his tiny wings. It fluttered up to my face, put a minuscule hand on my forehead, and said, "Just know that if you die in the attempt, the cheese in your bag will not go to waste."

I smiled awkwardly. How are you supposed to react to something like that?

"Come along, Reginald," I said, but he stayed put.

"I'm not going."

"Reg, you know what's going to happen if I move and you try to stay here."

"I'm willing to risk it. I don't want to go after no monsters!"

I shrugged.

"Suit yourself!"

I walked off in the direction the fairy had pointed. I'd only gone about thirty Beadledonian feet when *zing*!

"Ow!"

"Oof!"

Reginald crashed into my back—forced once again by the connection magic of the Stone of Eno.

"That is really annoying," groaned Reginald as he rubbed his head.

"All the more reason to get on board with this monster thing. We get the tooth, we get our stuff, and we get back on the road."

"But are we going to kill a monster? Is that part of your 'instinctual magic?' We don't have any weapons, and they didn't teach us anything about monster hunting in hero orientation."

The air was crisp and smelled faintly sweet. I continued to crunch through the fallen leaves without looking at Reginald—keeping an eye out all the while for a blanket of colorful mushrooms.

"First, shouldn't monster hunting be Heroing 101? Also, there's no monster."

"What do you mean there's no monster? You heard the fairy! The thing's got two heads!"

"No," I said as I held an arm out to stop him. We'd reached the edge of the toadstool forest. A significant swath in the middle had been crushed. "It's not one thing with two heads. It's two things, each with one head."

Reginald narrowed his eyes at me.

"How can you be so sure?"

"For one, I've studied The Archfiend's bestiary at length, and there is nothing in there with that description. And the other clue was . . . well, if you know, you know. But my money is on two humans sneaking into the forest for a lunchtime quickie. Fairies are more dusk-to-dawn creatures. They don't see as well in broad daylight. I think they saw what they thought they should see."

"And if you're wrong?"

I nodded slowly.

"Then we run like hell and figure out some other way to get our stuff back."

Reginald studied my face for a beat.

"Do I want to know why you were studying The Archfiend's bestiary 'at length'?"

"Reginald—"

"Okay, okay."

He held his arms up in front of him, then plopped down on the forest floor. I sat down beside him.

"And now we wait," I breathed.

"So what do you think about this other demon thing now?" Reginald nearly shouted.

I pinched the bridge of my nose.

"Reg, in order for this to work, we are going to have to be silent. Not conversational. Not quiet. *Silent.* They cannot know that we're here until they are practically standing on top of us, or else we'll scare them away. Do you understand?" Reginald opened his mouth to speak, and I quickly covered it with my palm. "Si-lent."

I could tell from his eyes that this was going to be torture for him. But he nodded and pushed my hand away. I cleared a space and started picking up and examining small rocks and pebbles from the ground. He selected a stick from the litter beneath us and peeled away the bark until he held a bone-colored shaft. He relieved fourteen other sticks of their outer-wear before we heard it. Sitting bolt upright, we trained our ears in the noise's direction. It sounded like a crazed boar on the loose, crashing into trees and making many loud grunts and groans. But then—

"Did I just hear a giggle?" Reginald whispered.

I turned and shushed him, but my eyes were triumphant.

Sure enough, crashing through the trees were two young lads of about nineteen, all love bites and tangled limbs with not a thought to anything aside from each other. One had bronzed skin and golden locks that fell to his shoulders. The other was pale, with hair so black it almost looked blue in the tree-filtered midday light. Both were near-perfect human specimens in their own way, and I wondered how this would have gone down were I five-hundred-and-some years younger.

I let them stumble right to their usual spot, and just as they were angling toward the ground, I stood up and stepped out from behind a tree.

"Gentlemen," I said and made a shallow bow.

"What the—" the dark-haired one managed, and they toppled over onto the mushrooms.

"My name is Lord Malgon, and this is my colleague, Sir Reginald."

"Hello!" said Reg, waving and smiling at them from his spot on the forest floor.

"Hello?" said the blond one, though it sounded more like a question. I strode toward them, face as solemn as a judge.

"Under normal circumstances, I fully support these kinds of extracurricular activities, but in this case, I cannot let them continue. You have—inadvertently, I assume—been performing your relations on a toadstool forest belonging to fairy royalty."

Both their mouths dropped open.

"Quite. You've destroyed much of their harvest," I said, motioning to the flattened toadstools. The two lads jumped up and away immediately.

"We didn't know!" said the dark-haired one.

"Honest—we didn't!"

I held up a hand for them to stop speaking.

"I assumed as much. But there is still a price to pay for your negligence. I will need a tooth from one of you. You have one minute to decide whose mouth I will remove it from."

They both turned slightly green.

"A tooth? You're just going to pull it out?"

"Right here? From one of our mouths?"

"I am a demon in the fairy's employ. I have been authorized to do so."

The blond one started to cry.

"Mal! Are you serious?" asked Reginald

I nodded gravely.

"Quite serious, Sir Asstradle."

The two young men were holding each other's shoulders, searching each other's eyes, wondering who would give in first. The only sound was the sniffling of the blond boy. It was as if the entire forest were holding its breath, waiting for their decision. I looked at Reginald—he was so tense that he was barely breathing. I couldn't take it any longer.

"I'm just kidding!" I said with a swipe of my hand in their direction. "You should have seen your faces!" I laughed so hard I bent double and wheezed. "Can you imagine? Just reaching in and grabbing your tooth?" All three humans turned stony expressions on me, but I couldn't stop laughing. They'd been so terrified!

Eventually, I wiped the tears from my eyes and calmed myself down enough to scowl up at them.

"You three are no fun."

"The thing is, though . . ." Reginald dropped his volume and muttered out of the corner of his mouth. "We promised the fairies a tooth."

"And they shall have one!" I said, producing the stone I'd gathered from the forest floor with a flourish. It was long and curved—jagged on one end and smooth on the other. I almost lost it again as the lovers flinched away from me but held it together.

"Now, if you gentlemen would be so kind as to take your revelry far away from this spot, we'll consider the matter settled."

"Absolutely!" they cried in unison and nearly tripped over one another to hurry away. I tossed the "tooth" up into the air and caught it in my palm.

"That was so clever of you to find a rock that looked like a tooth," said Reginald as we started back toward the fairies.

"It'll have to do," I said, holding it up between two fingers and inspecting it as we walked. "I didn't have pliers on me, otherwise I would have taken a real one. I mean, who carries pliers on them all the time, right?"

Reginald looked like he was going to be sick.

"Do you think it'll fool them?"

"Of course it will! Without a doubt."

IT ONLY TOOK a few minutes to arrive back at the fairy settlement. Long legs and all that.

"They have returned!" came the soft yet commanding voice of the fairy king. "But have they returned triumphant?"

"Indeed, we have," I announced. I palmed the tooth off to Reginald. He looked at me, confused. "You're the hero, Reg," I whispered. "This will be better coming from you."

"Right," he said hesitantly. "Oh, Fairy King! We have . . . uh . . ."

"Felled," I whispered.

"Felled!"

". . . the beast . . ."

"The beast!"

". . . and brought back its tooth."

"And brought back its tooth!"

He held it up in a shaft of sunlight for all to see.

The fairy monarch fluttered toward us and examined the tooth, squinting his eyes in the brightness. Whatever he saw, or didn't see, seemed to satisfy him because he cried,

"They have slain the beast!"

A flurry of movement and murmuring captured my attention, and at once an entire community of fairies sharing their thanks and congratulations surrounded us. A small group broke off and came back with our bags. We took them, slinging them over our shoulders.

"Well, now that that's done, we must move on. Quest things. You know how it is."

The fairy looked upon us with eyes so earnest I almost felt guilty about lying.

"Thank you again for your help. Our forest is safe once more!"

After some bowing and goodbye-ing, we extricated ourselves from the group of fairies and set off in pursuit of our sleeping accoutrement.

"Why are you jogging?" asked Reginald as I speed-walked us back along the mushroom trail to our bedrolls.

"If I said, 'For our health,' would you believe me?"

"Mal..."

"Okay, fine. I'm not entirely sure how long the stone ruse is going to hold up, and I'd like to be as far from here as possible when they realize we have duped them."

"I thought you said it would work!"

"I did. But I was lying."

As if on cue, a high-pitched but angry cry sounded from far behind us.

"Run, Reg! Run!"

I thrust him ahead of me, and we dashed the rest of the way to the fairy circle. Leaning in, we grabbed our bedrolls midstride, then wound our way back to the road. Not wanting to chance it, we sprinted a little farther on, our bedrolls streaming out behind us like flags in the wind. When we arrived at a crossroads, we finally stopped to catch our breath.

"Well, you're right about one thing," Reginald gasped.

"What's that?"

"You don't have to have magic to be a you-know-what."

I winked at him.

"Will I ever be welcome anywhere in Widdershins after traveling with you?" Reginald gasped.

I leaned over and put my hands on my knees.

"Doubtful."

Reginald clasped his hands and rested them on top of his head.

"Splendid."

"If it helps—I literally cannot help myself. They spawned me to be the right hand of evil. Well, in my case, it's more like the left pinky toe. But still—mischief is at the very core of my being."

"It doesn't really help."

"Yeah. Thought not."

Reginald squinted up at the sky, then pulled a circular brass object out of his back trouser pocket and flicked it open.

"You have a pocket time wheel?"

He looked up.

"Yes."

"Why didn't you say so before?"

"Did we need it before?"

I mentally scrolled back through the past days to see if we could have avoided catastrophe if we'd only known the time. The answer was no.

"I guess we didn't."

"Well, right now it's ten minutes to three in the afternoon."

I rifled around in my bag until I found the map. Rolling it out on the ground, we tried to get our bearings.

"So, where are we now?" he asked.

"This is where we went off the road." I pointed to a spot in the illustrated trees. "And I think this," I pointed to a crossroads on the map close to that spot, "is where we are now."

"Are you sure? I thought we went off the road here." He pointed to a spot on the opposite side.

"No, I'm certain that this was it. But honestly, either way, we've made almost no forward progress."

Even at a decent clip, we couldn't arrive at the Empty Plains before the evening, as we'd originally intended. We were nearly a full day behind schedule and we'd only been on the road for one day. I was starting to think that Reginald's grandmother was a portender of doom.

"Well, we can't stay here in the middle of the road. Let's at least go in the right direction, and we'll see what we shall see."

"All right. But are you definitely sure that you're reading this map right?"

"Reginald. I am the navigator and I take that job seriously. This is the way we need to go—right at the crossroads."

We made the right and started off again.

In entirely the wrong direction.

CHAPTER 3
THE INN

We didn't realize I'd led us astray until we reached the Inner Sea and caught the scent of salt on the air. A cluster of fishing huts hunched over the shoreline like ravenous beasts at their kill, and an eerie mist hung low to the ground, adding to the misfortune of it all.

"Fuck-ing Hell."

"This is not the Empty Plains, I take it?"

"I really thought we were headed the right way."

"You seemed very certain."

I pulled the map from my pack once more and dropped to the ground. Sitting cross-legged, I examined it while Reginald looked over my shoulder. His expression was so calm a dropped pebble would have made ripples in it. It made me want to ring his neck.

"'Life's a journey,' right, Reg?" I asked, trying to get a rise out of him.

"It sure is, Mal."

I frowned.

"You have nothing to say about the fact that we just wasted another hour heading in the wrong direction?"

He shrugged.

"You are the navigator."

I closed my eyes and rubbed my temples.

"Do you ever get mad?"

"I guess."

"About what?"

"Things."

I was going to ask him to expound upon "things" when a breeze caught the map and whipped it away toward the water. Maybe it was the weather and the quiet playing tricks on me, but I had the distinct impression that there was something in that water that I didn't want to find out about.

I shot to my feet and sprinted after the map. Just as it was about to sail out over the sea, I snatched it out of the air.

"Gotcha!"

My upper body tipped precariously over the water, but I pulled back just in time. After I'd regained my balance, I walked back to where Reginald was standing, inspecting the map as I went.

"I see where I went wrong," I called out to him. "We just follow the road back and then bear right a little past the crossroads."

Reginald hiked his bag into place on his shoulders, and I refolded the map.

"I'm not sorry to be leaving. This place is pretty creepy," he said as we started back the way we came.

"Me too. Visiting here once is one time too many."

I set a brisk pace in our new direction, forcing Reginald to keep up lest we get magically smashed back together.

"We never got to talk about the other demon again," Reginald said.

I winced.

"That's because I don't want to talk about it."

Reginald jogged to come alongside me.

"So you *do* think they saw another demon!"

I paused in the middle of the road and turned toward him.

"I don't know. Logic says that there's just me. But the description of the other demon was . . . uh . . ."

"Oh, my gosh, you know who it is!"

I avoided looking at him by examining my fingernails. "I don't know who it is, Reg. Like I said, logic says there is no second demon. But the description of the probably nonexistent creature sounded a lot like . . . my brother."

"Your *what*?"

I sighed.

"Ugh. See? This is why I didn't tell you sooner. I knew you'd overreact."

"I didn't know you had a brother! Did I know you had a brother?"

"I have three brothers, actually. But this would be my oldest one—Tannith."

"Three older brothers. Wow. I don't have any siblings. That must have been exciting—growing up in a big family."

Cringing, I started walking again.

"You could say that."

"So—but wait," said Reginald, grabbing my upper arm to halt me again. "Say the people at the tavern and the fairies were right. A portal was flickering in and out near the Forest of Arden, and they saw your brother. What if he actually came out of it? What would that mean?"

I pulled my arm out of his grasp and kept walking.

"It means that it's even more important for us to get to Headmaster Steadly as quickly as possible. If breaking the Stone of Eno somehow caused a weakness in the magic that keeps our worlds separate, then Widdershins is about to be in for a terrible time. Because if you think I'm bad—wait till you meet the rest of my kind."

"So, is that what it does? It keeps our worlds separate?"

"How am I supposed to know? Nobody knows! All I know is

that Quill Valor stole it from the dryads centuries ago, then lost it. It must have turned up in Beadledom, though, since the committee gave it to you to return for your first quest."

Actually, "quest" is not really the best way to describe it. If Reginald's hero paperwork had been perfect, then he would have simply taken the sack with the unblemished stone to the forest, handed it to the dryads, and returned home. Heroes these days were just glorified mail people. It wasn't until Reginald summoned me via paperwork error and I showed up in that park that it really turned into a "quest."

We walked for another hour, exchanging arguments about the validity of the second-demon rumors, when suddenly—

"Bloody, fucking hell! Is this a cursed map? How did we get back to this creepy village?"

"I think it's because we took a right instead of a left at that intersection. And we should have gone left initially as well."

"Why didn't you say anything?"

"Well, first, because you're the navigator and you take that job seriously. Second, because life's a journey, right? Plus, you would never have listened."

"I *might* have listened if I'd known I had Sir Reginald P. Asstradle, Patron Saint of Fucking Map Reading, with me!" I yelled.

Reginald cocked an eyebrow at me, and I deflated.

"You *may* be right. I *might* not have listened."

"Would you like to see if third time is the charm?"

I narrowed my eyes at him.

"Are you making fun of me? I'd like to see you do better. Here—" I stuffed the map in his hands. "Let's see what you've got."

At that moment, the water near the shore bubbled and gurgled.

"Did you just see that?" whispered Reginald. I had. A smooth hump had briefly surfaced and dived again.

I nodded.

"What do you think it was?" asked Reginald, eyes wide with panic.

I scrolled through a list of things it could have been. The Black Squid, the Midnight Whale, the Morally Gray Sea Turtle.

None of them were good.

The water frothed and churned near the shore.

"I don't know, but it's time to go, Reg!"

A roar sounded behind us and we set off at a run, our packs bouncing on our backs.

"I'd never realized how much running questing involved!" shouted Reginald.

"Maybe there's less running if you're better at it!"

We hit the road, our feet pounding against the dirt until we could no longer see the water. Finally we slowed, and Reginald consulted the map, plotting a course. To my deep annoyance, we reached the edge of the Empty Plains in the early evening. I was in a dark mood as we approached them. I didn't love the idea that Reginald—who had never even left Beadledom before we met—could navigate the wilderness better than I could. But my mood improved slightly with the unexpected sight of an inn. We were on the boundary between civilization and a part of the world people tended to avoid, but there it was: thatched roof, plank siding, and light pouring from every window. It sat sentinel at the edge of the dry expanse, like a watchman who'd forgotten he was off duty.

"I thought people avoided the Empty Plains," said Reginald.

"Maybe they avoid everything after this? Looks pleasant enough, and we still have some money." Reginald opened his mouth to protest. "For food! And a bed! And maybe just one drink. We can stay here tonight and get an early start tomorrow."

Reginald's rumbling stomach could not have piped up at a better time.

"I *am* hungry."

"I know, Reg. You're always hungry."

FOR AN INN on the Empty Plains—it was bustling. The din of the rowdy crowd reached us before we even entered the building. Pushing through the swinging door, a familiar scene met us. A bartender poured a steady stream of ale for a veritable army of busty barmaids making their rounds. Regulars took it in turns to chug their drinks or make drunken dares. The place smelled of old beer and fetid breath. A fiddler was doing her best to entertain us with a lively tune, but aside from the highest notes, it was all but drowned out by the jovial crowd in the dining room. These folks were here for a good time.

"What can I get for you?"

A curvaceous server with deep-brown skin appeared in front of us, batting her eyelashes coquettishly. She had her empty tray under one arm and her full bosom in my face— which is standard greeting protocol for barmaids at inns. When she caught sight of my eyes, her templated grin turned wide and wicked. "Well, I'll be. A demon and a human walk into a bar. Sounds like the beginning of a joke. It's been a minute since you all were topside, hasn't it?"

"Five hundred years."

She pushed some loose hairs off her forehead with the back of her hand and gave a low whistle. "Like I said. It's been a minute. Rumor was you were going up the coast road along the Inner Sea." She inspected my face. "And that you had a pretty nasty scar."

I grimaced. They have a saying in Widdershins: "Thrice makes the truth." We'd now heard the demon rumor three times. What's worse, if this rumor was to be believed, he'd escaped the portal and was running amuck in Widdershins. My stomach dropped.

"Still," she went on, "we're prepared. Got beer for the lad," she said, nodding her head in Reginald's direction, "and a bottle of Satan's Piss for you, if you're partaking, sir." She performed the barest hint of a curtsey.

Satan's Piss is the brand. Not the contents of the bottle. In the Underworld we call it firewater. They can't actually get it in Widdershins, but they approximate it. Other brands include Demon's Delight, Devil's Brew, and Lucifer's Liquor. Satan's Piss was one of the better fabrications.

"Oh. I am," I said, shaking off my unease, reaching out, and taking one of her hands in mine. I leaned down and kissed it gently. Her skin was softer than I'd imagined for someone who used their hands all day. It made me wonder how much smoother the rest of her might be. "Lord Malgon Belroth Kirranith, at your service, ma'am."

Reginald, who'd been gawking unapologetically at her breasts, took this moment to find his voice.

"He's also the Collapser of Soufflés!"

She giggled. I tried to crush him with my mind.

"Well, whoever you are," she said, ushering us in, "you're both welcome here."

She found us a table at the opposite end of the room from the fiddler near the staircase, and after stashing our bags beneath it, we drank. It took just one mug of ale before Reginald was humming tunelessly along to the fiddler's jig. After two mugs, he had his shirt off and was challenging the surrounding tables to arm-wrestling competitions. After three drinks, he fell asleep with his head on the table, hand still wrapped around his mug. Settling his discarded shirt across his back, I surveyed the room. I'd had my fair share of firewater as well, but I wasn't really here for the drinking. I was more curious about the *company* available. Across the room sat a devilishly handsome silver-haired gentleman whose eye I'd been trying to catch. Finally succeeding, I grinned wickedly at him, and he cocked an eyebrow while angling his head toward the stairs in invitation. Our server returned, and I nudged my head in her direction. The silver-haired gentlemen gave a quick nod.

The server smirked at Reginald's placid form as she collected our glasses.

"I see you two are enjoying yourselves."

I cut my eyes toward Reg, then back at her.

"I could think of a few ways I might enjoy myself more," I said, taking her hand again and laying butterfly kisses in a line from her hand up to her elbow. I caught the eye of the gentleman across the room once more, and she followed my gaze. Spotting my mark, she grinned.

"It's mad in here—why don't we go upstairs where it's a little more private." Winking, she deposited her tray on our table, grabbed my hand, and motioned toward the gentleman to follow.

So it was that the three of us made our way to a room right at the top of the stairs, where we lost no time in disrobing. The barmaid, her dress torn open to expose her bosom, sandwiched herself between me and the silver fox. He was down to just his trousers and I was standing in stockinged feet with my shirt unbuttoned as we began our carnal dance. We were a tangle of half-unclothed, writhing bodies when *zing!*—

Disoriented and collapsed beneath a heap of bodies, I took a moment to understand what had happened. Lifting an arm that did not belong to me, I realized we were piled on the small stage downstairs, along with the fiddler.

And Reginald was squashed beneath me.

"What's happening? *What is happening?*" screeched Reg. Though he was at the bottom of the pile, he scrambled out first. He stood bug-eyed and swaying, clearly still drunk—watching us disentangle ourselves with judgmental fascination.

I'd forgotten all about the fucking connection magic.

My companions were screaming and covering themselves with the minimal garments still on their person. Reginald, who at first couldn't look away, finally covered his eyes and turned his back to our disarray.

The dining room, however—which had been silent from the moment we landed downstairs—erupted into enthusiastic applause.

I grabbed hold of Reginald's arm, and the two of us raced through the crowd. At the bottom of the staircase, I leaned over to swipe our bags, but as I pulled Reginald up the stairs, he fought me. His eyes were wild like a caged animal's.

"Why are we going upstairs?"

"Not for sex, you asshat," I hissed. "I need my pants!"

We took the stairs by twos and retrieved my bottoms. Then, having absolutely no interest in returning to the scene downstairs, we climbed out of the bedroom window onto a low roof and jumped.

I don't know exactly why the spell didn't pull us back together immediately. I can only surmise that at our original table Reginald was the perfect distance away from my frolicking upstairs but that when he ascended the stage to sing a ballade with the fiddler, it was just a hair too far for the spell.

Either that, or the magic of the Stone of Eno has a mind of its own and it's a jerk.

Anyway, we landed on the ground with a crash. Since we'd arrived at the inn, the sun had ensconced itself beyond the horizon. Beyond the halo of light cast by the inn's interior lights lay the vast, almost palpable darkness of the plains.

"This was an earlier start than I'd intended," I muttered.

"Me too. We didn't even get to eat."

Just then, the bartender swung open the door, waving his towel.

"Oy! You didn't pay your tab, you wretches!"

Reginald pulled the purse out of his bag and tossed it overhand to the bartender. The bartender caught it and looked inside.

"This doesn't cover even half of what you owe—never mind what I should charge you for that stunt back there!"

I grimaced.

"So sorry about that," I called, putting a hand on Reginald's back and urging him forward. I leaned close to his ear and whispered, "Run, Reg! Run!"

We sprinted as fast as we could straight into the Empty Plains. Pounding footsteps and shouts sounded behind us for a while, but eventually they faded away. Like I said, most people avoid the plains.

Finally, when it was safe enough to stop, we collapsed on our backs in the grass and heaved in lungfuls of air. As we lay there recovering, the stars mocked us with their steady, noncriminal twinkling.

"I don't feel so good, Mal."

I smacked my forehead.

"Please try not to throw up right now. Think nonvomity thoughts."

"Too late!"

I heard the telltale sound of Reginald's insides lurching forth and screwed up my mouth. When he finished, we gathered our belongings and moved several yards away. The wind whipped away the warmth of the day, and a chill settled into our bones.

"It's kind of cold out here," said Reginald.

"Mmm," I replied and rubbed my hands along my upper arms to encourage them to warm.

"What about a fire?"

I shook my head no, but realized he may not see it.

"It'll lead them straight toward us."

"Right."

Reginald sat up and rummaged around in his pack for a bit before he pulled out the blue blanket, then unhooked his bedroll and laid it out on the ground.

"What are you doing?" I asked.

"Are we going to walk in the dark?"

"No."

"Then I'm going to bed."

He settled himself under the blanket and lay down. I had too much pent-up energy to sleep, though. First there'd been the promise of sex, next the threat of violence, followed swiftly by a quick sprint across one of the most inhospitable places in the world. So I sat on the hard ground next to Reginald, hugging my knees to my chest and thinking about what the other demons would have to say about my journey thus far.

But I didn't have to wonder. I was an embarrassment to my kind even before this quest. I hadn't earned my tail or horns yet, and I looked, as Reginald had put it when we first met, "like a fine gentleman," aside from the eyes. That was all unfortunate before the debacle with the Stone of Eno, but understandable, as demons were no longer welcome in Widdershins. But to have the opportunity to wreak havoc and fuck it up?

My subconscious, in a voice that sounded uncannily like my father's, whispered, "Maybe you're just as bad at being a demon as Reginald is at being a hero."

"Shut up!"

I thought I'd said it in my head, but apparently I'd said it out loud.

"I didn't say anything," came Reginald's sleepy reply.

I sighed.

"Not you, Reg. I was . . . never mind. Go back to sleep."

CHAPTER 4
THE CENTENNIAL STORM

I didn't remember falling asleep, but since I woke up spooning Reginald in broad daylight, I had to assume that it happened.

"Satan's ball sack!" I screamed and scrambled away through the tall, dry grass.

"What is it? The bartender? The sea monster? Fairies? Dryads? The—"

He'd sat straight up and was spinning his head from side to side as if evaluating our position in case of an onslaught.

"No. What? No. I just thought I saw a . . . snake. But it was nothing."

Reginald put his hand to his heart.

"You had me worried for a second."

I ran my hand through my hair.

"Sorry about that. It was . . . a disturbing experience."

"I'll bet."

Reginald unwrapped himself from his evening's cocoon and folded his blanket. Gazing out at the expanse of strawlike weeds and grasses, I could already see a shimmer of heat blanketing the ground. I shuffled on my knees over to the packs and unclasped a canteen from the side of mine. The water swished pathetically around the bottom.

"We should have gotten water at the inn."

It was the wrong thing to say. In an instant, the atmosphere between us went from companionable to uncomfortably quiet. It was as if I had beamed our little corner of the world into the vacuum of space: it was both silent and seemingly devoid of air. Reginald suddenly found a thousand interesting things to focus his attention on, and none of them were me. Why did I have to bring up the inn? Eager to restore the equilibrium between us, I said, "It doesn't *look* like a two-day journey to the mountains from here, does it?"

Reginald looked north and his mouth dropped open.

"Those are the Giant's Fingers? They're massive!"

"Yes, well, they are mountains."

He scowled at me.

"I've seen mountains before. You can see the Stone Rot Mountains from my house."

"The Stone Rot Mountains are *rotting*, Reg. It's right in the name. They're half as tall as they used to be. These are veritable mountains."

"But how are we going to cross them? We don't have any climbing gear—not that I'd know how to use it anyway."

I clipped the canteen back to my pack and tossed the whole thing over a shoulder.

"Don't worry about that. The golden-age heroes made a pass through them." I was neglecting to mention that I had absolutely no idea where this pass was, but we would cross that bridge when we came to it.

"Thank goodness," said Reginald, looking relieved. He was stuffing the last of his belongings inside the green backpack.

"Ready to go, then? We've got a long journey and not nearly enough to eat or drink. We'll be able to get water near the mountain, and I daresay there will be something edible that way. But right now we've got to find the road and hoof it."

"I want it on record that I'm not happy about this."

The unspoken words were "I'm not happy about the way we had to leave the inn, thus depriving us of food, water, and a decent night's rest."

"Noted. Now—come along, Reginald."

———

HE PAUSED and squatted down to examine something unseen at the side of the road.

"I swear on my mother's tit, Reg, if you're about to help another animal across this thoroughfare, I will smite you where you stand."

He frowned and stood, adjusting the bag slung over his shoulder.

"I would if you would stop trying to step on them on purpose."

"They're ants, Reg. It's practically impossible to avoid ants. And anyway, these are supposed to be the *Empty* Plains. I was just trying to help them live up to their name."

"Whatever. And anyway," he continued, "you *won't* smite me because we don't know if that will smite you too. Or is it smote? Smitten?"

"Yes, yes, all right," I interrupted, waving my hand in his direction. "Don't hurt yourself. I get your point. But *my* point is that we need to move faster. We're still two days from the foot of the mountains. We only have food for one, and at this rate it will take us a week to make the crossing."

Sir Reginald P. Asstradle looked down at the ground and scuffed his shoe in the dirt.

"Yeah. All right. But I think you should know—you make it hard to be magically connected to you."

My eye twitched, and I smacked it with the palm of my hand.

"I? I make it hard? We left the Forest of Arden only a handful of days ago, and they have been the longest of my 550-year-old life."

"What? What did I do? You're the one who got us lost for an entire day!"

"First, we traveled miles out of our way for food—"

"For the greatest duck wings in Widdershins—"

"For sus-ten-ance. Which we could have gotten at half-a-dozen places along the way. Then you started in on the stories about your dog."

"Bitsy Wigglebottom! I miss her so much."

"I am *aware*. Then there were the fairies—"

"Not my fault—"

"And the . . ." I caught myself this time. I was never bringing up the inn. Ever again. "Anyway," I continued. "In summation—"

I didn't have a conclusion to my rant, so I turned on my heel and hurried ahead, only to feel the zinging sensation that meant I was about to be thrust back into his orbit.

"Ouch!" we both cried and toppled to the ground.

"This! This is what I am trying to avoid. Several lifetimes of this zinging and crashing and having to be within a few yards of you while you relieve yourself."

"It's not a treat for me either, you know."

I cocked an eyebrow at him and stood, dusting myself off. He held his hand up for me to hoist him up, but I just walked on. I heard him climb to his feet and jog after me.

"You know, I've been thinking a lot about this, and I don't see what's so great about being immortal."

I gaped at him.

"What are you talking about? Everyone wants to be immortal. Not only do immortal beings live forever—we're perfectly crafted, *if you know what I mean.*" I gestured groinwards and Reginald rolled his eyes. "Plus," I continued, "There's a rumor that Quill Valor traded his soul for immortality!"

"Well, not me."

"Why not?"

"You're immortal and you are the crankiest person . . . demon . . . whatever that I've ever met. If immortality is so great, why are you so angry all the time?"

I opened my mouth to answer but couldn't think of a reply.

"Okay," I finally said. "Well, you're just proving my point, Reg. I annoy you, you annoy me. Plus, there's the slight possibility that in breaking the stone, we have inadvertently doomed all of Widdershins to the whims of a fully realized demon. Or by now, it could be a whole horde of them for all we know! We. Need. To. Move."

"That's right. I forgot about that. Well, I didn't *forget* about it. But the ants . . . Anyway, we should hurry," he replied and increased his pace slightly.

"Actually, wait," I said, looking up at the deep indigo creeping across the sky.

"What?"

"It's getting dark. We should stop for the night."

Reginald blinked at me several times before saying, "So this is how it's going to be?"

I shrugged, palms up.

"What can I say. Immortals are also capricious."

THE THING about fire in the Empty Plains—even magical fire—is that it's very easy to set the entire landscape ablaze. The plains are 90 percent kindling and 10 percent dry-ass dirt. I wouldn't have chanced a fire at all, but I was fucking freezing. Also, we were both starving and thirsty, so I thought it best for morale if we were at least warm.

"It's got to be perfect, Reg. Make sure it's—"

"Found a spot!"

Reginald stood on a bald spot of dusty dirt amongst the tall grasses. I circled it twice, appraising its suitability. It was perfect, of course. But I wasn't about to let Reginald know he got it in one.

"I guess it'll do."

I dropped to a squat and coaxed a small flame into existence. It wasn't a lot, but it threw off enough heat so that we wouldn't freeze to death. We pulled out our bedrolls and the last of the flatbread and cheese—both of us so exhausted and hungry that not even Reginald had the energy for conversation. Once we'd eaten, though, he perked up a bit and started an interesting line of questioning.

"Dryads. They're like you, right?" asked Reginald.

"They are absolutely nothing like me."

"I just mean that they are magical creatures."

"Oh. Then, yes. They are exactly like me."

"And you can 'instinctively' make fire. So why couldn't they 'instinctively' fix the stone themselves?"

It caught me off guard. It was a *good* question. He kept going.

"They must have made it—otherwise, why would we be returning it to them?"

I cocked an eyebrow at him.

"I don't know. But the more pressing issue at the moment is figuring how you were body-snatched without my knowing. Because I'm really not used to this level of deep thinking from you, Sir Asstradle."

He scowled at me.

"I'm not stupid, Mal."

I smirked.

"Not entirely, anyway."

He tore a handful of strawlike grass from the ground and tossed it at me, but a slight breeze caught the strands and they flew back into his face. I didn't even try to stifle my laugh.

"Whatever," he spat, pulling a piece of grass out of his mouth. "I'm going to go to bed."

"Oh, come on, Reg. Even you have to admit that was funny."

Apparently, he did not have to admit it. He turned away from me and the fire and curled around his pack. I continued to watch the flames and ponder Reginald's atypically thoughtful questions.

Why couldn't the dryads fix the stone? Who made it if not them? And for that matter—what did it even do? Did it really have something to do with the Underworld?

Reginald snored, and I silently thanked Lucifer that we didn't have to worry about bandits or carnivorous beasts in this destitute place. He would have led them straight toward us.

THE FIRE HAD GONE OUT in the night, so we rose at dawn stiff and chilled through. If you ask me, the Triplets must have been high when they created a world where the more scorching a place was during the day, the more freezing it was at night. Actually, come to think of it, that's the exact kind of nonsense that happens by committee.

Reginald was still sore from our conversation the night before, so we walked in silence. He thought he was punishing me, but I was elated. No stupid stories, no complaints about how hungry he was. We were even focused more on speed than scenery. In fact, we were cruising right along when something in the distance caught my eye. There was a dark smudge on the horizon and it was moving. Quickly.

"I know you're mad at me, Reg, but it's been a while since I was topside. I was wondering—does campfire smoke usually barrel toward one at unbelievable speed?"

Reginald stopped short and bent over with the pretense of retying his boot. He still didn't even want to look at me, so I decided now was not the moment to remind him that his boots didn't have laces.

"Not that I know of. Sounds more like a Centennial Storm than smoke."

The smudge had morphed into an ominous cloud. It flickered with purple lightning and was hurtling toward us at a breakneck pace.

"Mm-hmm, Mm-hmm. And what, pray tell, is a Centennial Storm?"

"Remember, my gran mentioned them at the Cock o' the North? I've never seen one myself. We don't get them back in Beadledom. But Gran says it's a storm 'so violent it could depose a dictator.' They only muster up the energy to occur once every hundred years. Nasty things. Apparently they've been known to pluck the feathers right off a chicken."

"How convenient. And, in your professional opinion, based on your gran's vivid imagery—is that," I pointed at the darkness ahead, "a Centennial Storm?"

Reginald finally looked up, and his face paled to the color of spoiled milk.

"Oh no. That's not good."

A wall of gray as tall as a mountain was pushing toward us.

"Terrific!" I yelled. "That's fucking terrific. Just my luck. I've been here for a week and I've been saddled with you and have made enemies of myriad magical races. And now we're walking across the Empty Plains where there is nowhere to hide as a Centennial Storm heads our way!"

"Plus, there was the inn . . ."

"We are never speaking about the inn!"

The wind picked up, and my cravat fluttered up into my face. Thunder rolled, and we felt the vibration in our bones.

"Mal?"

"Yes, Reg?"

"What are we going to do?"

A light rain began to fall. I turned on the spot, looking in every direction. The landscape was flat for as far as the eye could see.

"I . . ."

I wanted to tell him that if he was so smart, he could think of a plan. But then thunder boomed, and we jumped into each other's arms like frightened children.

"Are we going to die, Mal?"

His eyes were wild, and in their reflection, I saw that my expression mirrored his.

"Um . . . maybe?"

"What do you mean 'maybe'?"

The rain was falling harder now. It ran in little rivulets around our feet, and the temperature dropped several degrees.

"Just what I said! Maybe! How am I supposed to know?"

"Oh, man . . . I think I'm going to throw up."

I made a strangled noise and said, "Why is vomiting your default reaction to unpleasant situations?"

"I don't know! I guess humans weren't 'perfectly crafted'!"

"Clearly!" I shouted. "Just don't do it into the wind. It's bad enough to watch you. I don't want to be covered in it."

The gale whipped around us as we stood, shelterless, watching the full strength of the storm head our way. There was something majestic about it. Nature—a power unto herself.

Lightning struck a league away and we both screamed. I changed my mind. Nature was a dastardly, dramatic little bitch, and she could kiss my immortal ass.

With the arrival of cloud-to-ground lightning came the deluge. It was as if someone had turned on the meteorological bathroom tap to full blast and forgotten to turn it off again.

"I've never been this wet in my life," sputtered Reginald. "Is it possible to be more wet on the outside than I am on the inside?"

But I couldn't answer. The previously parched ground couldn't take on all this water. And these were the Empty Plains; they were flat. The water had nowhere to run. So instead it was rising.

"Mal? Are you okay? Oof . . . what are you doing?"

I was doing the only sensible thing I could think of: climbing up onto Reginald's shoulders.

"Mal! I can't . . . gosh . . . Hey, you're going to make me drop my bag!"

"Demons don't swim, Reg! I don't know what happens to you if I drown! I might be saving your life right now!" I shouted down from my perch.

"But . . . what? Am I supposed to just stand here?"

"Stand. Move. I don't care. Just as long as I'm far away from the water."

Reginald stood, feet shoulder-width apart, but even with the combined weight of the two of us, the wind was too much. It howled in our ears as we watched lightning hurl itself down between us and the mountains.

"On second thought, I'll take my chances with the flood," I yelled and clambered back down him. I'd forgotten that lightning liked to strike the highest point. "I thought I saw a patch of dry earth before I climbed down. Let's make our way over there!"

Reginald nodded, and we struggled against the wind toward the spot I'd spied. It wasn't even high enough to be considered a hill, and it, too, would soon be covered, but it would buy us a few more minutes.

We were both soaked to the bone and freezing cold. The wind whipped at our clothes; the lightning made horrible hissing noises wherever it hit.

"Mal, I'm scared!" Reginald shouted.

"Me too, Reg!" I shouted back.

"I wish I'd gotten to say goodbye to Bitsy Wigglebottom! I was only supposed to be gone for a few days!"

"Hrmn." I didn't know how to respond to human regrets. They taught little empathy in the Underworld.

"What about you?"

"What about me?"

"Isn't there anything you wish you'd gotten to do?"

There were so many things, really. I wished I'd gotten to spend more time *not* attached to a human. I wished I'd lived up to my title and familial expectations. I wished I'd earned my tail and horns.

"I guess I wish . . ."

But I never got to say what I wished. Instead, I yelped because the patch of ground next to us was moving—and I don't mean it vibrated with the violence of the storm, although it did that too. No. I mean that suddenly the patch of grass that had been next to us was removed by a door opening up from the ground. In its place was a gruff, ruddy-looking face with the most spectacular, raven-dark beard I'd ever seen.

"By the Triplets, but you two are a sight," said the dwarf, and I immediately started scratching my elbow. "The name's Elgar. Best come down before you're washed away." Lightning forked dramatically above our heads. "Or worse. You can wait out the storm with me."

His head vanished, and we both leaned over to peer into the hole. A rusted metal ladder led down into darkness.

"Now!" cried the dwarf again. "And close the door behind you."

Reginald and I exchanged a look.

"Can't be worse than this!" I bellowed.

Reg nodded and started down. I swung my legs in after him and pulled the grass door back over the hole. Then I, too, climbed down into the deep darkness of the dwarf warren.

CHAPTER 5
INTO THE DWARF WARREN

With my leather satchel slung over my shoulder and a smile on my face, I began my descent. With every rung down, I felt more at ease. The dwarves didn't live in the Underworld, strictly speaking, but they did live underground, and that was at least halfway home for me.

It didn't seem to suit Reginald at all, though.

"Ow! You stepped on my fingers again, Mal!"

"Then move faster, *Sir Asstradle*."

"I *can't* move faster. I can't even see my hand in front of my face. What if there are bats in here about to fly at my head? What if it's a thousand-foot drop? What if we've been tricked, and it never ends at all? I can't do this! I'm climbing back up!"

Elgar's voice echoed up from the inky depths.

"I've not tricked ya, lad. We'll be at the bottom any minute now."

I squinted down into the blackness and could, in fact, detect the faintest orange glow.

"See, Reg? We're nearly there."

"Oh gods, I think I'm going to . . ."

"Do not say throw up."

"I wasn't going to say that!" came Reginald's disembodied reply.

"What were you going to say then?"

"I was going to say . . . vomit."

I rested my forehead on a rung and growled.

"I have an idea for how to get you down quicker, Reg."

"What's that, Mal?"

"I can smash my boot down on your fingers until you let go. You'll be at the bottom lickety-split if you're free-falling."

"I'd really rather you didn't."

"Why not tell me your names to take your mind off the dark?" asked Elgar.

"Great idea. The frightened, vomit-y one is Sir Reginald P. Asstradle—a Hero of Widdershins, if you can believe it! I am Lord Malgon Belroth Kirranith of Artifice-on-Lethe, demon of the Underworld."

"Pleased to make your acquaintances, I'm sure." I heard a thump and understood it to mean our dwarf-friend had jumped from the final rung onto the firmament. "Here we are, then!" he called up to us.

"Almost there, Reg! Hold on to your lunch for a few more steps, and you'll be fine."

I heard a second thump and then several more thuds as Reginald lost his footing and tumbled onto the dwarf.

"Get off me!" yelled Elgar.

"Sorry 'bout that," replied Reginald.

I finally reached the end of the ladder and leapt gracefully to the ground. The light was dim, but I could just make out the entrance to a low-ceilinged, packed-earth shaft that led to a tunnel of the same composition. The smell of dirt was strong but clean. There was none of the mustiness that one would usually associate with being below the frost line.

Reginald and Elgar were already at the mouth of the tunnel. Elgar was standing comfortably, but Reginald was bent almost double. A short distance behind them, a torch cast a pleasant amber light across the walls.

"Finally," I said, brushing my hands on my trousers and ducking past them. "This way, then?" I started in the direction of the light, but Elgar held up a hand to stop me. He looked uncomfortable.

"Hold up there! Uh . . . a few things before we get going."

"Oh, of course," I said, tapping the heel of my hand against my forehead. "Where are my manners?" I drew myself up as high as I could in the low space and bowed deeply. "Our sincerest gratitude for your unexpected yet timely rescue. Now can we go?" I turned away again when Elgar said, "Well, if I'm honest, it wasn't entirely unexpected." He was wringing his hands. "I was sort of expecting a demon and a hero to be wandering the plains today."

Reginald and I exchanged a look.

"Why?"

Elgar smirked.

"My cousin was at the inn the other night."

As I was crouching, face occluded, in a dimly lit tunnel, Elgar could not see my pained expression. Thank the Lord of Darkness for small mercies.

"Ah," I said. "Well, that was all a bit of a misunderstanding, you see."

Elgar barked a laugh.

"A misunderstanding? Sounded like quality entertainment if you ask me! But anyway, that's not what I meant. You're about to enter the Realm of the Plain Dwarves."

Reginald's eyes traveled from Elgar's bald head to his enviable beard and down to his silver belt buckle.

"I wouldn't call you *plain*. That's a very fancy belt buckle."

The dwarf's brow furrowed.

"What? No. Not that kind of plain. Like the *Empty Plains*."

Reginald flushed.

"Oh. Yeah. That makes more sense."

"As I was sayin'," said Elgar, as his eyes found a fascinating spot on the ground. "You should know that we are craftsdwarves of the highest order, and everything you'll see in there is proprietary—meaning that it's secret and we don't want you two running your mouths about any of it above ground, you hear? Unless," his eyes darted between us, then focused back on the dirt, "unless someone asks you to, of course. Then you should probably listen and assist in any way you can."

"Sounds like a fair trade for saving our lives," said Reginald.

Something was off about this conversation, but I was willing to say anything to get us moving again.

"Completely understood," I replied as I crossed my fingers behind my back for good measure. I didn't know if we'd see anything worth blabbing about down here, but best to be prepared.

"Excellent!" said Elgar cheerfully. "In we go, then!"

Reginald and I followed the dwarf down the torch-lit hallway, but between our respective heights and the bag of rocks, it was slow going. The passage wound serpentine beneath the plains, periodically dipping so low that we nearly had to crawl. An indeterminate amount of time into our journey, we became so encumbered that we were outstripped by a snail.

It was more than I could take.

"How much longer is this fucking tunnel, Elgar?" I wheezed while squeezing sideways through a narrow crevasse. "The longer this goes on, the less certain I am that I'll be able to fulfill my dream of remaining a three-dimensional being!"

"The worst is over, m'lord. In fact—here we are."

"Oh, thank Lucifer," I gasped as I staggered out of the tunnel. A cavern with proper headroom opened out before us, and I winced as I straightened to full height. Stretching my arms up as high as they could go, I turned my attention to our capacious surroundings.

What I saw took my breath away. Mouth dropping open in amazement, I let my arms flop back down at my sides. Next to me, Reginald was still unfolding himself. I poked him in the ribs until he looked up.

"What was that for? I . . . oh," he said.

The surrounding cavern was lit more purposefully than the tunnel we'd just come through, and that purpose was clear. It was to highlight the gargantuan silver doors set into the rock before us. The sight rendered even Reginald and I speechless, which is—well, I guess it's not saying something—but it's still quite a feat.

Elgar grinned at our reactions as we gaped in awe. Then a thought struck me.

"If you can build something like this," I gestured toward the doors, "why do you leave the way in like that?" I pointed in the direction we'd just come from.

Elgar shrugged.

"Drama. Obviously."

I could appreciate that answer, actually.

"So what happens now?" asked Reginald.

Elgar smiled and cracked his neck with a fist to his chin.

"Oh, you'll like this part," he said with a wink and turned away from us. He strode to a spot right in front of the doors and spread his arms wide. He looked so small compared to the massive entryway.

"One might say that he's *dwarfed* by the doors, right, Reg?"

I beamed at Reginald, but he hadn't even heard my pun, so I scowled and crossed my arms over my chest. His attention was trained on Elgar, who looked as if he were about to perform a conjuring.

The dwarf took a deep breath and in a clear baritone bellowed, "Open, says-a-me!"

His voice echoed energetically around the cavern. But other than that, nothing happened.

"Hm. Okay," he muttered, "maybe it was—Abracadabra!"
Again, nothing.

Elgar turned his head in our direction. He smiled self-consciously and held up a finger.

"Just a moment, gentlemen."

Turning back around, he started rifling through his pockets. He pulled out three differently sized hammers before he found what he was looking for: a crumpled piece of paper. He unfolded it and started mumbling to himself. I turned toward Reginald and raised an eyebrow in question. Was this guy off his rocker? Reginald just shrugged.

"Aha!" cried Elgar in triumph. "I've got it! The magic word is —Please!"

"I could have told him that," murmured Reginald. "My gran's been drilling that into my head for twenty-two years."

The ground beneath our feet stirred as deep rumbling filled the cavern. It was a physical, chest-aching sound that rattled the bones. The doors were swinging rapidly toward us—the speed at which they were moving was incongruous with their size. The engineering prowess of the dwarfs knew no bounds, it seemed. I relaxed a bit, knowing that our guide was not the crackpot I'd briefly suspected him to be.

Well, I *was* relaxed. Until he started yelling.

"I forgot about this! We're too close! Run, run!"

I immediately saw what he meant. One door was on a collision course with Reginald. If it got much closer, it was going to squash him flat. Reginald saw it too, but he was frozen in terror and didn't move.

"Oh no! You don't get to die until I know if your death will kill me too!" I cried and hoisted him up over my shoulder on top of my bag. Sprinting after Elgar, we raced toward the entrance to the tunnel. When we reached it, I tossed Reginald and the bag down on the ground next to the dwarf. Then, shaking, I flopped down beside them as the doors finally stopped moving.

"A heads-up would have been nice, Elgar!" I gasped, gulping down air to catch my breath.

"I told you, I forgot! I rarely come in the front way."

Getting to my knees, I turned back toward the open doors. Beyond them was the dwarven equivalent of Reginald's sanctified anthills. Tier after tier of tunnels were stacked one on top of another—but all were open to a gaping chasm in their midst. Ropes, pulleys, and pallets laden with raw gems and precious metals were moving into and out of the pit with great care. In the tunnels and alcoves, dwarves were building, forging, eating, and training. There were thousands of them, each one of them busy as a bee.

"Reg, you've got to see this!" Despite my general disinterest in anything other than myself, I found it fascinating. "Reg?"

The sound of retching interrupted my observations, and I froze. There was a beat of silence. Then Elgar's voice echoed through the cavern.

"Ew."

My shoulders slumped and I shook my head.

———

AFTER THE CONTENTS of Reginald's stomach made their plea for freedom, the three of us struggled to our feet and officially entered the Realm of the Plain Dwarves. Well, I say the three of us. Mostly, Elgar and I got up and physically dragged Reginald and our bags behind us. We passed through the doors onto a grand balcony that overlooked both the mine below us and the surrounding warren of tunnels. I leaned so far over the railing that my head was almost level with my feet.

"How far down does that go, exactly?"

Elgar screwed up his mouth.

"Not *that* far down. We're not so foolish as to dig into the Underworld."

Feeling my bag slip from my shoulder, I swung myself upright again.

"Just wondering." I caught sight of Reginald's prone form out of the corner of my eye. He was always pale, but the events of the past few days were catching up with him, and he was white as a sheet. He stared, unblinking, up into the shadowy arch of the ceiling. I nudged him with a foot, but he didn't respond.

"Oi, Reg? Asstradle? Anyone in there?"

Nothing.

I turned to Elgar. "Any chance we could, you know, go somewhere where nothing will try to chase us, drown us, or squash us?"

Elgar glanced down at Reginald, then jumped into action.

"Yes, of course. Where are my manners? I invite you down here and nearly get you killed, and now here we are lollygagging at the front door. Your hero needs attention. Come, follow me. My chambers aren't far."

I peeled Reginald up off the ground and swung an arm around his shoulders. He had said nothing since the incident with the door, and though I would never admit it out loud, I was concerned for the lad. The thought stopped me in my tracks.

"Oh no," I said aloud.

"What's that?" asked Elgar, looking back.

"Oh . . . nothing. Never mind. Please, lead the way."

But it wasn't nothing. In the past five centuries, I hadn't concerned myself with anyone other than myself. I fervently hoped that this was a temporary insanity brought on by excessive stress and not the alternative: that our connection was causing him to rub off on me.

I shuddered.

"Come on, Sir Asstradle. We'll be sitting somewhere comfy soon."

Reginald made an unintelligible noise and allowed himself to be led forward.

———

It was fortunate that we had a knowledgeable guide in Elgar because we'd hardly taken three strides before I was lost. I'd already established that I was shit at directions, and this place was a maze. We'd just left a few hollowed-out sparring alcoves behind and appeared to be moving through an industrial area. The dwarves we passed were hard at work. Some were bent double over worktables, jeweler's loupes on their heads. Some were tempering metal over anvils while their furnaces burned bright. Others were tinkering with tools and machines. One tinkerer looked up from her work, narrowed her eyes at us, and swished a yellow curtain across her workspace.

"I'm sensing some animosity, Elgar."

"Yes. Well, strictly speaking, you shouldn't be . . . um . . . here."

"'Here' as in this tunnel, or 'here' as in this warren?"

"The . . . second one?"

More eyes narrowed at us. More curtains were tugged closed as we passed by.

"Then why, may I ask, did you bring us here?"

Elgar was wringing his hands again and picked up his pace.

"Can't I just be a good Samaritan?"

His voice shook, and it was the last suspicious straw. I paused, deposited Reginald against a wall, then reached forward and tugged Elgar back by his collar. He let out a strangled cry and struggled to free himself.

"What are you doing? Get off me!"

I slammed him against the wall next to Reg, who took no

notice. Leveling my head with his, I stared deep into his eyes. Without even thinking about it, I worked a small bit of magic.

"Is it getting darker?" whispered Elgar. "All I can see is your face."

"That's because I need you to give me your undivided attention. Right now I am being nice because you saved us from that flood—even if you did so, as I suspect, for your own nefarious reasons. But you are going to tell me right now what we are doing here, or I swear on my own damnation I will toss you over the railing into the mine below. I am a demon, which makes me a bloodhound for ill intent, and you don't smell so great. So don't give me any more of this 'good Samaritan' dragon shit. Why are we here?"

Elgar was shaking with fear, but he'd stopped struggling.

"Fine. Okay. Yes. I had an ulterior motive. I have this invention, see? And I need someone to take it topside and promote it on my behalf. I heard from my cousin that you were headed to Seven, which would be a great market for it. So . . . now you know."

I pulled back the magic and the light returned to normal.

"Oh. That doesn't sound so bad. Why all the subterfuge?"

Elgar's eyes darted back and forth down the tunnel.

"Look, I promise I'll tell you everything once we reach my place. It's just around the next corner."

I let go of his shoulder where I'd pinned him against the wall and tugged down the sleeves of my coat.

"Fine," I said, gesturing in front of us. "Lead on, then."

I turned toward Reginald and cocked my head at his bony figure propped up against the wall. He looked like a gangly rag doll but, Hell's Bells, was he heavy. I really didn't want to carry him anymore, so I lowered him to the ground, grabbed his wrist, and pulled. I paused for a moment, listening, but he made no objections, so I dragged him the rest of the way to Elgar's.

IF I COULD SUM the dwarven race up in a word, it would be *fastidious*, and Elgar was no exception. As we rounded the corner of the tunnel and entered his chambers, I marveled at the impeccable order before me. The back wall was hollowed out into cubbies of various sizes and shapes to accommodate plates, clothes, books, and close to three hundred hammers. Maybe. I didn't actually count. But it was a lot of hammers.

I peered into a few more cubbies as I passed by and saw a folded piece of parchment with the words PLAIN DWARVES WARREN stamped on top. A furtive glance showed me it was a map. I lifted it surreptitiously from its cubby and slipped it into an interior pocket of my waistcoat. That might have been ungrateful, but the way I saw it, our need was greater than Elgar's. He knew the place like the back of his hand, whereas Reg and I did not—and we'd gotten into the habit of needing a quick exit.

"Make yourselves at home."

I dragged Reginald to a small table in the center of the room and heaved him up onto a chair. The natural, familiar act of sitting in a comfortable chair as a normal human does must have been just what he needed, because he came back to himself. He blinked as he gazed around the spotless apartment, and his eyebrows rose so high they were at his hairline.

"Where are we? Also, how did I get here?"

I gestured toward Elgar.

"We're at Elgar's place. Do you remember Elgar?"

Reginald nodded slowly.

"Great. Then the answer to your second question is that I dragged you."

"Oh. Thank you? I guess?"

"You're welcome."

I settled myself into one of the other chairs and deposited

our bags on the floor next to me just as Elgar came over with three mugs.

"Tea for you," he said, setting the cup down in front of me. "Tea for me," he said, sliding a cup over to the empty chair. "And rootshine for you, lad." He slammed the mug down in front of Reginald.

"Why am I the only one with rootshine?"

"You're the only one that needs it, Reg."

I turned to Elgar and pointed down into my cup.

"Did you, perchance—"

"I put a tear in it from when you threatened me earlier. Still had one dripping down my cheek."

"Lovely. Thank you. It means a lot that you would remember demonic customs."

Elgar lifted his mug into the air.

"You are our closest neighbors."

I nodded in acknowledgment and took a sip.

"Huh. That tastes truly terrifying. I almost feel bad."

"Why did you threaten him, Mal?" Reginald was eyeing his own mug suspiciously.

"Oh, don't be rude, Reg. Just drink the fucking drink."

"I would. It's just, my gran told me this stuff will burn away my internal organs."

"It'll feel like it, lad," said Elgar. "But it won't truly harm ya. Not that much, anyway. You'll feel the burning, and then there will probably be a period of swearing as it moves through ya, and then you'll be right as rain."

Reginald? *Swearing?* That was a sight I needed to see. I spun my finger in a circle, indicating it was time to get drinking. His expression was one of a man on his way to the gallows, but he lifted the glass anyway.

"Bottom's up."

And then Sir Reginald P. Asstradle chugged the whole mug.

When he first set it down, everything seemed copacetic. But then . . .

"Is . . . is my body on fire? I think I'm on fire."

Reginald jumped out of his seat and started running around the room, screaming. Elgar leaned over and whispered to me, "That's the fire part."

This went on for an uncomfortably long time. Out of the corner of my eye, I saw Elgar raise his mug to take a sip of his tea. The motion also caught Reginald's attention, and his eyes flicked toward the dwarf. He prowled over to us, leaned across the table, and pointed a finger right in Elgar's face.

"*You!*"

"And," yelped Elgar as he backed away from Reginald's finger, "this is probably the swearing part."

I lounged back in my chair, hands clasped behind my head, a broad grin stretched across my face. I was ready for the show. If feelings was the Reginald thing that was rubbing off on me, then I felt sure that swearing was absolutely the gift I gave to Reg.

He paced across the floor, arms flailing over his head, and started yelling.

"You're a real donkey's uncle, Elgar, you know that?"

I stopped grinning. Donkey's uncle?

"Anyone serving this stuff should be thrown in jail on grounds of being a . . . a nincompoop!"

Nincompoop? I buried my face in my hands. Reginald was messing up swearing? What was it with this kid?

"That's really the best you can do, Reg?"

Reginald looked unsure of himself, then his face lit like a beacon. He faced Elgar again.

"I hope you get a sounder of boars up your backside!"

Reg looked back at me, the need for approval etched across his face.

"I give you a three for obscenities but a nine for enthusiasm."

"I can live with that," he said as he sat back down at the table.

Elgar looked daggers at both of us.

"So, is that over, then?"

Reginald looked up at the ceiling. Knowing him as I did, I guessed he was doing a mental inventory of the organs the rootshine had burned through and cataloguing all the pseudo-swears he knew.

"Yeah. I think that's it. Wow. I've never said so many bad words in my life."

"Reg, you didn't say *any* bad words."

He smiled gratefully over at me.

"Yeah. Right. Just don't tell my gran, okay?"

I sighed.

"You got it, partner. Now, for the answer to your other question—why *did* I threaten you, Elgar?"

Elgar peered sheepishly at the two of us over the rim of his mug. Then he sighed and rested it back on the table.

"My intentions in bringing you down here might not have been wholly selfless. Dwarves are, by their nature, a secretive race. We've created some magnificent art and ingenious inventions—but for what? They're all just collecting dust down here with no one to appreciate them, and now it turns out they've attracted a Grootslang!"

I sucked in a quick breath.

"Oh, that's not good."

"What's a Grootslang?" asked Reginald.

"Well, lad. I want to say it's a snake, but that's not exactly right. If a Grootslang is a snake, then a pebble is a boulder, if you take my meaning. It's bigger than any snake you've ever seen, I reckon. And they covet exactly two things: flesh and shiny things."

"Oh," said Reg. "That's not good."

"Exactly," said Elgar. "Anyway—I have this invention that I think could be a real game changer. It's a type of communication device, you see."

I furrowed my brow.

"So why don't you just go up and hock it yourself?"

Elgar nodded.

"For one—we're in pretty close quarters down here, so it's been tough sneaking out to try to sell it. Everyone's all, 'Where are you going, Elgar?' and 'What's in the bag, Elgar?' and 'Put on some pants, Elgar!'"

Reg and I blinked at him. Elgar flushed crimson when he realized what he'd said. We sat in awkward silence, digesting the vision of a pants-less Elgar, until he coughed once and continued.

"Plus . . . you may have noticed that I'm not exactly what you would call charismatic. I crumble under pressure, and when I showed it off in front of an audience, I couldn't explain myself properly. One time I got so nervous that I dropped a prototype into the Marais."

I shuddered.

"But," he continued, "when I heard that the first hero-demon duo in five centuries was headed my way, I got a great idea: celebrity endorsement! You two have got to be pretty popular, right? It's been five hundred years!"

I kept my face serene and agreeable, but Reginald was frowning. Not wanting to chance him opening his mouth to contradict Elgar, I kicked him.

"Ow!"

"What is it?" asked Elgar.

"Oh, nothing. Sorry. Bit my tongue," said Reginald, scowling at me.

Elgar looked back and forth between us a few times, then shrugged and went on.

"Anyway, that's when I went up top to see if I could flag you down and whatnot. Imagine my delight when you were sitting half-drowned right at the front door!"

Reginald is not usually one for sardonicism, but the lingering effects of the rootshine plus the kick had him in a saucy mood. His face remained placid, but he folded his arms across his chest, looked Elgar straight in the eye, and said, "Yes. I'm sure you were delighted."

Elgar grimaced.

"That's not what I meant, but see—you're proving my point! I'm bad at this. But if you two were to do this thing for me, I think it would sell like a half-priced Bronzon."

"Like what?" I asked.

"Bronzon? The best hammer a dwarf can . . . oh, never mind."

I tilted my head, considering. There was nothing saying that we couldn't be celebrity endorsers and get ourselves to Seven. I quite liked the idea of being adored for no reason other than being myself. Plus, I had to think about my life after we returned the Stone of Eno—assuming we eventually returned it.

In the deepest recesses of my mind, a thought was scratching at the walls of my consciousness. What if this screwup was just too big? My parents had barely smoothed over everything that followed in wake of my failed maneuver to fix the Hero contract in demons' favor. (Lucifer had not been pleased at my "meager effort.") I never thought I'd get a chance at redemption, but then Absentminded Asstradle had summoned me, and I'd gotten a second chance. The performance of the first significant act of demonic evil in half a millennium had been in my grasp, and it slipped away. Plus, there was still a chance that being connected to Reginald would have adverse, anti-evil effects on me. I might not even be allowed back home.

"Okay. I'm listening. Tell us about this communication device. Does it translate languages? Interpret babies? What is it?"

"Those are both . . . fantastic ideas. Wow. But no. It's a rectangular handheld apparatus with a few methodically honed gems. The gems catch certain vibrations in the air—specifically voices. So say you and I each had one. If I talked into mine, you could hear me in yours—even if you were as many as forty leagues away! With these devices, people can be in touch with their friends and loved ones no matter where they are in Widdershins. You can stay connected forever!"

Elgar's face was alight with pride and purpose.

Mine was carved in disbelief. I blinked twice at Elgar to give him the opportunity to tell me he was joking, then laughed. No, actually, "laughing" is too tame a term. I howled as Elgar's face fell from pride to befuddlement. Seeing that it was entirely lost on him why I was in hysterics, I calmed myself enough to explain.

"Elgar. I have to say. We are the worst possible people to rope into this scheme."

"What? Why's that?"

"The reason we are headed to Seven is that we mistakenly destroyed the Stone of Eno." I gestured to my bag. "And now the two of us are going to be 'connected' forever if the wizards can't use their magic to separate us again. And trust us—connection is not all it's cracked up to be. In fact, this might be the stupidest idea I've ever heard. Which is saying something because I have to listen to Reginald's ideas all day." I turned to Reg. "No offense."

He squinted at me.

"Offense taken."

"Right," I continued. "Seriously, Elgar. In what realm do you think someone would voluntarily stay connected to other people? People are the fucking worst! They say the word 'literally' when they actually mean 'figuratively,' they talk in the privy, they fight each other over absolute nonsense. At least demons have the decency to own up to what they are. Humans are duplicitous, back-stabbing little shits, with less self-awareness than worms."

"I mean, some of them. But not all of them. Plus . . ." said Reg, stroking his chin.

"No, Reg . . ."

"It would be nice to stay in touch with my gran. And Bitsy Wigglebottom. If Bitsy had one, I could talk to her right now."

"She's a dog, Reg. She's not going to—"

"My supervisor, my school chums, my neighbor Adolph Brownoser. Wow, Elgar," Reginald said. "This is a terrific idea. You could learn a thing or two from Elgar, Mal. Maybe people wouldn't be 'the worst' if they weren't so lonely and cut off from the people they care about. You know what we have now for communication? A couple of amaranthine galloping around the world on horseback. That's not exactly immediate."

Reginald looked pointedly at me, so I mimicked him sarcastically.

Elgar cut in.

"I'll give you twenty percent of the profits!"

Reginald's eyes grew wide.

"Is that a lot of money?"

Elgar opened his mouth, then closed it again.

"I don't really know. It depends how well it sells."

Unfortunately, that seemed to be good enough for Reginald.

"Okay. We'll do it!"

I narrowed my eyes at him.

"You're serious? You really want to help Elgar? A few minutes ago, you were calling him a nincompoop!"

"That was the rootshine talking."

"No. That was the truth. All the rootshine did was drown

out the pious brainwashing your uncultured upbringing saddled you with."

Reginald thought about that for a moment.

"Can't he be a nincompoop *and* have a great idea?"

"I sure can," interjected Elgar before I had time to argue anymore. "It's settled. Here are the prototypes." He placed two rectangular objects on the table. "You'll sell them in the City of Seven and get twenty percent of whatever you make. Now," he let out a dramatic yawn. "I'm exhausted, and you two look about done in. How about a quick bite and then some rest?"

"That sounds excellent," said Reginald.

My mind itched to be going, but my body wouldn't follow.

"Fine. But just for a bit. Then we really need to be on our way."

Elgar hopped up from his chair and started bustling around the tiny kitchen. It was just a potbelly stove, a counter, and an icebox, all set in a row against the wall. The sound of earthenware plates clattering and a knife hitting a cutting board provided a domestic soundtrack to our continuing conversation.

"So you broke the Stone of Eno, huh? And you think I'm stupid."

I sighed.

"Now, Elgar, don't put words in my mouth. I didn't say *you* were stupid. I said your *idea* was stupid."

"That's not a lot better," he grumbled.

"Elgar," Reginald interrupted, "do you know anything about the stone?"

He shrugged, then put some purple potatoes and carrots on a plate.

"Not much. I know it was given to the dryads for safe-keeping and that Quill Valor stole it from them."

"So they didn't make it themselves?" asked Reginald.

"That's not how I heard it. But who knows with the old tales, right? Hard to tell truth from fiction sometimes."

"Hard indeed," I mused. "But assuming your version is right —you don't know who gave it to them? Or what it does?"

Elgar set plates of root vegetables and jerky down on the table in front of us.

"Sorry, fellas. I don't."

Reginald attacked the food as if he hadn't eaten in days. Which, I suppose, we hadn't. We'd had nothing but flatbread and cheese since buying them days ago, and the last of our paltry supply had run out the night before—plus, Reg had upchucked in the cavern earlier. But I had too much on my mind to eat, and frankly, I was just too tired. I leaned back to close my eyes and contemplate everything I'd just learned and was asleep in seconds.

CHAPTER 6

A GROOTSLANG AND A CONFESSION

"Where is he? That scoundrel is at it again!"

I sat up with a start and wrenched my neck. I was still bone-weary, so we couldn't have been asleep for long.

"Who the fuck was that?"

Reginald lifted his head from the table where he, too, had fallen asleep. There was a piece of jerky stuck to the side of his face. I peeled it off and tossed it on a plate. The voice boomed again.

"Elgar Dishonorable Dwarfson!"

We turned our heads toward Elgar.

"Oh no," he said.

Elgar's shoulders sagged, and he hung his head wearily as a fierce-looking dwarf with an eye patch came thundering around the corner. She was Elgar's opposite in every way. Where he was pale with a rich black beard, she was sable-skinned with cloud-white hair. He was diminutive, and she was nearly the same height as Reginald. He was forgettable. She was formidable.

"Rumor has it you've got yourself another pair of strays in here. And, ah yes. Here they are."

"Another?" I said to Elgar. He cringed.

"I might have tried this once or twice before."

"Ha!" barked the visitor. "At least." She prowled around our table, never turning her ireful stare from Reginald and me. As she walked, she bounced the shaft of her axe against her hand. "A demon and a hero walk into a dwarf warren. Sounds like the beginning of a joke. But how does it end?"

"Why do people keep saying that?" I whispered to Reg. He shrugged but didn't answer.

"Sir Reginald. Lord Malgon. Let me introduce the head of my clan, Gerta Dwarfson."

"Charmed," I said, not rising from my seat or breaking eye contact with Gerta. Reginald moved to stand, but I placed a hand on his shoulder, and he lowered himself back down.

Gerta tossed her axe down on the ground so she could splay both hands on the table. It was a scare tactic I'd used myself occasionally.

"Let me guess. Elgar here wants you to take his invention and sell it topside. Well, I absolutely forbid it."

I arched an eyebrow.

"You *forbid* it?"

She sneered at me.

"Are you deaf, demon? Yes, I forbid it. What has topside ever done except belittle us? While they're up there telling short jokes, beneath their feet is an ever-expanding wonder that they will never see. The collections we have amassed— including Elgar's communication device—will stay here where they are appreciated appropriately, as is our law. Elgar is trying to circumvent bureaucracy, and I won't stand for it!"

"What about the Grootslang?" I asked.

A flicker of fear crossed her face, but it was gone in a flash.

"We have it under control," she said with what anyone could see was false confidence.

"Gerta, was it? Here's the thing—I've lived underground all my life, and I can say with unerring certainty that no one but the Archfiend himself has ever had a Grootslang 'under control.'"

At this point, I'd heard enough. Did I think Elgar's invention was stupid? Yes. Was I going to take it anyway because authority could go blow me? Yes. Yes, I was.

I unfurled myself from my chair and stood to full height. Well, almost to full height. Honestly, the intimidation I'd intended was lessened by the fact that I could not stand upright in Elgar's apartment, but I was still a full head taller than Gerta.

"The situation is this, *dwarf*. You may not stand for it, but I will."

Gerta and I stared at each other for so long that her eyes watered. That's when I shouted,

"Run, Reg! Run!"

Mercifully, he must have read the room, and he was ready. Pocketing the prototypes and dragging the bags, he dashed out the door with me on his heels. The axe made a *thunk* as it sunk into the packed earth beside me. Gerta growled in frustration, but I paid her no heed.

Catching up to Reg, we ran comically side by side, half-hunched over.

"Why did you decide to help him?" panted Reg.

"Because rules are for the weak-minded and unimaginative. Now—do you know how to get out of here?"

Reg tried to turn his head to look at me, but it was no use.

"Me? You're the one who said 'run.' I assumed you did."

"Oh, right! The map!"

I felt around in my pockets for the map, marveling at my forethought about taking it. The pounding of many boots sounded behind us, and we quickened our pace.

"Should you really be the one with the map?" Reginald yelled.

"Too late to switch now!"

Taking random lefts and rights as the paths forked before

us, we tried to shake off our pursuers, but we hadn't lost them yet.

"So I think—ow!" I yelled as I smashed my forehead into a rogue root sticking out of the ceiling. "If we take the next two lefts, that should lead us to a tunnel that leads topside."

"You know what's kind of funny?"

I couldn't think of anything that might seem funny at the moment.

"No, what?"

"I'm twenty-two years old, and I'd never even heard the word 'topside' until I met you!"

We took a left.

"We may need to talk about what constitutes humor, Reg."

The way got even lower, and we ended up crawling. But we took the next left, crawled a few more yards, and felt a change in the air. After a few feet, we emerged into a cavern. The perimeter and ceiling were cloaked in darkness, but there must have been light coming from somewhere because the center of the space was flat and open aside from a few russet boulders that looked like they'd probably descended, at haste, from the ceiling at some point. The air was cooler, and I caught the faint sound of rushing water nearby. Hearing it gave me a sudden realization.

"Reg, stop moving and listen."

He stopped.

"I don't hear anything."

I grinned at him.

"Exactly! They've stopped following us! If we can just find the exit, we'll be home free!"

I pulled the map in front of me again, and Reginald turned to examine it as well.

"Now, I think we're here," I said. "And if I'm correct, that means . . ."

"Do you think that's the Grootslang?"

"What?" I peered down at the map where there was a hand-drawn squiggle. "Oh. That's probably just decoration."

"No, not there. *There.*"

I raised my head slowly and saw that Reginald was not looking at the map but at a snake as tall as a tree. Its scales were such a deep emerald that out of the light they appeared black, and its eyes were brilliant and auriferous and trained right on us. Long fangs protruded past its bottom jaw, and a forked, crimson tongue flicked out of its mouth. Aside from that, it was motionless, but there was no doubt that it had noticed us.

"Yes, Reg," I gulped. "That is the Grootslang."

———

THE GROOTSLANG BROUGHT ITS VAST, serpentine head down to our level and hissed. They say that at these moments, sentient beings submit to either their fight or flight instinct. But our bodies rebelled against such mundane evolutionary traits and instead experienced paralyzing indecision. Frozen in place like a pair of scared mice, we silently willed the creature to seek something else for lunch. The chance of being squashed by a rogue ceiling boulder suddenly seemed like a much better way to die.

"Maybe if we don't move, it won't see us," whispered Reginald. Even as he said it, his shaking knees caused the bags to shift noisily against his shoulder.

The Grootslang hissed again and brought its head even closer.

"I don't think that's how it works with a Grootslang, Reg."

The creature began circling us with its massive body. Grootslangs, we were discovering, like to play with their food before they strike. I closed my eyes so I wouldn't have to watch, but that only amplified the swishing sound of impending doom.

"I guess this is the end," Reginald whimpered.

"I guess so."

We let that sink in as the Grootslang picked up speed around us.

"Do you have any regrets, Mal?"

"Some. Right now I'm regretting that we're alone in this cavern, so there will be no songs sung about how we died."

"I could sing a song right now, if it would help."

I smiled then. Not a smirk. Not a sly grin. An *actual* smile. Even if we didn't die in the belly of the Grootslang, I was fucking doomed.

"Reg?"

"What's that?"

I sighed.

"I need to tell you something."

The Grootslang was tightening the circle. I took a deep breath and spoke my confession on a whoosh of air.

"The reason I don't have a tail is because you have to earn your tail and your horns—they are a badge of honor that says 'I'm Lucifer's fav' and I've done nothing to warrant them and my whole family is really embarrassed about it and I don't really know why I'm telling you this but I guess it's because I'm about to die an absolute failure to my kind and I thought someone should know."

Reginald was silent for a moment.

"Wow. There's a lot to unpack there."

I opened my mouth to retort but was interrupted.

"No need to unpack it yet, friends."

A wee figure materialized out of the darkness at the edge of the cavern beside us.

"Elgar!" Reg shouted past the Grootslang.

"Are you here to save us?" I shouted as well.

"That's the idea," he called back.

"So I just confessed my deepest, darkest secret for nothing?"

"It appears that way."

"Well, that's just my luck," I grumbled.

The Grootslang paused its circling, unsure how to proceed with its dinner split into two courses.

"Oi! Grootslang!" called Elgar. "I'll make you a deal."

The monstrous snake cocked its head to one side, listening.

"Let these two go, and I'll give you these shiny diamonds." Elgar held out his hand and wiggled his fingers, revealing a palm full of translucent, sparkly gems.

The Grootslang swung its head back and forth, looking from us to the diamonds. It was clearly a tough decision.

"I'll even throw in this ruby," said Elgar, producing a red gem the size of his fist from a pocket.

I was feeling a little bad about how I'd treated Elgar. He was bartering a small fortune for our release—and it was working. The Grootslang slithered over to Elgar and put its head down on the ground. Elgar dumped the diamonds and the ruby into a small sack and hung it on one of its fangs. It lifted its head, hissed menacingly at Reg and me, then slithered away.

"We don't have a lot of time," whispered Elgar. "Come this way."

"Are the other dwarves still after us?" asked Reginald.

"No. They gave up as soon as they saw you were headed for the Grootslang."

"So why don't we have a lot of time?"

"Because what I actually gave the beast was a combination of rock candy and cut glass—so let's go!"

We heard a roaring, crashing sound behind us and high-tailed it out of the cavern. Fortunately, Elgar knew how to get us to the exit.

"Here's the tunnel. It's a steep climb, but it will take you right to the foot of the Giant's Fingers."

The walls of the tunnel were vibrating, and bits of dirt and rock were falling from the ceiling. We all looked up at it, shielding our eyes from the debris.

"Yup," said Elgar. "Grootslang's mad."

"Are you going to be okay?" asked Reginald, eyes wide with worry.

"Oh, I'm not afraid of the Grootslang. Gerta, on the other hand . . ." Elgar grimaced and his eyes unfocused. He was imagining some horror that awaited him when he made it back to his clan. Then he snapped back to the present and shooed us up the tunnel. "Go, go! Get out of here!"

I put a hand on his shoulder.

"I might have misjudged you, Elgar."

He grimaced.

"You can repay me by selling my invention. Now, run!"

We took off up the tunnel at a sprint, leaving Elgar to deal with the mess we'd left behind.

BY THE TIME we reached the end of the tunnel, we were wheezing, sweating, and exhausted. Reginald in particular seemed unsteady on his feet. He let the bags drop from his shoulder and leaned against the wall.

"Are muscles supposed to wobble like this? I've never been this tired in my life. Or this hungry."

"You just ate!"

"That was last night! At least, I think it was. Plus, it was mostly carrots!"

I was hungry too. Starving, actually. But neither of us could afford to think about that now.

"We've just . . . got to make . . . it out," I panted. Bent double with my hands on my knees, I felt the world spin and closed my eyes. We just needed to get to the top of the ladder, and that would lead us back up into the sun. Presumably. Unless it was nighttime. Anyway, we'd be back in Widdershins, and considering the horde of angry dwarves and the furious ancient beast we'd just left behind, it was where we needed to be.

"Come on, Sir Asstradle. Time to hero up."

Reginald groaned but reached for the ladder. I swiped the bags from the floor before following him, and rung by rung we climbed out of the dwarf warren and into the Giant's Fingers.

CHAPTER 7
THE CHARITY RUN

"Merciless Satan, am I glad to be out of that cursed warren."

I winced at the sunlight as Reginald and I pulled ourselves up out of the dwarf door and back into the wider world. Sprawling like a couple of sunbathing butterflies on a stone, we basked in the warmth and fresh air.

"I'm not sure I'll ever be able to move again," said Reginald.

I craned my neck in his direction and spotted a bush just beyond his head.

"Oh, I think you will, Reg."

"No, Mal. I'm not sure my arms even work anymore."

"What if I told you there was a black currant bush just past that rock over there?"

Reginald was on his feet, quick as a jackrabbit.

"Food! Glorious, tiny, purple food!"

I was starved too. Enough to take a gander at the berries as well. Rolling over onto my front, I pushed myself up off the ground with a groan and curved a finger around the straps on our bags. Getting to the bush was a struggle that elicited a grunt with every step. I picked a handful of berries and popped one into my mouth. It was so tart my lips puckered and a shiver went down my spine.

"I didn't think you'd be able to eat these."

Reginald's mouth was full of currents so it sounded more like, "Ah umm mh uuliss."

"There are a few exceptions to the preparation rule, actually. For example, if the food item is torturous to eat all on its own, then I can consume it. Also, I still have some of these from your gran." I held up a few packets of demon dust.

"Why did she have those, anyway?"

I winked at him.

"Oh, Reginald. I think there might be more to your gran than meets the eye."

He opened his mouth, then closed it. I didn't think he was ready to contemplate just how *worldly* his grandmother might be. He cast his eyes anywhere but at me and, in doing so, gained a new appreciation for the next leg of our journey.

"Golly. Those are some tall mountains."

We'd been so relieved about getting out of the warren and finding some food that we really hadn't taken in our surroundings. The Empty Plains were mercifully behind us, and we were on a round hill at the foot of the Giant's Fingers. Gray rock faces loomed above us, their tips shrouded in clouds. They seemed impossibly tall, and I felt less certain about trying to cross them.

"They looked big from the other side of the plains, but now they're unreal," said Reginald.

I'd been having the same thought.

"And you're sure there aren't really giants there?" he asked.

"The giants died out centuries ago, but the mountains jut up from the ground tall and columnar, so they *look* like a giant's fingers. No. The dangers before us are freezing or falling to our deaths. But no matter their size or the risk," I said. "Crossing them is our next step. So stop gorging yourself on currants. It'll give you a stomachache, and who's going to be the one to deal with it? Me. That's who. Probably will have to carry you through the pass, won't I?"

Reginald flopped down on his back next to the bush and rubbed his belly.

"Too late."

I rolled my eyes and finished my handful of berries. Then I laid back down as well. A granite boulder behind the currant bush partially sheltered us. The shade from the shadow it cast plus the relative safety had me more relaxed than I'd felt in over a week. I was just drifting off to sleep when Reginald said, "So about what you said when we thought we were going to be eaten by a giant snake . . ."

I groaned.

"I was hoping you'd forgotten about that."

"Come on, Mal. You're the one who brought it up—why *don't* you have a tail or horns yet?"

My stomach felt queasy. For some reason, I felt uncomfortable telling him about it.

"I know that the standard picture of a demon, according to you humans, is horns, tail, pitchfork, right? But actually, not having them isn't uncommon. It's just uncommon for a Kirranith, like me."

"A Kirranith?"

I shook my head in resigned frustration.

"Sometimes you really are a brainless twit. That's my name. Malgon Belroth Kirranith. Anyway, demons with those additional appendages have differentiated themselves from the run-of-the-mill demons—the appendages are a reward from Lucifer. My brother, for example, entered into a contract for a quest to destroy a magical mirror. The payment he extracted was cursing a princess to sleep for a hundred years. It was particularly evil because she not only had been engaged to a politically satisfactory prince but loved him as well. The Archfiend took notice and, as a reward, granted my brother a tail and horns."

Reginald's eyebrows rose.

"Wow. That is horrible."

I nodded.

"Yes. It's a high honor. My entire family is exceedingly evil. But I..." I trailed off.

Reginald shot me a small smile.

"You're not that bad?"

Maybe it was the fatigue or the relentless peril. Maybe Reg had found and pressed a hitherto unknown insecurity button deep inside me. Either way—out of nowhere—I exploded.

"Didn't you just hear me? My family is basically second in command to Lucifer himself! I understand that you've personified me—that you consider me a kind of wayward but otherwise acceptable human. But I am *not* a human. I am a demon and demons have two priorities. The first is to look out for themselves. And when all things are satisfactory in that camp, their only other function is to make as much mischief as fucking possible. That's it! You want to know the real reason I haven't earned my tail or my horns? It's not because I don't have the spine for it. I assure you that if the opportunity presented itself to burn Beadledom City Hall to the ground, I would do so and then dance in the ashes. If it were possible for me to turn all the gold of the world into dragon pellets and cackle at the rich as they scrambled through bank vaults full of shit—I would do it in a heartbeat. No, it's because I wasn't privy to the best hero missions back in the golden age. Those all fell to the older generations. While I was helping some low-rung hero steal a purse back from a thief, my father was helping Valor retrieve treasure from a dragon's horde! How was I supposed to compete with that? I tried with the Hero contract but . . . Anyway, when you summoned me, I thought, *This is it. This is finally my shot.* But no. You've gone and fucked that up for me as well. So don't go acting like you know me or my life, *human*. You don't know the first thing about it! I am a Kirranith and I am evil to my core."

I was panting by the end of my rant, but Reginald just got up and stretched his arms toward the sky.

"Strong words, Mal. But every family's got a black sheep. Or a white sheep in your case, I suppose."

I growled. I wanted to rage, but Reginald was so passive that it was impossible to pick a fight with him. Stomping back to the dwarf door in a huff, I got too far ahead and felt the familiar zinging sensation just before we collided painfully together. Rubbing a growing lump on my head, I felt all my anger drain away, replaced by a limp emptiness. I blew out a long breath and said, "I'm not really a lord, you know."

Reginald's head cocked in my direction as if nothing I'd been saying was surprising to him at all.

"Oh?"

"Well," I corrected, "I am. I just mean that it's a pity title. Artifice-on-Lethe is on the farthest outskirts of Hell. There's nothing there. It doesn't need a lord. My parents convinced Lucifer to bequeath it to me so that they wouldn't have to be embarrassed by my complete lack of personal achievements. Lucifer granted it on the condition that I confine myself to that place forever and never try to 'help' ever again. He was . . . not overly excited that I botched up the Hero contract assignment."

"Oh," said Reginald.

"Yes," I said. "He will not be too pleased with me about all this, I think. I just wish I could do something worthy of being a Kirranith. Even something smallish, like casting a town into infinite darkness—"

"That's smallish?"

"—then maybe my parents would come around. Then I could be more than the Collapser of Soufflés or the Giver of Papercuts."

"Don't forget the humblebrag."

My mouth formed a sad smile.

"How could I?"

"Hey," said Reg, resting a hand on my shoulder. "Don't be so hard on yourself. Papercuts are a b . . . b . . . well, anyway, they're a bummer."

I blinked at him.

"Did you just try to say that paper cuts are a bitch?"

He grimaced.

"Yeah. I did."

"You tried to swear. To make me feel better."

Reginald shrugged.

I put a hand on his shoulder as well.

"You don't know how much that means to me, Reg."

He opened his mouth to reply, but we both stilled, then hit the ground as the sound of voices reached us from the other side of the boulder.

"Who could that be?" I whispered rhetorically. Together, we belly-crawled to the rock and peered around the side. To our astonishment, there was a temporary-looking tent town down the hill from us. Garnet, crimson, and ruddy umber tents all flew slim scarlet flags in the fading light of dusk. Some tents were obviously for sleeping, but others appeared to be for bartering and selling. I saw a man on a stool under a wine-colored awning with barrels full of spices in every color imaginable: canary yellow, cerulean blue, deepest eggplant, and more. The tent next to him had steam curling in fanciful tendrils from its peak. People, dwarves, trolls, and other creatures wrapped in towels entered and exited at intervals, and I took it to be a sauna.

"But people avoid the plains," said Reginald, confused. "And we have firsthand knowledge as to why. They are terrifying. So why are these people here?"

I scanned the tents and crowds for weapons. A couple of

knives shoved into belt loops, a stone-tipped spear leaning up against a tent pole, and a man stumbling down a wide avenue in the center of the tents, holding a mug in one hand dragging a broad sword behind him with the other. That was it.

"I don't know, but I only see a handful of weapons. It seems pretty safe. And it's getting dark. Why don't we go check it out."

Reginald pulled his head back from the boulder and studied my face in the dim light.

"'Only a handful of weapons?' That doesn't sound safe to me. But say they are nice—are you going to steal from these people? Or pretend you're going to pull out their teeth? Or do some other nonmagical mischief making?"

I gaped at Reginald in mock astonishment.

"Who—me? Of course not!"

He cocked an eyebrow and crossed his arms.

"Okay, probably. But I don't set out to do these things, Reg. They happen *organically*. And hey—is that guy selling roasted pork?"

Reginald was back to craning his head around the rock in an instant. Spotting the pork vendor, his pupils dilated, and he turned his creepy eyes on me.

"Fine. We will go down. But we are doing this my way. And by my way, I mean the nice, polite way."

I held my palms up.

"Nice and polite. Got it."

We struggled over the boulder—and I mean struggled. I felt as if my muscles had been petrified. Every motion was agony. But eventually we were down the hill, entering the makeshift village near the spice trader's tent. I wrinkled my nose as the scents of cinnamon and lavender wafted over us.

"Greetings, travelers," the spice man said with a smile bright enough to rival his wares. He had a round, friendly, deeply tanned face. His outfit was simple, beige homespun.

Traders—even poor ones—were usually dressed to the nines to give the impression of success and wealth. Not this one.

I found myself mirroring the man's smile unintentionally, so I smacked myself on the cheek to dislodge it. The act didn't seem to phase him. "You two look like you've traveled a tough road recently. Your auras are looking pretty dim."

I scowled at his use of "aura"—a thing I do not believe in—but looked down at myself, anyway. My usually spotless ebony morning coat was dusty and pilling, and my boots desperately needed a shine. A gust of wind blew down from the mountains. It whipped at my cravat, and I saw it was fraying—thin, dark threads unspooling in the wind as if trying to escape. Reginald's once-white shirt was a disgusting, multicolored chronicle of all our adventures. Green grass stains from the fairies and muddy brown dirt smudges from our time crawling into and out of the dwarf warren.

"We've had a bit of a week," I said.

The round-faced man nodded in sympathy and eased himself off his stool.

"Then, come. Have some food, enjoy the warmth of a fire, and rest a while."

Reginald looked stricken.

"We wish we could," he said, eyeing the pig on a spit a few tents down. "We *really* wish we could. But we don't have any money."

The man smiled again.

"That's nothing to worry yourselves over. This is the Charity Run. We're not expecting payment."

"The Charity Run?" The word "charity" tasted weird on my tongue, so I muttered a few curse words under my breath to cleanse my palate.

"Between the Inner and Outer Sea there are a bunch of nomads, runaways, and just plain lonely folks like you living along the base of the mountains. Three times a year we make the journey to see if there's anything we can provide to make their lives a little easier."

"Are you Threeists, then?" asked Reginald, and I elbowed him while surreptitiously scratching behind my ear.

"Oh, no," the man said with a laugh. "Not that there's anything wrong with that, mind. Sometimes I wish I was. It would be a comfort to think that something bigger than me had my best interests in mind. But no. We're just a group of people who've had it hard in the past and have the means and opportunity to help others now."

"That sounds s—" I was about to say "suspicious," but I caught sight of Reginald shaking his head at me. "—sweet of you."

He shrugged.

"All we can do is our best."

"That is so true," I replied, and Reginald rolled his eyes so dramatically I'm surprised he didn't lose his balance.

We chatted and walked along with the man—whose name turned out to be Alowe—until we reached a roaring fire at the center of the tent city. He sat us down on a log beside it and hurried away to get us some food and blankets.

"What luck is this?" Reginald asked as I rubbed my hands together and held them up to the fire. "Free food, free fire, free rest? Not even you could deny that this is wonderful."

I wasn't ready to call it a win yet. An entire group of cheerful people who lived their lives on the road, slept in tents, and did good deeds? I'd never met anyone who was that nice— no matter what Reginald said.

"Don't get too comfortable, Reg. I still haven't ruled out the possibility that this is a cult," I said grimly.

Reginald laughed.

"Always assuming the worst."

I lifted a shoulder and let it fall.

"Yes. Well. At least I'm better prepared for disappointment that way."

A memory flashed through my mind. I was kneeling before the Archfiend. My parents were standing on either side of him, and he was berating me for what the humans were doing to close the loophole I'd created in their Hero contract.

"Sorry, that took a minute. I wanted to make sure you had some of everything," said Alowe, coming up behind with a plate for each of us. I couldn't really see what we were eating, but Reginald was too hungry to care, and I was too tired. Pulling a packet of demon dust out of my bag, I sprinkled it liberally over the food and tucked in.

"So where are you from?" asked Alowe as we scarfed down our dinners. Reginald's mouth was too full to answer, so I said, "Far from here."

"Oh, I know *you* are. You're a demon. Though," he frowned, "not the one everyone's been talking about up the coastal road, I don't think. Is it possible that after five hundred years there are two demons in Widdershins?"

I sighed.

"It seems to be the case."

Alowe examined my face—eyes searching mine—and apparently found whatever he saw satisfactory. He smiled again, and while I wanted to believe there was something afoot here— it seemed genuine. In fact, I sensed nothing suspicious at all. Could Alowe and the Charity Run really be what he claimed?

"We're trekking west toward the Outer Sea. You're welcome to come with us, if you're running from something."

Reginald swallowed his mouthful of food and said, "That is really generous of you, but we have to cross the Giant's Fingers so we can get to the City of Seven."

Alowe's warm smile faltered.

"The Giant's Fingers? You cannot go that way."

"Why not?" asked Reginald, wiping his pinky in some sauce on his plate and licking it off.

"The people who go up there—they do not come back. They say the ghosts of heroes past haunt the old pass."

Even in the flickering firelight, I could see Reginald's face pale.

"I'm sure that's just an old wives' tale to scare off curious children or something," I said.

Alowe shook his head emphatically.

"No. I mean it. We sent someone up to it when we came by last year. They never returned."

"Huh. Interesting. And where is this pass, exactly? Is it far from here?"

Reginald turned his shocked face toward me.

"You took us all the way here, and you don't even know where it is?"

I put a hand up to forestall any further comments.

"I know approximately where it is."

"How approximately?"

"It's approximately . . . somewhere on this side of the mountains."

Alowe tilted his head to the side.

"But the mountains run all the way between the two seas. That's hundreds of miles of terrain to check."

"Which is why I am asking *you*, Alowe!"

"Well, I mean . . . It's close to here, actually. Maybe a league back east? There's a tree at the start that's impossible to miss. All the branches and leaves points up toward the pass. But are you sure you want to go that way?"

I said yes at the same time that Reginald said no.

Alowe looked between us and shrugged.

"It's up to you, I guess. But I at least insist that you stay here tonight."

"Now that is something we can all agree upon."

Alowe and some of the other villagers pitched a crimson tent for us. The group's seamstress brought us hot water and soap, and she washed and dried our outer clothes for us while we cleaned up. Once we were scrubbed, she led us to the sauna, where we got our sweat on for a while before exiting back into the brisk wind. The sauna part was amazing. The leaving-the-sauna part was awful. They told me it was good for my health. But what did they know about best practices for the health of a demon?

After that, we stumbled back to our tent. Alowe or someone else had left our bags propped up against the center poll. We pulled out our bedrolls, and for once, both Reginald *and* I were asleep before our heads hit the ground.

THE SOUND of hooves pounding the dirt outside our tent woke us.

"Did you buy me a pony, Gran?" Reginald asked, rubbing his eyes.

"Definitely not," I whispered and pulled my morning coat on. There had been an urgency to the sound that I sensed even in sleep. I pulled a tent flap open and looked out.

It was dark outside, but I could still see the snout of the proud, chestnut-colored steed that was level with my nose. On its back was a rider cloaked in black with the hood up, obscuring their face.

"Are you Malgon Belroth Kirranith?" a muffled voice asked from beneath the hood.

"Depends who's asking," I said. I was just wondering if I'd actually been right to suspect these people when Alowe came hurrying up.

"Who are you? What's this all about? Why are you disturbing our guests?"

The rider didn't answer. Instead, they gracefully dismounted the horse, landing noiselessly on the ground. The movement was so fluid—and I realized I'd seen it before.

"It's all right," I said, relaxing slightly. "It's okay, Alowe. It's an amaranthine messenger."

The courier removed their hood, and I could see that it was the same individual who had delivered the message to the baker near the Cock o' the North. She was even more lovely in the predawn light. Large, lilac almond eyes looked out from a heart-shaped face framed by star-white hair. She pulled a sizable onyx crystal out from a pocket in her cloak and handed it to me.

"You were difficult to find. I am Osa, messenger to all. Here are your tidings. I must be away."

And, just as before, she swooped back into the saddle, reared her horse, and was gone in the blink of an eye.

Reginald emerged from the tent.

"What's going on?"

I stared at the crystal in my hand. It was polished enough that I could see my reflection in its dark surface.

"I've had a message," I said.

"From who?" he asked.

"From *whom*," I corrected. "And I don't know."

"Well . . . how do we find out?"

I turned the crystal over in my hand until I saw a few words etched into the raw base. It said, HOLD THE CRYSTAL UP IN FRONT OF A LIGHT SOURCE. SAY YOUR NAME AS THE MESSENGER SAID IT TO YOU. YOUR TIDINGS SHALL BE REVEALED.

The sun was brightening the sky, but it was still far too early for it to be considered an appropriate light source.

"Nothing for it, I guess," I said, looking at Reginald. I produced a small flame in my hand, and Alowe whistled. Then I held it up to the crystal and said my name just as Osa had said it to me. Light suddenly shot through the opaque crystal, revealing the echo of a humanoid form standing on the other side. It was tall and broad and had a scar running from its forehead, across its eye, down to its ear. The figure wore an ebony morning coat like mine, a pitchfork strapped to his back, and a vicious smile on his face.

It was Tannith. My brother.

CHAPTER 8
THE HERO'S PASS

"Little Malgon." His voice was saccharine, but I could still see the wickedness behind his eyes. "I hope this message finds you reveling in the knowledge that you have finally made your family proud. Since coming topside, I've heard much about your quest to return the Stone of Eno and after. Had to torture a dryad and a fairy to get it, but it was worth it."

I gulped but continued to listen.

"Who knew that the Stone of Eno was responsible for the barrier between this world and our own? The timing of it all makes that pretty clear. Though with the portal fading in and out, I've been the only one able to come through. I'm sure that's why you're headed to Seven now—to extract the information on how to stabilize it from the wizards. Not to fix the stone, as rumor would have me believe. Why would you do that when stabilizing the portal would earn you your horns and tail?"

I stopped breathing. All demons were self-serving, narcissistic assholes hell-bent on sowing discord—but my brother more than most. Was he serious? Had Reginald and I been right about the Stone of Eno? And if I fixed the portal—would I really earn my tail and horns? I broke into a smile at the thought of seeing my parents at a ceremony in my honor.

The thought of Widdershins invaded by a horde of demons interrupted my vision. Reginald, Reginald's gran, Elgar, Alowe —they'd all be under the thumb of a much crueler sort of evil than I'd ever managed.

"But if you *are* in Seven to fix the stone," continued my brother, his voice deepening to a growl, "know that I am on my way there as well. Not only will I stop you, but I will make sure you can never set foot in the Underworld ever again."

Then, quick as a flash, his devilish smile returned.

"But I'm sure the rumors are mistaken. A Kirranith would never take a stand against the Archfiend—and for all your failings, you are still a Kirranith, little brother." His eyes swiveled toward someone or something to my left, and I turned to look, forgetting for a moment that he wasn't really standing before me. "I'm being told that this crystal is nearly full, so I'll just say how much I'm looking forward to our reunion. See you in Seven, Malgon."

The echo faded away. It was over. I stared unblinking at the spot where the image of my brother had been.

"Mal?" came Reg's soft voice. I sensed his hand hovering over my shoulder, but the touch never came. I spun around without looking at anyone and ducked back into the tent. Inside, I tucked the crystal into my backpack and lay face down on my bedroll.

I'd just gotten the best news of my whole life.

And I'd never felt worse.

"MAL. TALK TO ME."

Reginald was sitting on his bedroll, and from the tension in his voice, I could tell he was one loud noise away from a panic attack. I knew how he felt. If my intention was to fix the stone, then we needed to get to Seven before my brother, which meant that we needed to get up and out of this musty tent immediately. But if we fixed the stone, then everything that I had ever wanted in my 550 years of life would be forfeited.

"What do you want me to say?" I said, head still facedown on the bedroll.

"I want you to tell me what you thought about your brother's message."

I growled and pushed myself up to a sitting position.

"I don't know what to think. It will not surprise you that Tannith is both a liar and a bully. Maybe the entire point of his message was to give me a false sense of hope so that when I do return, I'll be horribly disappointed that none of it was true. Or, maybe it was true, and everyone is really proud of me, and I've instigated a deed so evil that it will earn me my horns, my tail, and the respect of my family."

"And what about us?" he whispered, and I felt a pang in my chest. "If you do what he says . . . what will happen to us?"

I closed my eyes and raised my face to the ceiling.

"Nothing good."

There was a beat of silence, and then Reginald said, "I thought not."

I opened my eyes and looked at him. He was hugging his legs, chin resting on his knees. He looked fragile and terrified. I told myself it didn't matter to me. My father's voice screamed in my mind that I was a demon and I needed to act like it. I took a deep breath, squared my shoulders, and stood.

"I've come to a decision, Reg."

He looked up at me, and I recognized the expression he wore as his "if this is bad news, I'm going to throw up" face.

"Grab your bag. We've got to get to the pass."

I picked up my satchel and was mostly through the tent flap when I heard him say, "To find out how to stabilize the portal?"

I paused and poked my head back in.

"To get to Steadly before my brother and get him to fix us and the stone."

TRUTH BE TOLD, I wasn't 100 percent certain that "fix the stone" was my definitive answer, but it was certainly the one that motivated Reginald to get his ass in gear. He was out of the tent and standing next to me in seconds.

"Friends!" we heard Alowe call, and we both turned. "Before you go, please take these." There were two packets of food wrapped in cheese cloth; inside were dried meats and a wrinkly, yellow fruit.

"Thank you," said Reginald, reaching for the packages.

"Consider it a token of good will," said Alowe. He shot me a nervous smile and lowered his voice so that only I could hear what he was saying. "I probably only understood about half of what that message meant—but I can tell you one thing. Even though it was through a crystal—or possibly *because* it was—I could sense that your brother's fate is set and that he is on a dark path. It wasn't surprising to me. He is a demon. But your aura . . . it changes. Sometimes it's inviting. Sometimes it's skeptical. I believe that in the future, you will be forced to make a choice. I hope you remember the kindness of the Charity Run and of your friend there when you do."

We swiveled our heads toward Reginald. When he saw us looking, he smiled and gave us a finger wave. Alowe squeezed my shoulder once, then let go.

"Don't let me keep you. Be safe in the pass. My good thoughts go with you."

I bowed my head slightly in his direction as Reginald ran up and hugged him.

"Thanks for everything, Alowe!" he cried. "Maybe we'll see

you again someday."

Alowe raised a hand in farewell, and Reginald and I took off east, leaving the ruddy-colored tents huddled against the wall of gray stone above. I looked back over my shoulder. The serpentine flags on the stalls and tents whipped back and forth indecisively, snapping in the freezing wind. It felt like a warning, but I wasn't sure which path I was being warned about.

"What was Alowe talking to you about?"

The truth threatened to bubble up out of me, but I swallowed it down just in time.

"He was just reminding me what the tree at the bottom of the pass looked like."

The answer satisfied Reginald, and he launched into a long monologue about what a strange concept he thought the sauna was. As we walked, I took in the pitch of the mountains, and my throat tightened. The peaks were still invisible in the dense cloud cover, and while I was certain the mountains sloped, from our perspective they were more like a shear wall of granite stretching impossibly high. Every once in a while, the clouds would break, and the sunlight would pour down, highlighting an outcrop or a tenacious pine tree growing alone on a small ledge. But mostly it was just flat stone all the way up.

"That's got to be the tree, right?" I heard Reginald say. I'd tuned him out and lost myself in thoughts about the diverging paths before me—but that snapped me back to the present. The tree was exactly as Alowe had described it.

"Wow. It really is pointing up the mountainside," I said as I examined the obviously magical tree bent almost parallel to the ground. The trunk was still upright, but every branch and leaf was trained upward, as if pulled by an invisible force.

"The leaves aren't even rustling in this wind," said Reginald —who I now noticed was traveling with the blue blanket wrapped around his head and shoulders, and I cursed myself for not asking Alowe for some warmer cloaks.

"As much as I'd love to stay and observe a motionless tree, it's time for us to set off." We rounded the trunk and saw a gravel path leading up through a crack in the mountainside. We picked our way carefully up the shifting slope to the entrance of the tunnel into the mountain. The air inside it felt stale, as if an unseen barrier had kept it from being cycled with the wind outside. It was also dark in a way that made you wonder if maybe your eyes had stopped working.

"This is a bit scary, Mal," I heard Reg say over the crunch of our feet on the uneven ground. I was reluctant to produce any light in case we disturbed any slumbering creatures. But he was right—it was creepy as fuck. And I didn't want us taking a misstep and falling down through a crevasse in the stone, never to be seen again.

I pulled a small flame into being and let it hover above my hand. It was dim—but whether that was because of my nerves or the air quality, I couldn't be sure. We could now see about a foot in front of us, which should have been a good thing, but it was not.

"Are those . . . bones?" whispered Reginald as we finally saw what our feet had been crunching on.

"I think so. But look at how small they are! Clearly whatever is eating these tiny creatures isn't up to a bigger meal like us."

"Or maybe it just hasn't had the chance for a bigger meal, and now we're walking toward it on a silver platter," he squeaked.

"Nonsense. You're letting your imagination get the best of you."

He was probably right, actually.

We passed by another tunnel entrance. It was much smaller and from it wafted a powerful reek. Just as we passed, we heard a long, sleepy hiss escape from it on a rush of wind that pushed at our backs. Judging by the strength of the exhale, something large was asleep down there.

It didn't follow us—but we instinctively understood that it would wake up eventually, and we didn't want to be around when it did. After that, I was a lot less cautious about the state of the ground. We increased our pace to a jog and kept it up until we saw a pinprick of light in the distance.

"We're almost through the tunnel!" shouted Reginald as we pelted toward the light. His words echoed thunderously off the tunnel walls, and I knew before the piercing cry that we were in trouble. The mountain shook and my flame winked out. The thing had awoken.

"You don't know how lucky you are that it would be inadvisable for me to kill you right now, Asstradle!" I shouted as we increased our jog to a sprint in the direction of the growing circle of light before us. The ground trembled again and I lost my footing. I tripped, but Reginald hadn't noticed and kept on sprinting. I was nearly to my feet when we got zinged painfully back together.

"Ow!"

"Get up, get up, get up!" I yelled, scrambling to my feet. I held out my hand to him and tossed a glance over my shoulder just as the light we were chasing fell upon the cave dweller behind us. Its body was round and hairy and its head seemed to be made entirely of eyes. Eight spiny legs protruded from its thorax. Spider legs usually look delicate and spindly but these were as thick as tree trunks and the beastly thing skuttled towards us with unbelievable speed.

"Back at the Cock o' the North I said there were spiders here! I was right!" cried Reginald as he jumped to his feet and we set off running again. The giant spider was close enough that I could hear the clicking of its fangs. But we were only thirty feet from the opening. Twenty. The spider snapped its chelicerae, but was too late—the mouth of the cave was just feet away. We were running, running . . .

And then we were falling.

DISTRACTED by our fixation on the outer world—a world without a massive arachnid in search of a meal—we forgot to look down. A crack lay between the tunnel and the world outside. It was wide enough for us to tumble into, but not for our pursuer. Just before we fell, I saw that there once had been stairs that led down into the darkness, but they'd crumbled away. So now we were free-falling. Reg had a death grip on my leg. I reached out on either side to see if I could catch hold of something to break our fall. All I snatched was air.

"Well, Reg," I shouted and, for what felt like the hundredth time since I'd met him, said, "I think our luck has finally run—"

Boing!

We hit the ground—but the ground was soft; buoyant, even.

"What the?" I heard Reginald say as he bounced up in the air again before landing permanently.

I stood up and studied the ground as I pressed the surface with my feet. Ripples appeared, and I rose up before sinking down again. Bending down to touch it, I saw that it looked just like rock but was pillowy soft.

"Hey, Reg. Look at this. It's been magically changed to soften our landing. This must be the proper start of the pass—" I said, clipping the last syllable. I'd just realized that though my flame had gone out long ago, I could still see. Glowing crystals illuminated a path into another tunnel—but this was no mere crack in the mountain. This had been purposefully carved, as evidenced by the two towering stone figures flanking its entrance. Their heads were missing and much of the detail had worn away. Bits of rubble and rock around their feet told the story of their demise.

"Who do you think they were?" asked Reginald, bouncing up beside me.

I shrugged.

"Probably whichever heroes originally created this pass."

"Wow," he said in childlike wonderment; then he hung his head. "I don't think I'd ever really understood the difference between me and the golden-age heroes until just now. I knew that the heroes of old didn't have to file paperwork and that they carried swords and slayed dragons and all that. And I knew that as a hero now, I was basically signing up to be some kind of trumped-up errand boy. But even knowing all of that, I still wanted to be a hero my whole life. Always—in the back of my mind—there was a thread or something that connected me back to the great heroes. I felt as if I was continuing their work, in a way. But this—" he gestured at the glowing opening before us. "The scale of this is beyond anything I could ever hope to accomplish." He took up a pebble and tossed it away. "I shouldn't be allowed to call myself a hero," he said, frowning.

My first thought was to tell him I'd been saying that since we'd met. But he looked so damn depressed. Clenching my fists with frustration at giving a shit, I said, "It's true that you're not strong or brave. You throw up at the drop of a hat and more often than not are falling over your own feet. But the way I understand it is that true heroes aren't heroes because they can do big things. Heroes are just people who do the hard stuff despite their . . . er . . . obvious limitations. So come on, Sir Asstradle! Pick that chin up and let's get moving. The stone isn't going to fix itself, and my brother fucks things up way less than we do, so he's probably closing in on Seven as we speak."

Reginald didn't look convinced, but he nodded once, and the two of us passed between the stone sentinels and onto the glowing path before us.

THE TRIP through the second tunnel took two days, but it was uneventful. We broke out the food that Alowe had given us and passed the time by describing our favorite moments of the journey thus far. Reginald had significantly more highlights than I did. He was just finishing his version of getting to see the inside of a dwarf warren when we emerged into the fresh air once more. The tunnel emptied onto a wide outcrop with narrow stairs off to the right that hugged the side of the mountain. Before us, the view was staggering. Mountains rose like columns from the ground and pierced the sky above. Dusk was falling, and it painted the gray granite in warm, rose-gold light. It was a stark contrast to the brutal wind that bit at our exposed skin.

"If it weren't so windy, I'd say we should stay here forever," said Reginald. I glanced at the stairs. We needed to go down to find the rest of the path.

"Well, we can't stay here forever, but we should probably stay here for tonight. Those stairs look perilous. If we don't get swept off them by this wind, we're sure to lose our footing in the dark. We'll leave at first light."

I led him back to the opening of the tunnel and made a small fire, which crackled comfortingly as the sun sank below the roots of the mountains. It was no lava flow or everlasting inferno, but it was fire all the same. I gazed into it and watched all the little flames spring to life, rise, and then inevitably fade into the night. Much like human life. The thought gave me a jolt of panic as I realized we still hadn't resolved the immortality question: What would happen to me if Reginald died?

I was so lost in my thoughts that I didn't even hear Reginald saying my name.

"Mal!"

I shook my head to clear it.

"What?"

"I've been calling your name."

"Well, what is it?"

Reginald was picking some of the dried meat out from between his teeth.

"Wasn't there a mountain over there before?"

He thrust his chin toward a blank spot on the horizon. I looked, but I'd been paying more attention to the stairs than placing the hundreds of mountains.

"Mountains don't move, Reg."

"I know that! At least, I thought I knew that. But the world has gotten very weird in the past nine days . . ."

A few rocks slid out of place somewhere above us and tumbled down the mountain in our direction. We spun our heads toward the sound, but thankfully they were not the heralds of a full-blown rockslide. A couple of small stones bumped and skipped down the slope to the side of our camp; nothing more. But the interruption had disrupted our argument, and neither of us had the energy to continue.

"We should get some sleep. With any luck we'll be able to make it the rest of the way across the pass tomorrow and into Seven."

Reginald yawned and stretched his arms.

"I'm excited to see a city run by wizards."

I settled myself into a ball on the rocky ground, a tuft of hearty mountain grass as my pillow.

"It's basically the same as any other city. Smelly. Crowded."

"But with magic," sighed Reginald.

"Yes. But with magic," I yawned. "So let's take this rare opportunity to get some rest while nothing hunts us."

Reginald didn't need telling twice. He was already snoring.

I was wrong, of course. I'd vastly underestimated our level of danger. If I'd been more alert, I might have noticed the odd way the shadows fell across the mountainside behind us, or heard the rhythmic crunching of stone against stone. But I was too exhausted and fell asleep immediately.

CHAPTER 9
GUILLFOYLE

I rarely dream, but tired as I was, I dreamed I was flying. And for a being who has spent most his life in what—let's face it —is basically an underground sauna? It was both terrifying and exhilarating. I was just getting the hang of this cerebral soaring when, predictably, Reginald spoiled everything.

"Mal!"

I sat bolt upright at the sound of my name. My first clue that something was wrong should have been that he had woken me up and not the other way around, but I was groggy and disoriented.

"What? What is it?" I rubbed my eyes, and blinked in the early morning sun. "Reg, if you woke me up for something ridiculous, I'm going to flatten you into a leaf and use you to wipe my ass."

"*Mal.*"

He wasn't yelling; he was whispering. I lowered my hands from my eyes and really looked at Reginald's face. He was still as a statue except for his eyes. Those were darting from side to side. I turned my head to follow their path and saw—

"We're in a *cage*?"

Reginald nodded. The cage was enormous. The two of us

were like mice compared to its size. It was round, with thick wooden bars wide enough apart to see through but not quite wide enough to squeeze through. A square door on wooden hinges blocked my view on one side. Above us, the bars joined into an arched roof of sorts—if a bunch of sticks that didn't completely cover our heads could be considered a roof. The floor was strewn with wood shavings. I didn't have a good feeling about this.

"Why are we in a cage?"

He shrugged.

"How'd we get in a cage?"

"Search me. I was sleeping."

I shook my head, still trying to clear it and make sense of this situation.

"Well . . . who put us in the cage?"

"You're going to like this," he said with a grim smile. Reginald cocked his head to the side. I peered between the thick wooden bars next to the wooden door of our enclosure. There was a roaring fire not fifteen feet away.

And on the other side of the fire was a stone giant.

I gulped.

"So, Mal?"

"Yes, Reg?"

"Remember when you told me that the Giant's Fingers were called the Giant's Fingers because they were big like a giant's fingers?"

"Uh huh."

"And not because there were giants here, because there were no giants anymore?"

"I remember saying that."

"You were wrong."

"Yes, I can see that, thanks."

"What are we going to do?"

We were high in the mountains—higher than we'd been

when we exited the tunnel. Snow dusted the craggy peaks and pine trees. The weak winter sun provided little warmth. If not for the giant's fire, we would be frozen solid. I did not know what we were going to do, but that's never stopped me from taking charge before. I was about to open my mouth to deliver some bullshit when the giant moved his head slowly in our direction.

"So . . . you . . . are . . . awake?"

"Uh, yes. We are awake."

"Then . . . eat."

With glacial slowness, he unlocked the cage door, reached a hand toward us, and deposited a pile of food within reach. I mentally catalogued some roast rabbit, a handful of apples, and a few flat pieces of wheat cake as he closed the door again.

"Meat!" cried Reginald and grabbed frantically for the rabbit.

"Wow," I said, selecting a cake and sniffing it. "This is unexpected. If I'm honest, demons wouldn't feed the people they keep in cages."

"Be quiet, Mal," Reginald hissed before gnawing on a leg. "So what if it feeds us?"

"I . . . believe . . . in . . . humane . . . slaughter."

Reginald stopped eating.

"I'm sorry, did you say 'slaughter'?"

"Yes," said the giant across the fire. "You . . . eat . . . rabbit. I . . . eat . . . you. Circle . . . of . . . life."

Reginald turned green.

"I just forgot. I'm . . . er . . . allergic to meat, actually."

"You don't want to eat us anyway," I said, panic rising in my chest. "Look at me! I'm basically a toothpick to you!"

Reginald looked like he was going to be sick, and for once, I didn't blame him. I whipped my head around, looking for inspiration to buy us some time, when the giant's face broke slowly into a grin, and he laughed. The sound was like an avalanche.

"Just . . . kidding. Giants . . . only . . . sometimes . . . eat . . . humans."

Generally speaking, the assumption that I am human irks me to no end. Here, I was willing to let it slide.

"Splendid news. But uh," I tapped on the wooden bars before us, "why are we in a cage, then?"

"So . . . you . . . don't . . . run."

Reginald and I exchanged a look.

"If you don't want to eat or hurt us, why would we run?"

The giant hung his head.

"They . . . always . . . do. In . . . the . . . end. I'm . . . always . . . alone."

"You're lonely?" asked Reginald in that way that made me suspect he was about to rope me into something that was going to piss me off.

"Family . . . far. Visitors . . . few. Life . . . lonely."

"I understand how you feel," he offered. "Where is your family?"

"Near . . . the . . . sea. And . . . some . . . in . . . Stone Rot."

My eyes roamed from the top of the giant's head down to its gargantuan feet.

"But you're, like, a hundred feet tall," I said. "It will take you about fifty steps to get to the sea."

"Slow . . . slow . . . steps. Long . . . time."

"So instead you're going to cage us to make us be your friends."

The giant was silent for several minutes. He was probably just taking a breath, but it took so long that I taught myself how to say the alphabet backward while I was waiting.

"Exactly."

I threw up my hands.

"Great. Perfect. It's fitting, really, that we would be caged in a friend-prison by a slow-talking giant. This feels right for us, doesn't it?"

"Mal," Reginald said, turning to me.

"No."

"You don't even know what I was going to say!"

"I don't need to. The answer is no."

"But what about Elgar's invention?"

I snapped my head toward him, eyes wide.

"Reg—what about Elgar's invention?"

He rolled his eyes.

"I just said that."

"Excuse me—giant!" I called, waving to get his attention.

The giant swung his head in our direction.

"Guillfoyle."

"Great," I continued. "Guillfoyle. Good news: it turns out the fates have intervened. We have something in our possession that can solve your problem."

"How?"

"Well, it just so happens that we were recently given a set of devices that will allow you to talk to people . . . er . . . giants far, far away." I rummaged around in Reginald's bag—which was mercifully in the cage with us and not back at wherever our campsite had been—until I found the prototypes. "Here! See?"

The giant made his way over to us. In the interim, Reginald and I played sixteen rounds of "Rock, Parchment, Broadsword," and then I took a brief nap.

"How . . . do . . . they . . . work?"

I started, waking from my rest and realizing all over again that I was stuck in a cage. "Well . . ." I also realized that in my complete disinterest in the communication devices, I'd ignored everything Elgar might have said about them. I did not know how they worked.

"Like this." Reginald and grabbed them away from me and

moved a dial on each device. Then he handed one to the giant. "Put it up to your ear."

The giant complied and stood straight. At this height, Guillfoyle was nearly thirty yards away from us so it was a fair demonstration of the device's efficacy. Reginald spoke into one gem.

"You can use this to talk to your family far away," he said.

A smile broke across the giant's face.

"What . . . magic . . . is . . . this?"

"Dwarf stuff," I cut in. "Very expensive. But if you let us go, we'll let you have them for free!"

The giant inched back down toward us until his face was level with the cage, and held out his hand. Reginald and I exchanged delighted looks as he handed the second device over to Guillfoyle. The giant closed his fingers around it, straightened up, and said, "Still . . . no . . . though."

"No?" asked Reginald.

"What do you mean, 'no'?" I asked.

"No. Still . . . far . . . from . . . family. You . . . stay. Be . . . friends."

I flopped down on the floor of the cage and watched the giant lumber back to his seat by the fire. As he walked, he called back over his shoulder.

"So . . . why . . . you . . . in . . . mountains?"

I sighed.

"This," I said, holding up my bag. "A blasted stone." I thought about that for a moment and added, "No offense."

"We have to get to the City of Seven," explained Reginald. "We broke a connection stone, and we need the headmaster at the academy to help us fix it so that we're not stuck together forever—and also so that Widdershins isn't invaded by a demon horde."

"Which . . . stone?"

My head snapped to Guillfoyle.

"What do you mean, 'which one'? There's only one."

"There . . . are . . . three . . . stones."

I sat, dumbfounded.

"Three? There can't be three. Can there?"

The giant took several heartbeats to shrug.

"Eno . . . Nie . . . Sunu."

He counted off on his fingers as he named each one.

"How do you know this? Do you know what they do? Why do they exist? Do they really keep the Underworld from mixing with this one?"

Right now, all I had to go on was Reginald's and my guess about the timing of the stone breaking and the portal appearing . . . plus that message from my brother. If Guillfoyle could confirm what they actually did, we'd finally have something definitive.

The giant threaded his fingers together.

"They . . . connect."

"They connect what, though?"

He shrugged.

I let out an exasperated noise, but honestly, it was probably for the best that the giant didn't know more. Having a conversation at this snail's pace was giving me an eye twitch.

Reginald turned to me.

"Do you think the dryads knew there were three?"

I shook my head.

"I do not know."

"Do you think your *brother* knows there are three?"

I gave him palms up.

"You . . . have . . . traveled . . . far. Tell . . . me . . . a . . . story."

I was about to tell Guillfoyle that we didn't share stories with jailers when I got an idea.

"Reg—give me your shirt," I whispered.

He backed up, holding his shirt in place as if I would whisk it off of him.

"No! Why?"

"Shh . . . just do it. And then . . ." I continued in a much louder voice, "Reg-in-ald! I think Guillfoyle here would thoroughly enjoy the story of Bitsy Wigglebottom and her altercation with the mayor of Beadledom. Would you be willing to tell it?"

Reginald's eyes bugged out, and he beamed as he stripped his shirt off and handed it over.

"Would I?" he yelled. "Absolutely!" Then he turned to the giant. "I have this adorable fluffy puppy named Bitsy Wigglebottom. She's funny and feisty and just the best pet that a guy could ask for. Gosh, I miss her. Anyway, this one time I was out walking her highness—that's my nickname for her—and this frog crossed the road right in front of us! We . . ."

The suggestion that he tell this story was a risky move on my part. I was counting on the story being just as annoying to the giant as it was to me. So annoying, in fact, that he would let us go. But just in case, I was going to turn Reginald's shirt and the blankets from our packs into a rope. You never know when a bit of rope will come in handy.

The sun was at its zenith as Reginald described the spotted pattern on the back of the frog that had apparently crossed his path that day.

The sun was toying with the idea of setting when he described the one blade of grass on the mayor's lawn that was taller than all the others.

The sun had finally dipped behind the mountains, and Reginald was still talking when he was interrupted by a low, booming voice.

"*Stop.*"

Reginald stopped so short he nearly choked. Guillfoyle turned his head slowly in my direction.

"Does . . . it . . . ever . . . end?"

I squinted my eyes and cocked my head.

"Depends what you mean by 'end,' I suppose."

The giant doubled slowly over and held his head in his hand.

"I . . . can-not . . . stand . . . it. Maybe . . . I . . . should . . . eat . . . you . . . after all."

"Welllll, that backfired," I said, tying off the last knot on a bar near the door.

"Mal?" Reginald's voice quavered.

Guillfoyle stood to full height and plodded over to our cage. Beside me, Reginald was shaking like a leaf. I didn't have a plan, but I leaned over anyway and whispered into his ear, "I know you're scared, Reg, but we're not eaten yet. Be ready to run when I say run."

He was still white as a sheet but he nodded mutely.

The sound of stone on stone was deafening as the giant leaned over to unlock the cage. The door swung open, but before Guillfoyle could reach inside and grab us, I tossed the rope out of the opening and shoved Reginald toward it. He started down, but it wasn't long enough to reach all the way to the ground.

"Mal!"

"Just jump!"

He hit the dirt around the cage hard just as I swung the bags over my shoulder and started down myself. I landed next to him a moment later and shouted, "Run, Reg! Run!"

We sprinted away from the fire toward the freezing peaks. I had no way of knowing if the path that led away from the giant was part of the hero's pass, but the important thing now was to just get away. A line of pine trees looked like snow-tipped toothpicks ahead of us, but I thought that if we could just get to those trees, maybe the giant wouldn't be able to follow us.

"Wait!" called Guillfoyle. "Come . . . back! I . . . promise . . . not . . . to . . . eat . . . you . . . yet!"

The giant was after us now, though; his slogging steps

pounded against the mountainside and dislodged rocks ahead of us. With every shake of the ground, we struggled to keep our footing—which was hard enough while trying to swerve around the avalanche of rocks and boulders Guillfoyle was causing.

"He's right behind us, Mal!"

It was dark now—our way was lit by moonlight—and so cold that moving was difficult. A rock the size of a house was tumbling down the mountainside straight for Reg, and I dove into him and pushed him out of the way just in time to avoid it. It smashed against Guillfoyle's knee instead.

Guillfoyle roared his frustration, and I felt him clip my coat as I scrambled back to my feet, pulling Reginald up with all my might. A cramp formed at my side, but I ignored it and ran as if my ass were on fire.

"If we can just make it to that turn beneath the line of trees, it looks as if the path narrows!"

We made our way between two boulders, and Guillfoyle reached forward one last time. His fingers closed around Reginald and began to gradually lift him up into the air. I saw his mouth open and heard Reginald's blood-curdling scream. Not knowing what to do, I threw our bags with all my might at his face. Thankfully it was still fairly close since the giant had crouched down to catch Reg. Otherwise I don't know if I could have reached. Guillfoyle started back in surprise and dropped Reginald. The two of us bolted beneath the shadow of the trees and onto the narrower path where Guillfoyle could not follow. Running along a little while longer to be certain, Reg finally bent over and gasped.

"We're safe!"

"From the giant, maybe." I eyed him critically. The skin on his arms was turning blue, which was not, as I understood it, a normal human color.

I was conflicted. On one hand, it was against my nature to

help anyone other than myself. Plus—my waistcoat. This may sound silly, but it was like an appendage at this point. Was I even myself without it?

On the other hand, I still didn't know if his death would take me down as well, so helping him *was* helping me.

"Fine! You win!"

"What do I win, Mal?" Reginald asked, teeth chattering.

"What? No, not you. But you can have my morning coat. *For now.*"

"Oh, wow," he said as I pulled it off and handed it over. He slipped it on. It was big on him, but he didn't look half bad in it. "It smells like sulfur."

"That's brimstone. And it smells like home."

"Oh," he said. It was one of those polite 'ohs' that lets you know a person was about to say something disparaging but thought better of it.

"Anyway, now we're both half-frozen, which seems fair and appropriate."

Reginald let out a hysterical little laugh and wrapped the coat tighter around his front.

"You know what I'm confused about?" he asked as he stomped heat into his feet.

"What's that?"

"Why would *stone* giants eat *people*?"

"I'm not well-versed in their biology, Reg. Perhaps they aren't made of stone through and through."

"Oh. I hadn't thought of that."

I rubbed my hands together, inspiring them to warm.

"Come on, Asstradle. If we don't get to Seven soon, we'll both freeze to death. Plus the stone . . . oh no."

"What is it?" he asked, rubbing his arms vigorously.

"I threw our bags at Guillfoyle's face. The stone was in my satchel."

Reginald went green, but to his credit, he did not throw up.

"What are we going to do?"

I tapped my chin in thought.

"Stay here—I'm going to see where they landed."

I backtracked to where we'd entered the trees. Luckily it wasn't far enough to disturb our magical connection. To my colossal disappointment (pun intended), Guillfoyle was still there and was now holding our bags hostage.

"Come . . . get . . . bags . . . human! Can . . . wait . . . all . . . century!"

"Dammit."

I jogged back to where Reginald sat, huddled against a tree. He'd coaxed dried pine needles into a pile to sit on and was regretting it.

"Ow—geez. Pine needles are pokey."

If we'd had time, I would have thrown a barb his way about the idiocy of trying to get comfortable on a pile of something that had "needles" right in the name, but we didn't. Every single moment that went by was one in which my brother was moving toward Seven and we were not. We had to get those bags.

"Guillfoyle is sitting around that corner with the bags piled right beside him."

Reginald winced as another pine needle poked through his pants. As he gave up and stood, he said, "What do we do? Wait for him to fall asleep? That could take hours."

"I know. And we need to get going. No, we've got to get them now."

"So what's the plan?"

"You're not going to like it."

<hr />

"Mal?"

"Yes, Reg?"

"This is a terrible plan."

"Do you have a better one?"

". . . I do not."

We were peering at Guillfoyle from around the boulder that marked the entrance to the pine forest. A clump of snow dislodged itself from a pine bough and landed on Reginald's head.

"Gah! Bad words!"

"Reginald, when this is all over, remind me to teach you how to swear." He spluttered and wiped snow off his face.

"How do we know the magic will work like this?"

"We don't, really. But it's powerful magic. There's at least a fifty percent chance of this working. You ready?"

"No."

"Time to go anyway!" I pushed him out from behind the boulder, and he staggered in front of Guillfoyle. He looked shrunken and pathetic in my overcoat—and so breakable.

This better work.

"Oh no! Guillfoyle! You are still here! I had no idea!"

If Guillfoyle didn't see through Reginald's terrible acting, he was blind. If he did, we were sunk.

"Yes . . . I . . . am . . . , human."

With that, he snatched Reginald up again and started slowly back down toward the fire, thankfully leaving the bags behind. I ran up, snatched them, and tossed them into the forest. Then I came back out and waited for the zing.

A moment later, we smashed together—not just me and Reginald, but Guillfoyle as well. The giant hit the ground and released his grip on Reg. I was almost certain that I'd cracked a rib careening into a stone giant, but there was no time to think about it.

"Time to go, Reg!" I said, and the two of us sprinted into the trees again, grabbed our bags, and ran until we could no longer hear Guillfoyle's angry yells. We were out of the pine trees and back in the open air. The moon hung low like a giant yellow face, laughing at our misfortune. Or was it smiling at our luck?

"The pass! Reg! Look!"

To our right, not a hundred feet away, was a path lined with the same glowing crystals we'd found in the mountain tunnel. We hurried toward it as fast as two squashed, exhausted creatures could manage.

So it was—semiclothed and befuddled by the anatomy of giants—that we navigated the treacherous, frozen peaks of the Giant's Fingers. As dawn dawned around us, we rejoiced. The pass was finally angling down the other side of the mountain range, and it favored us with the sight of the City of Seven below. Tomorrow we would find Headmaster Steadly—and all would be back to normal.

CHAPTER 10
THE CITY OF SEVEN

Half-frozen and in need of a full wash, we stumbled down the foot of the mountain.

Seven perched on the edge of nowhere. The mountain range on our right stretched west all the way to the sea, and to the north there was nothing but squashy peat bogs and a few man-made paths as far as the eye could see. But to the east, the City of Seven shone like a beacon. Vast stone walls surrounded it on all sides, and the only entrance was through the arched gateway on the road before us. Beyond it, the High Street wound from the half-timbered lower city up through stacks of manor houses and finally to the academy at the peak of the hill. The two wizard towers—one slightly taller than the other— were attached via a covered sky bridge and haloed in a golden haze of magic.

"Oh, sweet, corrupt civilization," I said as I collapsed dramatically to my knees before the walls.

"I thought you didn't like people," said Reginald.

I stood back up and brushed off my trousers.

"I don't like people, Reg. But it turns out I like giants even less. In fact, I really prefer any sort of creature that doesn't want to eat me, so I'm glad to be out of the mountains."

"Me too," said Reginald, rubbing his arms to keep warm. "I still can't believe what you did to my shirt."

"It was for the greater good. We'll get you a fresh shirt."

"Where?"

"I don't know. At a tailor's, probably? All I know is we can't show up looking like we do right now to ask the wizards for help. Your gran said they are a bit of a touchy lot, and in my limited experience, they're a bit pompous. Seven is a cosmopolitan city—we'll figure it out."

"I'm hungry too."

"We'll get some food."

"And tired."

"We'll find a place to stay."

"How?"

"What do you mean?"

"With what money?"

"We'll . . ."

That one stumped me. We didn't have any money, nor did we have anything to trade with. All we had in our possession were a couple of bags and some rocks. We didn't even have Elgar's stupid communication things anymore. In the Underworld, this would not be a problem. We would just take what we wanted from whoever had it. Topside conventions and the watchful eye of Saint Asstradle dictated that we be a bit more civil about it.

"I haven't quite figured that part out yet, but I'm sure something will present itself."

Reginald groaned.

"Couldn't we have a proper plan for once?"

"Oh, just come on, will you?"

I stomped between the walls and into the city, Reginald shuffling wearily behind me.

WHEN APPROACHING a city for the first time, the organs one activates in order are eyes, ears, nose. Most cities can be seen from leagues away; thus, the eyes are first. The City of Seven is particularly eye-catching, as it is overrun by magic. Shimmering haze surrounds the hilltop towers of the academy, and it's not unusual to see both hats and horses floating above the perimeter walls as a result of rogue, wild magic.

Ears: cities are home to lots of people and people make lots of noise. Within Seven, this includes the normal bar-side brawls, clucking chickens, and screeching children. Other sounds particular to Seven include the thousands of tinkling bells to ward off pixies, the dramatic casting of spells, and the occasional explosion from the school.

Finally, there's the nose. There is a particular stew of smells that only a bustling metropolis can produce, and the City of Seven is no exception. A dash of horse, a jigger of alehouse, and a healthy dose of refuse were three of the principal ingredients. But today, as we ambled onto the High Street that wound up to where the wizards dwelt, Reginald and I caught a whiff of something entirely new.

"What is *that*?"

Curious, I sniffed the air and followed my nose to our left. Almost hidden amongst the olfactory onslaught was an unfamiliar smell—rich, robust, and oddly comforting. As the aroma grew stronger, Reginald and I heard a disembodied female voice calling, "Magic bean juice! Get your magic bean juice here! Free bean juice!"

We wandered toward the sound and found a wooden stall at the side of the street. There was such a tight throng of humans and dwarves around it that we could only see the sign up top. The letters C-O-F-F-E-E were painted upon it in a scrolling, black script. Reginald and I exchanged a look and mouthed the word at each other. Through a brief break in the crowd, we could see that the table held a steaming black cauldron. A hand set a mug down beside it, and a dwarf near the front immediately snatched it up.

"Have you ever heard of 'co-ffee,' Mal?"

"I never have, no. Must not be very bad for you."

"I *am* rather thirsty." Reginald looked down at his bare chest beneath my overlarge morning coat. "And cold."

"I'm feeling parched myself, Sir Asstradle. Let us go and see what all the fuss is about."

We strolled across the cobbles to the stall and were about to push ourselves through when the crowd parted for us. At first, I assumed it was because of my natural air of authority. But as I watched their noses wrinkle, I remembered that Reginald and I hadn't bathed in a couple days and probably smelled like the back end of a donkey. Still, they didn't move too far away, and they stared at us unblinkingly.

"Uh, hello, miss," said Reginald to a harried young woman behind the table. She wore a taupe dress covered by a starched white apron. Her face was flushed, and a lock of flaxen hair fell out of her head covering as she dipped a ladle into the cauldron. "How are you on this fine morning?"

"I'm feelin' like I lost me marbles, honestly!" she spat. "Whose great idea was it to give out free samples of this stuff, anyway? Seems to me people'll pay up. They're downing it faster than a drunk drinks ale."

"Free, you say?" I interjected.

She looked up at me, studying my goldenrod eyes.

"New in town, eh?" Her eyes darted back toward the crowd. "Looks like you've got some admirers."

"Admirers?" I asked, glancing behind me at our wide-eyed observers.

"We don't get a lot of visitors round here. People are a bit starved for news and entertainment."

"Oh. I thought they did that because we smell so bad." Judging the distance between us, I realized she was awfully close. "Can't you smell us?"

She shook her head.

"Nah. Got struck by lightnin' when I was a child. Couldn't smell a horse dropping if ya waved it in me face."

"Lucky you," I said, and Reginald stomped on my foot.

"That's terrible," he said.

She shrugged and continued filling mugs.

"Can't hardly remember it now. But what about you two? Where'd you come from?"

"We just crossed the mountains," said Reginald.

Her eyebrows shot up, and she studied us more minutely.

"Did you now? I assumed you came east from Searfoss. You're in better shape than the last one to come through the pass."

"What happened to him?" he asked.

"He died just before the wall," she said, nodding her head at the towering structure we'd come through minutes ago.

"Oh."

"So," I said as casually as I could manage. "Does that mean there have been no other newcomers lately? No one with horns and a tail and a very obvious, angry-looking scar on his face?"

She laughed.

"No, not that I've heard—and I hear it all. But if you have a story about that, folks'll be interested if you have the time to share."

"We're on an important quest with a ticking time wheel, so probably not," I said. Then she handed each of us a mug. I sighed as the warmth seeped into my hands.

"Well, welcome to Seven anyway. Coffee's on the house."

I furrowed my brow.

"You already said it was free."

She winked at me and turned toward the cauldron. Then she spun back. "Oh wait! I've got somethin' I'm supposed to tell you before you drink it. The wizards created it to help you stay awake and such, and people really seem to like it, but there's some stuff you should know about it first."

She pointed at a sign next to the table with her thumb and went back to ladling. We stood to the side next to the placard, and a rush of people pushed in to fill the gap we'd left. They were still careful to give us a healthy distance, but they couldn't seem to help themselves. Out of the corner of my eye, I watched them sip their coffee while shooting us what they believed to be furtive glances.

"This is interesting," said Reginald. The sign read:

COFFEE

Coffee is a delicious new magic bean juice brought to you by the culinary wizards of the City of Seven. Excellent for use as a substitute for sleep or as a diuretic. Has been known to cause the following:

Sleeplessness

Anxiety

Low blood sugar

Increased heart rate

Increased appetite

Addiction

Excessive cheeriness

Excessive impatience

Boils

I shot a look back at the stall attendant and called over the heads of the crowd in front of her.

"The sign says you can get *boils* from drinking this?"

She made a dismissive gesture.

"One person got boils in the trials. It was probably totally unrelated, but they've got to list it if it happens."

I nodded thoughtfully and looked at Reginald.

"Shall we?"

Mugs in hand, we peered inside.

"It's . . . brown," he said. He sounded disappointed.

"Good thing. I can eat or drink anything as long as it's the color of shit."

Reginald narrowed his eyes at me.

"The loopholes to your eating habits get weirder all the time."

I shrugged.

"I didn't write the rules. Anyway, to not getting eaten by a giant!"

We raised our mugs and tapped them in a toast. Then we each took a sip and recoiled painfully.

"Ugh, that's disgusting—"

"It's so bitter—"

"It tastes like it's been burned—"

"It's like tar mixed with old hay—"

"It's so foul that . . . wait a moment."

We both stopped spluttering at the same time and examined the contents of our mugs again. I took another tentative sip. Reginald did the same.

"Actually," I said.

"It's not half bad, is it?"

"I was going to say the same thing."

We gulped the rest down and set our empty mugs on the table. The stall attendant looked at us expectantly.

"So? What'd'ya think?"

"At first it was terrible," said Reginald.

"But then it was less terrible," I said.

"And by the end it tasted fantastic," finished Reg.

She nodded knowingly.

"That's about the same story as everyone else's. Gross until it grows on ya. You want another?"

Reginald raised both eyebrows.

"We can have some more?"

She shrugged.

"Sure? Why not? Them's free samples, ain't they?"

I looked at Reginald.

"If it's free . . ."

He didn't need telling twice. We grabbed two new mugs and downed those as well. And then two more.

"I'd be careful," frowned the stall attendant as she watched us each consume a fourth cup. "People have been getting twitchy when they drink too much too quick."

"It's fine," I said. "I'm fine. We're fine. Everything's fine. Right, Reg?"

Reginald was grinning from ear to ear.

"I'm great, Mal. But . . . are you . . . *smiling*?"

I put my hands up to my face and massaged the corners of my mouth.

"Am I?"

"You're suffering from excessive cheeriness!" he said with a laugh. "That's one of the side effects!" Then he frowned. "Maybe we should be concerned about the boils after all."

My cheeks did feel strange. Sore, presumably from the smiling. They were also flushed and a bit tingly.

"Is this what it feels like to be a human? I have the energy of a thousand demons! Want to see me run?"

"Ooh! That sounds great, Mal. I'll run with you!"

I lifted a foot, about to sprint up the High Street, when the stall attendant clamped her hand down on my arm.

"Stop it, both of you." She pried the mugs out of our hands. "You're talking a blue streak, and you sound like a couple of brainless dolts. I'm cuttin' you off."

"You can't cut us off!" I cried.

"Oh? And why's that?"

I looked at Reginald.

"Because? Reg?"

"What, me?" he asked. "I don't know!"

"Oi! Finlay!" she called over her shoulder. At once, a fair-haired boy of perhaps seven or eight appeared at her side. There was a mischievous glint in his eye, and both his hair and clothes were rumpled. Some other creature's fur was mixed in with his own hair. If I had to guess, he'd just been tipping a cow or terrorizing some sheep.

"Take these two somewhere away from here where they can get washed up. Can't have them scaring away the customers."

There didn't seem to be any chance of that, but it was her stand, I guess.

"Hello—whoa!" said the lad, taking two steps back. At first he'd offered his hand, but he immediately snatched it back and used it to cover his nose. "You smell terrible."

I rolled my eyes.

"We know. Now if we're not getting a coffee for the road . . . ?" I cast my most pitiful expression over at the stall attendant, but she shook her head. My shoulders sagged, and I motioned for the boy to lead us onward. "Then I guess we'll be following you."

Finlay darted away like a field mouse winding through a wheat field. There was a dense crowd at the bottom of the town, so it was difficult to keep up with him. Plus, my ribs were in agony, and from the lingering wince on Reginald's face, getting manhandled by a giant hadn't done him any favors either. But we followed the boy as best we could until we arrived in a broad, cobbled square. Low, timbered shops with window boxes and steeply pitched roofs formed the perimeter. On one of the larger buildings hung a long, pointed banner in pale sage. Set upon it with golden embroidery was a shield flanked by two stags that appeared to fight over the crown atop it. On the shield were two fir trees under an umbrella of three stars, and beneath the shield were the words QUAERITUR ET QUARREL. It was technically the academy's emblem, but the people of Seven had adopted it as their own. At the center of the square was a tall fountain made of pale stone. The sky was clear azure, with not a cloud to be seen. A few people were visiting the modest shops, but otherwise, all was quiet. I looked at the boy, who continued to keep his distance from us.

"So where are we supposed to wash?"

"There."

He pointed at the fountain.

My laugh was incredulous at best and a little hysterical, at worst.

"You want us to bathe in a public fountain?"

"Where did you think I was taking you? A *spa*?"

His cheek was not appreciated, but I was too tired to fight.

"Fine. Come along, Reginald."

For reasons passing understanding, the boy shot us an impish grin before disappearing back the way we came.

A FUNNY THING ABOUT COFFEE, we discovered, is that after it invigorates you to the point of a heart attack, it sinks you right back down into fatigue. We still hadn't properly rested since our ordeal in the mountains, but there was no way we were going to go begging for our ever-growing list of needs smelling anything but our best. Or, at least, as close to our best as we could manage.

The fountain was maybe ten feet wide and eighteen feet tall; the pillar in the middle was carved into the shape of a half-naked woman reading a book. Reginald and I were splashing water over our faces when a girl of about five years with perfect, golden ringlets interrupted our ministrations. She wore a spotless blue dress and held a palm-sized package wrapped in twine.

"Excuse me, sirs."

I eyed the package suspiciously as she thrust it in our direction.

"What?"

Reginald looked at me askance.

"Manners, Mal!" He turned to the little girl, a disgustingly sweet smile spreading across his face. "What can we do for you, young lady?"

She placed the package down on the side of the fountain and pulled at one of her ringlets.

"This is from my mama. She mills soap. We could smell you from over there." She pointed her finger past the fountain and across the courtyard to a small shop with window boxes full of bright flowers.

"Oh," said Reginald, smile fading. "I was hoping it was food."

The girl wasn't paying any attention to him, though. She was studying my face intently.

"Why do you have yellow eyes?"

"Because I'm a demon. And they aren't yellow. They are goldenrod."

"What's goldenrod?"

"It's . . . yellow."

I heard Reginald huff a laugh.

"What's a demon?"

"A demon is a being from the Underworld."

"What's the Underworld?"

"It's a place where they send bad little girls who ask too many questions."

"Mal!" cried Reg.

"Kidding! I'm just kidding," I said, holding up my hands in defense.

"Who is he?" she asked, pointing a finger at Reg.

"I'm Sir Reginald P. Asstradle, Hero of Widdershins, m'lady," Reginald said with a bow in her direction. Unimpressed, she turned back to me.

"Why are you here?"

I sighed. Would she ever go away?

"To see the wizards."

"About what?"

My eye twitched.

"Sir Asstradle here accidentally summoned me. Then we broke a connection stone, and now we're magically intertwined until the end of time. We're hoping to get cleaned up, buy the hero a shirt, get presentable, and then ask the wizards to unstick us. Okay? Are you satisfied?"

"Do you like rainbows?"

"Nope. I'm not doing this!" I said, throwing my arms up. I took her by the shoulders, rotated her 180 degrees, and shoved her gently in the direction whence she'd come. "Please tell your mother Reginald thanks her for the soap, and go away."

She turned around once to stick her tongue out at me, then flitted away, though not towards the shop. Out of the corner of my eye I could see her going door-to-door and pointing in our direction as she told the proprietors who-knows-what story. Probably that I'd been rude to her.

"I wouldn't have needed to be so rude if she hadn't been so damn annoying," I grumbled under my breath.

Reginald picked up the package, sniffed it, then tore off the wrapping.

"Lavender, I think?"

"Lavender? Blech." I made exaggerated gagging sounds. Reginald rolled his eyes at me, but there was a hint of a twinkle in them as well.

"You're always so dramatic," he said.

I shot him a smooth smile.

"It's part of my charm."

I held out my hand for the soap.

"I thought lavender was—" He did his best to imitate the sounds I'd made.

"It is." Leaning over, I snatched the smooth bar out of his hand. "But it's what we've got."

We set to cleaning as many bits as we could reach without resorting to complete indecency, then waved our arms around in the brisk air to dry them off. It was not as cold in Seven as it had been in the mountains, but it still raised the hairs on my arms and chest.

"What do you think Steadly is like?" Reginald asked.

"Well, according to that brochure, he looks like a storybook prince. Chiseled jaw, broad shoulders. And that testimonial made him sound like just the sort of sap that would help us."

Reginald shivered as a gust of wind blew past.

"Is it weird that I can't wait to meet him but am also scared?"

I finished shaking out my hands and ran them through my hair.

"I think you'd be mad to feel any other way. He might be the nicest guy in the world—but he's still a wizard. He can probably squash us with his mind or turn us into fruit flies if the mood strikes him."

Reginald turned wide eyes on me.

"I'm kidding!" I said, punching him lightly in the arm. "Probably," I muttered under my breath.

"So, what now?" he asked as he slipped my morning coat on over his still-damp body. I yearned to snatch it back from him but reminded myself that things could go south for me, too, if he caught cold and died before we met with the headmaster.

"Well, we have," I reached into my pocket and pulled out some coins, "the equivalent of four half-rounds. That's enough for either food or a shirt, but not both. I'm starving so I vote food."

The space between Reginald's eyes creased in confusion.

"I'm starving too, but how do we have any money?"

I hitched a thumb at the pool behind me.

"I scooped it out of the fountain."

"What? Mal, those are people's wishes!"

"Yes, and now I *wish* to use them to get some food."

"No way! This time I'm putting my foot down. We are not stealing from these people!"

"Fine. We'll just sit here and waste away."

"Fine!"

"Fine."

Reginald took out his pocket time wheel, and we watched three full minutes tick by. Then his stomach rumbled so loudly that a group sitting on the other side of the fountain looked up.

"Lunch?" I asked.

He sighed.

"Okay, lunch."

WE FOLLOWED our noses toward the smell of cooking meat and ended up in a quiet alley off the High Street. Though it was sandwiched between two tall buildings that blocked the light, we still spotted the street vendor selling kebabs. His rickety wooden cart was on wheels to make it easy to move when the crowds thinned. Spears of the most perfect specimens of meats and vegetables were twirling in languorous circles on a spit on top of the cart.

"What can I get you two today? Chicken and vegetables? Or beef and vegetables?"

We stared hungrily at the food.

"Yes!" we both said. I slammed the money down on the cart, and the vendor reached down into the cart's interior and pulled out a couple of skewers. They did not appear as delectable as the ones on display, and they probably didn't taste as good either. The meat was stringy, and the "vegetables"—assuming that's what they'd been at one point—looked like they'd seen the inside of a blast furnace. Still, we were so hungry that we frightened the attendant by devouring them like ravenous wolves. He was so terrified, in fact, that he gave us each two extra kebabs for free and then scuttled off down the street, the wheels on the cart squeaking in protest as he ran. We made a mental note to always eat with vigor in the future.

"It's probably going to give me a stomachache, but it's worth it, really, for free food," said Reginald, swallowing the last of his meat cubes. "And it's not like we were *actually* going to hurt him. He just thought we might."

"I couldn't agree more," I said, tapping my fist to my chest to relieve some pressure.

Sated, we moved out of the alley, back into the late-day winter sunlight that bathed the cobbled High Street. Our attention turned toward the two towers cloaked in Rogue magic at the top of the hill. The magic gave the sky a greenish cast but did not mar the glowing whiteness of the school itself.

"It's hard to believe we're really here," said Reginald as we stared, mesmerized, up at the shimmering outline of the school.

"I know."

The entire journey to Seven, I'd been in a rush to get here. But now that we were just a hill climb from our goal, I was feeling jittery. I shook my head to clear it. Nervousness was a nonsense emotion at this moment. I was minutes from meeting the wizard who was going to detach me from Reginald, and we appeared to have beaten my brother to Seven. Delight was the only acceptable feeling.

Reginald pulled my coat tightly around him.

"I still don't have a shirt."

"I know," I said, still looking up at the school, "but I don't think we can delay any longer. We have to go see Steadly imme-

diately. That testimonial made him seem like the helpful sort—
he probably won't mind. You can do your apologizing thing."

"Yeah, all right."

Nodding at one another, we turned to hike up the hill. I'd just lifted a foot to start the journey when a voice sounded behind us, and I nearly toppled over.

"Not so fast, you two! You're not going anywhere."

CHAPTER 11
SAFFRON AND GOODFALLOW

"Ah!"

Both Reginald and I jumped, convinced it was Tannith. But as we turned around, we saw not one demon, but two humans. The speaker was a tall, fair male human wearing glasses. The other was a short, dark female human without glasses but with fabulous, curly, textured hair that stood out from her scalp in a glorious halo. Although they could hardly have been more different, they both had identical wide grins plastered across their faces.

"Sorry. We mean—you're not going anywhere without us!" exclaimed the female.

"Who the fuck are you?" I screeched, still breathless from the surprise. "And who introduces themselves by sneaking up from behind and saying, 'You're not going anywhere'?"

"Oh, right!" said the one with glasses still beaming. His spectacles slipped down his nose and he pushed them back up. "Where are our manners? My name is Goodfallow, and this is . . ."

"Saffron! My name is Saffron. We're so pleased to meet you," she said, nearly jumping out of her skin with excitement. "And you are Sir Reginald and Lord Malgon."

Reginald frowned.

"We are. But—I'm sorry. Who are you? I know you said your names, but I still don't get it," said Reginald.

Goodfallow and Saffron exchanged a look and laughed.

"Goodness, but we've gone about this all wrong, haven't we? We're students up at the academy!"

Reginald and I both stepped back to examine them. Now that they'd said it, it was obvious. They wore the shapeless robes of the academics, accessorized by messenger bags bulging with books that were slung across their bodies. Emblazoned on their ridiculous garb was the crest of the academy.

I'd never understood this particular fashion—if you can even call it that. Did robes prevent ridicule if one happened to gain a few extra pounds? Were all academics secretly badasses who carried concealed weapons in the endless yards of fabric? Perhaps the shapeless garment ensured that wizards focused entirely on their education. Because absolutely no one would want to have sex with a person who walked around in what was basically a nightgown masquerading as formal attire—I can tell you that.

"So why aren't you in class?"

"Headmaster Steadly sent us to fetch you. The way up to the school can be treacherous the first time if you're not students or professors," said Saffron.

Reginald and I exchanged excited looks.

"Headmaster Steadly knows we were here?"

"He does, indeed," said Goodfallow.

Saffron and Goodfallow were *still* smiling, and it was getting on my nerves. They weren't the manic smiles of two people who'd been forced to show us a good time under duress. They were the smiles of genuine interest and helpfulness. It was unnatural.

"It's rare that we get newcomers in the city, you know," said Goodfallow. "Your arrival added some significant grist for the rumor mill, if you know what I mean." He elbowed me good-naturedly in the ribs, and the pain radiated throughout the rest of my body. I lifted my arm to smack him, but Reginald put his hand out and lowered mine slowly back down. "Finlay is one of the academy's finest little rumor-mongers. Gives good money-trading information."

"Ah," I said, now understanding Finlay's mischievous fucking twinkle. "Well, let's not keep the headmaster waiting!"

"Hold on," said Reginald, throwing an arm out to halt me. "Didn't you say something about treachery?"

"Not 'treachery.' I said the road is 'treacherous,'" said Saffron. "It only looks like the road runs to our front door. There's an invisible magical maze that winds from here to the outskirts of the school in which both mages and nonmagicians alike have perished."

Reginald and I both gaped at her.

"*Perished?*"

"*As in dead?*"

For the first time, her smile faltered in favor of an expression of earnest concern. "I know. It's tragic." Then she hitched it back on and said, "The purpose is to keep those of ill intent from visiting. But once you've proven yourself to the maze, you are free to come and go as you please. So that's why we've come to get you—to get you through that first time."

"Or to watch us disappear in a puff of smoke if the maze doesn't deem us worthy?" I added snarkily.

Saffron nodded.

"Or that."

I exchanged a look with Reginald. The skepticism written on his features mirrored my own. Being a demon, I was particularly concerned, but I didn't think we had other options.

"Well?" I asked.

"I guess," said Reg.

"Only if you want."

"Well, we have to."

"Then it's settled."

I turned to Saffron and Goodfallow.

"Okay. I guess we're going with you."

Our guides just blinked at us.

"That was amazing," breathed Saffron. "Is this what all the hero-demon duos were like back in the golden age of heroes? The two of you are so in sync—it's like you have your own language."

I grimaced. Being "in sync" with Reginald was not a life goal of mine. I shot him a glance and saw that he clearly thought the same about me. At least we weren't so far gone that we were the same person. Yet.

"Quite. Anyway, let's get started."

I took three steps up the hill when I felt two sets of hands on my shoulders, and I lurched back.

"Not that way!" Goodfallow and Saffron yelled together.

"What? Why?"

Saffron scooped a loose pebble up from the cobbles and tossed it a few feet in front of where they'd stopped me. There was a slight disturbance in the air—like transparent ripples on a pond—and then it was just . . . gone.

"Fuck me," I whispered and shrugged their hands off.

Saffron was suddenly all business.

"Here's how it's going to go. Me, then you, my Lord, then Sir Reginald, then Goodfallow. You will walk exactly where I walk. It will tempt you to reach out and touch things, but you will not do so. You will not speak unless I tell you to speak. And you will, under no circumstances, curse. The wizards who created this maze were of a pious sort and an ill-timed expletive could land us anywhere from the Stone Rot Mountains to an entirely different dimension."

"Shit, seriously?"

Saffron raised an eyebrow.

"Sorry," I said, holding my palms up in front of me. "Last one. I promise."

She gave us each a stern look, then organized the four of us into a line. And in that way—looking like the world's strangest caterpillar—we inched our way up the street, through the maze, to the Academy of Magic at the City of Seven.

THE MAZE DID NOT RUN ALL the way up to the front door. A second wall ran around the entire campus. Once we made it there, we were through. But even with competent guides, we barely emerged unscathed. Well, I was barely unscathed.

"Mal?"

"Yes, Reg?"

"You're on fire."

"Seriously?"

I glanced down at my trousers and slapped at the flame licking up my right-hand pocket. Reginald's hair stood straight out from his scalp, and his coat—no, *my* coat—was coming apart at the shoulder seam. I glared at him and growled.

"That was harrowing," said Reginald, trying to pinch the arm of the coat back together.

"Yeah," I said, thinking about how I'd nearly put my right foot into a churning silver void by mistake. Luckily Saffron closed it up before I fell through. The world had looked different in the maze. Distances felt impossible to measure. The sky was sometimes disconcertingly beneath us instead of comfortingly above. The road warped and buckled. Our surroundings shifted from bright neon to deep purple to shimmering glass to burning flame. Reality bent nearly to the breaking point. Or at least that's what it felt like. But at every dip, turn, and near-death-experience, Saffron was there to keep the worst from happening. "You know a lot of magic for a twelve-year-old."

Saffron furrowed her brow, probably wondering if I was joking.

"Goodfallow and I are both seventeen," she said, deciding I was just bad at estimating ages. She brushed down her robes, though she showed no signs of dishevelment. "The first time we came through just as you did, with the help of a more advanced mage. But we all learn pretty quickly once we're enrolled. The magic is obvious once you know what to look for."

I marveled at her condition. Even Goodfallow had a few postmaze adjustments to make, but not Saffron. She was probably one of those insufferable people who color-code their calendars and arrive early for appointments. Those people annoyed the piss out of me. It's one thing to be organized. But to be organized *and* respectful of others? That's just showing off.

Goodfallow pushed his glasses up the bridge of his nose, then shook out his sleeves. His robes were just a few inches too long for him, and it lent him a slightly juvenile, boyish air.

"Right! Shall we get going, then?" The unnerving journey behind us, his enthusiasm snapped back into place.

The towers of the academy loomed large now. I looked over at Reginald, whose eyes were glassy and unfocused, as if he were reliving the moments of near dematerialization we'd just experienced.

"You okay to walk, Reg?"

His eyes cleared, and his eyebrows raised in surprise at my question. Actually, he probably didn't find the question as surprising as the questioner did—but thinking about his needs was a nasty new habit I'd formed. I was hoping our magical separation would break it.

"Yeah, Mal. I'm okay."

As we strolled up the rest of the winding road, we noticed

that the surrounding buildings looked different than those down the hill. While the lower town was constructed of mostly half-timber structures, the middle and upper districts had row homes of brick and stone. Near the peak of the roof on many of the houses nearest the school were signs with a few letters in another language.

"What do you suppose those are?" whispered Reginald. "Magic spells? Keep the . . . uh . . ." He looked suddenly sheepish, and I flashed him an evil grin.

"You were about to say 'to keep the demons away,' weren't you?"

"I . . ."

"No worries, Reg. It's a good thought. But no. In fact, it is an absolute miracle that the folks in those houses haven't summoned a demon by accident. The groups who live in those houses are called 'fraternities.'"

"Oh."

I looked sidelong at Reginald. My explanation hadn't helped.

"You know? A fraternity? A group of like-minded intellectuals who get together and destroy all their brain cells with alcohol consumption? You might get on well there. I hear they throw up a lot."

"Ha, ha," he said without humor.

"I heard once that it was three students from one of these frat houses that opened up the first portal to the Underworld," said Saffron.

I nodded.

"I wouldn't be surprised if it were true. Magic, alcohol, and early adulthood make a dangerous cocktail."

"Can you imagine?" asked Reginald.

"Imagine what?" I asked.

"How much simpler my life would have been if they'd left well enough alone?"

I smirked.

"How about you two?" I asked. "Are you two in a fraternity?"

Their expressions changed to ones of forced nonchalance. I was familiar with the reaction—one often uses it when one is lying.

"What would we need a fraternity for?" asked Saffron.

"We have all the companionship we need between the two of us and Lady Learning," concluded Goodfallow.

I wrinkled my nose.

"'*Lady Learning*'? You mean you rushed, but no one would have you?"

Goodfallow's shoulders slumped so low his knuckles nearly dragged on the ground.

"Yes."

"I was a pledge for a while. But I don't even want to think about the terrible things they wanted us to do. This one time we had to steal a sheep and sheer it, then wear the wool around for two days. I almost failed my classes that quarter because all I could say was *baa*."

I cackled and Reginald punched my arm.

"Ow—what?"

"He said it was terrible!" he hissed.

"Can't it be terrible *and* funny?"

"But it all worked out for the best. We met when we were assigned seats next to each other in Elementary Elements and realized that we didn't need anyone else," said Goodfallow, patting Saffron's shoulder affectionately.

"Except Lady Learning," I said.

"Oh yes. Except her," said Goodfallow.

I rolled my eyes.

We walked along in silence for a minute—the maximum interval Reginald can go without speaking—then he filled the void by asking, "What's magic like? I mean, I've seen

Mal do some magic. And we saw you doing some in the maze. But what is it actually *like*?"

Saffron and Goodfallow looked at one another in silent conversation.

"Imagine the hardest thing you've ever done," started Saffron.

"Then make it five times harder," said Goodfallow.

"Then do it while standing on one leg . . ."

". . . and drinking your favorite wine."

Reginald and I exchanged perplexed looks.

"So, what are you saying? It's . . . fun?" I asked.

In defiance of traditional human biology, their grins widened even further.

"Oh yeah. It's awesome."

"If you say so," said Reginald under his breath.

"Speaking of awesome," said Saffron. "Here we are! The front door."

"WELL, FUCK ME SIDEWAYS."

Calling it a "door" didn't really do it justice.

It was a massive ivory gateway into the main tower, with intricate gold filigree. The pattern that swirled up from the base of the mammoth opening looked like puffs of smoke or eddying wind. The doors were set into a tower of stacked stone bricks that shone pale gold. A conical turret covered in silver shingles graced the top of the structure.

I originated in a place of devilry. I possess some craft myself. But this was one of the most enchanted places I'd ever been. I could feel it in my bones.

"It's supposed to be magic," said Goodfallow, following my gaze. "The pattern on the doors, I mean. Doesn't really look like it to me, but I don't suppose I could do any better."

"I don't really care what it looks like as long as it leads to the wizards," I said, leaning forward to push the door open.

"What are you doing?" asked Saffron.

"I'm going in," I said, indicating toward the door.

"We can't take you in yet."

"Why not?" asked Reginald.

"Well, meaning no disrespect, but Sir Reginald is shirtless under a dilapidated morning coat, and a few minutes ago your pants were on fire." She said it with no judgment. These were simply the facts. I looked down at the collection of charred holes in my pants while Reginald started playing with the coat again.

"I see your point," I said.

"Come this way, and we'll find you something appropriate to wear," said Goodfallow.

Saffron and Goodfallow led us around the enormous tower. Ever the tour guides, they began narrating our journey.

"We refer the taller tower to your right to as 'The Wizard's Tower,'" said Saffron. "That's where the seven Grand Wizards work and teach. The smaller tower is the Mage's Tower. We have some classes there as well, but The Grand Wizards dedicated the top seven floors to the library. They built both towers around the hollowed-out husks of twin fir trees that once stood on this spot. It is supposedly one of the most magical locations in all of Widdershins."

"Must have been some trees," I said.

"They were of the *Prodigious* variety and originally stood twice as tall as the towers."

"Was Seven named for the number of wizards, or was the number of wizards determined by the name of the city?" asked Reginald.

I was still doing the mental gymnastics to understand his question when Goodfallow smiled.

"Noticed that, did you? Seven is named for the number of

Grand Wizards. It's one of the more powerfully magical numbers, though three is the most magical. When the school was established and started to grow in renown, the people changed the name of the city to honor them."

"What was the name before?" I asked.

"Bogwittle."

"So no real loss there," I said, rubbing my eyes. The haze of magic was thicker up here than in the lower town, and it made my eyes itch so intensely that I wanted to claw them out. Even breathing was troublesome. It was like breathing in smoke or dust if smoke or dust made your head feel as if it were floating around somewhere north of your body.

"What connects the towers?" asked Reginald.

Goodfallow looked up at the structure suspended between the two towers.

"That's the dining hall."

"Did you hear that, Mal?" Reginald asked. "The dining hall." He grinned and rubbed his hands together in anticipation.

We passed the small—I mean the *Mage's* Tower—and rounded the corner to an empty courtyard.

"Where is everyone?"

"The library, of course," said Saffron.

"It's only a few days until the end of term. Got to cram in all the studying they can," finished Goodfallow.

"And why don't you have to cram in all the studying *you* can?"

They exchanged an incredulous look.

"We do. But when the headmaster calls, you answer."

We crossed the courtyard to a three-story annex behind the towers that was still within the walls of the school. Constructed of the same pale gold stones as those of the main buildings, the annex looked smooth from far away, but up close you could see divots and pockmarks on its glowing surface. At the summit of the building was a wall-walk, and I idly wondered if it was for recreation or defense.

"Here are the dormitories," said Saffron as we crossed the threshold into a low-ceilinged atrium, where we paused in the entryway. At the far side of the space, two sets of stairs winded up in opposite directions.

I pointed toward them.

"What's that? Boy's side and girl's side?"

At my comment, Goodfallow—who had continued walking toward an open cabinet at the side of the room—turned back, eyes wide, and said, "Surely even a demon knows that the world is more complicated than that."

I shrugged one shoulder.

"In my experience, humans value predictability."

He made no further comment but ducked his head inside the cupboard. We could hear him banging and muttering until he pulled himself back out.

"Ah ha! Here we are!"

Across each of his arms was a swath of black fabric. I immediately held my hands up to wave him off.

"No. No, no, no. Absolutely not. I am not wearing those amorphous circus tents you call clothes."

Goodfallow and Saffron looked down at themselves as if they'd never considered the fashionability of their uniforms before.

"They're not so bad," said Saffron.

"That's correct," I said. "They're not so bad. They're worse than bad. They are downright terrible."

Goodfallow screwed up his mouth, which made his glasses fall down his nose. He tilted his head back so he could still see us.

"Well, it's this or nothing."

"Nothing would be preferable."

"Mal."

"Don't you be reasonable, Asstradle!"

"At least they're black."

"Don't care."

"Think of all the fountain change you could hide in there."

Saffron and Goodfallow exchanged inquisitive looks but said nothing.

"Still no."

Saffron spoke up.

"We could send your clothes to the thaumaturgic tailor while you meet with the headmaster?"

The three of them looked at me expectantly. Growling, I stared each of them down before stomping over to Goodfallow and snatching up the robes.

"Let it be known I am doing this under duress," I hissed as I grabbed Reginald by the arm and stalked away to a shadowy corner to change.

———

"Reginald?"

"Yes, Mal?"

"You look ridiculous."

"No more ridiculous than wearing a half-shredded coat."

"Not *a* coat. *My* coat."

"Regardless of whose coat it was, it was a mess."

"You're sure you got everything from my pockets?"

"Yes."

"Even the tiny interior one that's only big enough for a single pin?"

"Yes!"

I crossed my arms over my chest as we walked back to the Wizard's Tower to meet with the headmaster, but that seemed to exaggerate the dramatic flow of the fabric train trailing behind me, so I dropped them back to my sides.

"He's never going to take us seriously in these. I can't believe you talked me into wearing this."

Reginald looked shocked.

"Did I? I don't think I've ever talked you into anything before."

He strode slightly ahead of me, and I consoled myself by making faces at his back.

Goodfallow was at the front of our mini parade as we arrived back at the ivory doors.

"Now, before we go in, there is something that you should know."

In books, a character that is eager to get a move on is often described as "hopping from foot to foot." Hopping is not really my style, though. So I grabbed my hair and screamed out one long, frustrated exhalation. Then I turned politely to Goodfallow and said, "And what might that be?"

Goodfallow and Saffron looked as though they'd just had a close, personal encounter with a wild animal.

"Just that it's a spiral staircase. And . . . there are a lot of stairs," whispered Goodfallow. Saffron nodded her head emphatically.

"Well," I continued in my most civilized tone, "if there's one thing that has improved since the start of our journey—Reginald and I are now cardiovascular titans. Please, after you."

I motioned toward the door with a slight bow.

"Okay, then," said Goodfallow, turning toward the doors. He pointed two fingers on his right hand skyward, then did a complicated twisting motion. There was a rumbling, and we watched as the ivory gateway to the Wizard's Tower opened inward.

We were about to meet the wizard.

CHAPTER 12
WITH ALL THE POWER OF A STRUCK GAVEL

As we ascended the many stairs, I waged an inner war. For a few steps, I would convince myself that I was definitely going to ask the headmaster to fix the stone. Then, for the next few stairs, I was planning to hold him out of a window and force him to tell me how to break the barrier to the Underworld, winning me fame and praise. These were hard decisions.

"Do these stairs . . . ever end?" asked Reginald beside me, wiping the back of his hand across his forehead. School banners and the occasional bulletin board crammed with parchment notices saying things like JOIN THE CULINARY WIZARD'S CLUB and BE SUBVERSIVE—STOP JOINING CLUBS! broke up the constant spiral of the staircase. Doors appeared at landings, and through them we could hear classroom arguments crescendo and diminish as we passed. But though these interrupted the monotony, they did not make the stairs less steep.

"We're not even going to the very top. The headmaster's office is just below a meeting room on the top floor," gasped Goodfallow.

For all my bragging, all four of us were winded and

sweating when we reached it, and I had a numb spot on my back where the stones in my bag had been bumping against it.

Goodfallow knocked on the door. He and Saffron stood before us like herald trumpeters, announcing our presence. They even had the silly outfits. Though, so did we.

The door swung open, and at first I thought we had the wrong room. Or the wrong school. Possibly the wrong world. The only word I can use to describe the person who opened it is—*bulbous*. A bulbous man in cream-and-gold robes stood before us. Presumably. I couldn't actually see his feet. But the more I looked, the more I saw the echo of a powerful jaw and a princely countenance. Still, he greeted us with less enthusiasm than I'd been expecting from a man who'd sent us an escort.

"All right, then. Come in, come in," said Headmaster Steadly, ushering us into his office. "No, not you two!" he said to Saffron and Goodfallow, who'd followed us in. They bowed their silent apologies and backed out into the hallway, closing the door behind them.

"Sorry about the mess. Can I get you both some coffee? It's this new drink that the culinary wizards concocted. I should warn you—it's nearly unpalatable until you get used to it."

Reginald and I exchanged eager looks.

"Coffee would be amazing, thanks," said Reginald.

Steadly nodded, then busied himself at the sideboard. I took the opportunity to examine the office. His desk and floor were bestrewn with teetering piles of scrolls and tomes, like a miniature paper city ready to topple at any moment. The wide oak desk sat in front of three paned windows overlooking the city. Behind that was a veritable throne—an indigo wingback chair outlined with gold upholstery tacks. In front were stationed two basic, more utilitarian wooden seats. I took the one on the left and Reginald sat down to my right.

The smell of fresh coffee wafted over to us as I eyed papers filled with diagrams and notices. I was about to reach forward and dislodge one about the upcoming Yulesticetide Festival from its precarious stack, but the clink of mugs on saucers roused me from my observations, and I pulled back my hand.

"Do you take milk or sugar?" asked the headmaster as he placed a steaming cup in front of me.

"Brown is fine, thanks."

Steadly nodded and handed the other cup to Reginald. He waddled his ample form around to the other side of the desk and wedged himself into the wingback. It groaned and cracked under his weight but didn't collapse.

"Headmaster, I don't think I have properly introduced us. My name is . . ."

"Lord Malgon Belroth Kirranith. And this one," he said, gesturing to Reg, "is Sir Reginald P. Asstradle."

I blinked blankly at him.

"How . . ."

He eyed me behind his coffee cup, then put it down on the desk.

"Look, I'm going to cut to the chase, boys," he said. My back stiffened at being referred to as "boy," but this was a little early in the conversation to be making a scene. "I know why you're here and that you've come a long way to see me—but I'm sorry to say, I can't help you."

I stopped breathing.

In my mind, the sound in the room went whisper-soft, and all I could hear was the roar of blood pumping through my veins and an incessant ringing in my ears. Out of the corner of my eye, I saw Reginald go rigid—hands so tight on the coffee cup that I thought he might crush it. Neither of us had considered the possibility that the wizards would not want to help us.

"I'm sorry to have gotten your hopes up by bringing you here. Honestly, I would have refused to see you at all, but your grandmother being who she is . . ."

Reginald regained his mobility and shook his head.

"Gran? *My* gran? What's she got to do with this?"

The headmaster looked perplexed. He pulled a rumpled white handkerchief from the folds of his robes and dabbed at his forehead.

"My apologies. I thought you knew. She is one of our most generous benefactors and was also a very fine student."

I turned to Reg. His face was beet red, and he crossed his arms over his chest as he slouched back in his chair.

"Of course she was. Why doesn't anyone ever tell me anything?"

"Never mind his gran—what do you mean you can't help us? We read the pamphlet! You're the most powerful wizard in all of Widdershins, and you helped a guy walk straight again!"

Steadly looked at me as if I'd suddenly started speaking an unfamiliar language.

"I don't know about any pamphlet, but there are at least half-a-dozen reasons I can't help."

"But there are at least half-a-dozen reasons to help us as well! The most important being that Reginald and I are entangled for eternity if you don't. Well, that's the most important to me. But there's also that breaking the stone seems to have put the barrier between the Underworld and Widdershins on the fritz. There's a demon on his way here right now who will torture you for the information on how to make it permanent and—Satan's uncle. I just realized that I want to fix the stone."

I let out a little laugh at how easy the decision ended up being, but Reginald sat back up.

"What do you mean, 'you just realized'? You decided back at the Charity Run."

I tilted my head to the side and donned what I presumed was a guilty expression.

"Well . . ."

"Oh, my gosh! Are you ever not lying? Not fixing the stone would be horrible for all of Widdershins!"

I narrowed my eyes at him.

"It's not that simple and you know it."

He stared back at me, equally annoyed.

"Actually, it is that simple, but you just don't see it."

"Boys," interrupted Steadly. "While I admit a second demon is problematic, I don't see how the stone has anything to do with it."

"No?" I said, voice dripping with sarcasm. "The all-knowing, all-powerful headmaster doesn't understand that a day or so after we broke the Stone of Eno, a portal to the Underworld started flickering in and out? You don't see how the two events might be related?"

Steadly frowned at me.

"That's enough, Kirranith."

"Yeah, Mal," said Reginald. "We're never going to convince him to help us if you're mean to him."

"You're never going to convince me anyway," said Steadly. "And it's not because I don't have sympathy for your situation or that I'm not concerned about this other demon. It's the magic itself that is the problem. The type of magic necessary to assist you is not a type of magic I can allow. To lift the connection magic from you, place it in the stone, and repair the stone—that would require Change magic. We would fundamentally change the nature of both you and Lord Malgon," he nodded in my direction, "and the stone itself. And that's to say nothing about the rogue magic floating around this place. It would take an immense amount of power, and it would be irresponsible of me to permit it."

I glared at him.

"Just when I thought that humans were worth saving, you go and prove just how stupid you are all over again. Maybe I should have hung you out the window after all."

"Mal!"

Steadly ignored my comment and disencumbered his chair of its load by standing.

"This conversation is over. It's time for you to leave my office." He spoke with all the power of a struck gavel.

"Please, Headmaster," cried Reginald. "We've gone through so much to be here. We've tricked fairies, survived a Centennial Storm, and been chased by dwarves, a Grootslang, and some kind of mutant spider. We were nearly eaten by a giant and almost froze to death to be here. And Mal's brother is on his way here right now to get the stone! Can't you do anything to help?"

Steadly arched an eyebrow at us.

"Mal's brother? Well, that's a twist I wasn't expecting." The headmaster sighed. "There's nothing I can do that I know of. But you may stay and search the library. If you find a way to fix this without using Change magic, I will consider it. But until then, 'no' is my final answer."

He struggled, wheezing, over to the door and opened it. Saffron and Goodfallow were standing against the opposite wall. I stood and grabbed my bag but hardly registered that I was moving. Numb from head to toe, I shuffled through the door in time to hear Steadly say something about the library. Then I was on the landing outside his door, which was slamming in my face.

Everything we had been through—everything we'd survived—had all been for nothing. And all of Widdershins would pay.

"Mal?" asked Reginald, waving a hand in front of my face.

"What is it?" I answered without looking at him. We were walking away from the headmaster's office. I heard my footsteps echoing in the stairwell but felt unconnected to my feet.

I'd considered—and dismissed—the possibility that Steadly might not be able to help us. It had never occurred to me he wouldn't even try.

Reginald placed the waving hand on my shoulder.

"This isn't the end. We're going to figure this out."

I couldn't look at him. Seeing him made me feel angry, guilty, and confused.

"How?"

"You heard the headmaster—you can stay here as long as you like and use the library," interjected the unnaturally cheerful voice of Saffron. "He's even excused us from exams to help you!"

That snapped me out of my trance.

"He has? Why?"

Saffron and Goodfallow suddenly had the most interesting footwear in the universe.

"Well," said Saffron, eyes downcast, "the thing is . . ."

"We're rather good at school," said Goodfallow, crimson blooming on his high cheekbones.

"And we explained to him that even if we failed all our exams . . ."

"We would each still end the term with a one-hundred-and-twelve percent average."

"You really didn't hear them arguing?" asked Reginald.

I shook my head.

"Well, anyway, that's great news for us, isn't it, Mal?"

Reginald's exaggerated "isn't it, Mal?" implied he expected a response.

"Yes. Bully for us."

"The headmaster can't be completely immune to our plight if he's letting us stay here and is giving us help."

I was in a foul mood, and Reginald's logic wasn't helping it. We finally reached the bottom of the stairs when Reginald held me up.

"Look . . . I'm sorry about what I said. I know that family stuff is complicated. And I know that your horns and tail have been something you've wanted your whole life. I'm proud of you for choosing to do the right thing, in the end."

"Yeah, well, don't hold your breath. I still might change my mind," I grumbled, but Reginald just patted me on the back and caught up with Saffron and Goodfallow.

"Where to now?" he asked.

"To dinner, via the gardens."

"Gardens?" I said. "No, thank you. Reginald and I met in a garden. A garden started this whole mess."

"Technically, we were in a park," said Reginald.

"Park, garden—whatever. There were gardenias. And I *hate* gardenias."

"Ah, but these are the *poison* gardens," said Goodfallow.

"Are you sure we should go to a place full of poisonous plants? Our luck is not that great. Plus—isn't this building connected to the dining hall?" asked Reginald.

Goodfallow looked uneasy.

"It is, but we were so caught up in the excitement of it all that we forgot to stop walking. There's a shortcut in the other tower, so we'll just pop through the garden and be on our way. Unless you want to climb back up again?"

"No!" Reginald and I shouted in unison.

"You know what?" I said. "I am in no state to make any kind of decisions right now, so . . . lead the way, Sunshine. But this is a quick visit, mind. I don't want to freeze my ass off over some flowers or whatever."

Saffron pointed at herself, and I gestured to the door.

"Oh, uh, yes. But it's Saffron, Lord . . ."

"Are we leaving or not?" I shouted.

She yelped and hurried out the door with Goodfallow close on her heels. I didn't have to look at Reg to know what his expression would be.

"I know, I know," I said. "It's not their fault, blah, blah, blah."

"They're only trying to help. And they're the *only* ones trying to help. Try to be nice?" he said, patting me on the shoulder.

The corner of my mouth tilted up.

"Yeah, all right. I'll try to be nice."

He smiled brightly, and we both left the building.

"IT'S WINTER, so you won't be able to see everything, but they are still fascinating," said Goodfallow as we walked down a flagstone path. Our breath puffed out before us in the chilled air, and I was secretly glad to be wearing the borrowed ten thousand yards of fabric.

"What kind of poisons will we be seeing?" asked Reginald. He still didn't seem too sure about this outing.

"Technically, it's not a poison garden. Well—it is. But it's not *just* poisons. It's full of all the herbs, fungi, and flowers needed for both the healing arts and the more dangerous kinds of magic."

"Like Change magic?" I asked, a snippet of conversation with the headmaster coming back to me.

Saffron's eyebrows grazed her hairline.

"Why, yes! That's one of them. Also, anything dealing with Rogue magic."

"I'm sorry—did you say the healing arts?" asked Reginald. "I thought these were poisonous?"

Goodfallow chuckled. Facing us, he walked backward and explained, "Plenty of poisons are used in healing. Foxglove for the heart. Poppy for pain relief. It's funny—sometimes a small amount of bad actually does a lot of good."

Hadn't that been Quill Valor's justification for summoning

demons? But as far as the rest of the humans were concerned—he'd been wrong. A little bad was so awful that they red-taped them . . . us . . . out of existence.

"Huh," said Reginald. "I'd never thought of it that way before."

The path narrowed between high boxwood hedges, then ended in an arched trellis. It was covered in vines that wove themselves like black serpents in and out of the latticework. Star-shaped, midnight-dark flowers burst into bloom, revealing sunlit interiors as we walked under the arbor. Beyond stretched dozens of beds filled with tantalizing buds that erupted with color even beneath their hoarfrost blankets. A hint of earthy richness hung in the air, and although gardenias made me gag, it was a comforting smell even to me. Goodfallow and Saffron strolled ahead of us.

Reginald nudged my arm.

"Would you look at this?" he said, sweeping his arm across the vista.

I smirked at his childlike enthusiasm.

"Catch up to them if you like. I'll keep up. Just remember that if we delay here, we delay dinner."

He called back as he jogged ahead, "You know I'd never forget that!"

I smirked and picked up my pace to keep our connection from pulling too taut.

"This one over here is my favorite," said Saffron as I pulled up. She paused to cup a violently orange bloom in her palm. "It's a variety that only grows here in Seven. It's called Duchess Alstroemerias, and it's used to lessen the effects of Rogue magic on inanimate objects."

Reginald was squinting at her.

"You've said that a few times—'Rogue magic.' What is it? Why is it so dangerous?"

She stroked a petal of the flower before letting it go and continuing to walk to the Mage's Tower.

"It's a by-product of human magic. Think of it like this: magical creatures just do magic. It's part of them. They do nothing other than what they are made to do. But humans—we are not magical creatures. We, for lack of a better term, *borrow* magic. And because it's not innate to us, we need to practice and experiment to get it right. All that practice, all those failed experiments, they have a by-product that can be extremely dangerous. If humans stopped doing magic today, Rogue magic would probably dissipate after a while—go back into the ether or wherever magic comes from. But it's built up so much over the centuries that you can see it all around us. It's the haze that surrounds the academy. And Rogue magic is like a powder keg in that it could reassign itself at any moment."

"Reassign itself?"

"There can be terrible consequences if it activates around you," said Goodfallow. "You could explode, devolve into a puddle of goo, or even turn into a pig. It's anyone's guess and impossible to predict."

"That sounds really dangerous," said Reginald, scratching the side of his nose. "Why risk it?"

"To learn! To expand our knowledge of the universe!" cried Goodfallow with the enthusiasm of a Threeist priest standing before a potential convert. "And, really, isn't everything danger-ous? I mean, even life kills you in the end."

I opened my mouth to argue, but from a human perspec-tive, it was true.

"Here's the exit," said Goodfallow as we reached another arched trellis. "Ooh, Saff! There's a Cracking Game going on at the Yards!" He craned his neck to see over a fence in the distance.

"Maybe another time," said Saffron. "It's freezing out here, and we promised them dinner."

"Yeah, you're right," he said, sounding disappointed. We exited under the trellis, and his eyes wandered back toward the Yards.

"What is Cracking?" asked Reginald.

"It's a wizard's game. There are two teams of five. You basically try to herd the other team into a spot on the floor that you've weakened by magic. You win when they fall through, into the deep pit below the Yards. They say it's so deep that it scrapes the ceiling of the Underworld."

"Unlikely," I said dryly.

"He would know. He is a demon," said Reginald.

Goodfallow shrugged.

"Still. It's pretty deep. One time, it took a team a fortnight to get out of the pit. We had to keep going out and tossing food down, hoping they could catch it. Ah, here we are."

We'd reached the Mage's Tower and the shortcut. On the outside of the tower, unseen from the city below, there was a small platform enchanted to bring people up and down, to and from the dining hall.

"After you," said Saffron, still so bubbly I thought she might boil over.

When all four of us were on, she made a lifting gesture with her hand, and the platform rose. Reginald, who was going green, shuffled closer to the wall. I moved to stand next to him.

"Hold it together, Reg. You've faced a lot worse than this."

He nodded, not wanting to risk a verbal reply.

But it was no big deal. In moments were back inside and entering the hustle and bustle of the dining hall.

The ceilings were at least three stories high and faded into shadowy arches, but that was the beginning and end of its grandeur. The tables and chairs were all mismatched and haphazardly placed. There was a smattering of wooden refectory tables, round kitchen-type tables, card tables—even a toadstool table. The effect was eclectic but also kind of cozy. Or at least, nondemons probably would have called it cozy.

"Food is that way," said Saffron, pointing at a counter to the right of the entryway that was filled end-to-end with steaming tureens. "Drinks over there." She indicated toward a set of shelves to the left.

"Drinks, you say?" I asked, hopes rising.

"No alcohol, if that's what you were thinking," she said.

"Oh," I said, hopes dashing.

We split up to grab our food. Saffron and I were done first, so we went to find a free table.

***

"So let me get this straight. Magic is dangerous on its own," I said as Saffron and I found a spot for the four of us to sit. "Then Rogue magic complicates it even further, and *then* you play games like Cracking on top of it?"

"What can we say?" said Saffron. "We like to live on the edge."

She deposited her plate on the table next to mine as I chucked the stones under my turquoise ladder-back chair. The paint was cracked and peeling, and a piece of it stuck to the black mass of fabric I wore. As I picked it off, I watched Saffron take a full minute to adjust the placement of her napkin, utensils, and cup until everything was perfectly aligned.

"Yes. You seem the thrill-seeking type," I said.

Reginald settled down across from Saffron.

"You know what's funny?"

"What's that?" she asked as Goodfallow joined us as well.

"This is the first time I've been in a dining hall that's in an actual hall."

Saffron, Reginald, and Goodfallow had a good laugh at that, which annoyed me. They suddenly all seemed so young.

"Can we get down to business," I spat as I pulled a packet of demon dust from a fold of my robes. I tore it open and dumped the contents indiscriminately onto my food.

"What is that?" asked Goodfallow, his finger slowly approaching my plate. I swatted it away.

"It's nothing you need to know about until we come up with a plan."

He shook his hand to relieve the pain and nodded.

"Fine—let me see if I have this right. You broke the Stone of Eno, a magical connection stone. The connection magic then flowed into you. Now you two are connected, and the stone is in pieces."

"Yup," said Reginald with a mouth full of meatloaf.

"Hm," said Saffron, tapping the tip of her chin with the tip of her finger. "That sounds like Change magic."

Reginald swallowed.

"Well, that's not going to work. Steadly implied that doing Change magic is the whole reason he won't help."

Saffron and Goodfallow exchanged looks.

"Researching and doing are two different things," said Saffron. "We can do the research and see if we come up with some kind of work-around. But we should also comb the books for more information about the stone. Figuring out the nature of the Stone of Eno may help us uncover other solutions. What do you know already?"

"Not much, honestly," said Reginald. We filled them in on what little information we had. "The dwarves believe it was given to the dryads, not made by them. And the giants believe that there are three stones. Eno, something, and something."

"They're named 'Eno, something, and something'?" asked Goodfallow.

"They're named Eno, Nie, and Sunu."

Reginald looked at me, eyes wide.

"How did you remember that?"

"Well," I said, straightening my unruly robes as best I could, "we demons have a lot of names and temperamental tendencies. So we've developed excellent memories."

Saffron was scribbling in a notebook.

"What are you writing?" I asked, craning my neck to see.

"Oh, nothing," she said, not looking up. "Just everything you say."

"What? Why?"

I was half-flattered, half-concerned. She looked up.

"It's been five hundred years since a demon stood in the City of Seven. Five hundred is more than enough years for information to be lost, altered, or misremembered. I want the truth."

"Oookay," I said, taking the charcoal from her hand and placing it on the table. "Back to the matter at hand. How do we get started? Walk into the library and check the catalog for 'S' for 'stone'?"

Our guides broke out into hysterics. It was as if they'd never heard anything so funny in their lives.

"For what it's worth," said Reginald with a fork full of green beans halfway to his mouth, "I didn't think it was funny at all."

Saffron took a deep breath to calm herself and wiped at her eyes.

"I'm sorry. That was just such a ridiculous thing to say!"

Goodfallow saw my expression darkening and jumped in.

"Just leave it to us! We'll meet tomorrow at breakfast."

"*Excuse me.*"

A quiet voice interrupted our conversation. The four of us looked up in unison to see that it belonged to a painfully thin young man with an equine nose and a slight hunchback.

"Gerard," said Saffron with a nod.

"Are these two Lord Malgon and Sir Reginald? The demon and the hero?"

"We are," I said. Who speaks about people who are sitting

right in front of him? He was obviously an ill-mannered, ill-considerate . . .

His body folded awkwardly in my direction, as if he were trying to simultaneously bow and curtsy.

. . . respectful, wonderful young man.

"Your room has been prepared. Please follow me."

I looked at Saffron and Goodfallow.

"How will we find you?"

Saffron inclined her head toward a giant time wheel on the wall of the dining hall.

"Meet us for breakfast at half past seven?"

"Isn't that a little earl—" Reginald started, then gasped when I stomped on his foot.

"Half past seven is the perfect time. Thank you."

Reginald grumbled but stood, and after bending to retrieve the bag, I did the same.

"See you tomorrow, then," said Goodfallow, and both he and Saffron waved enthusiastically. Gerard didn't make a move. He was just staring at us.

"What are you waiting for, a cracker? Let's go!" I said to him. At that, he sprang into action.

"Of course. Right this way."

We strode at a decent clip to the other end of the hall. Students enjoying their suppers stopped eating to gawk at us.

"What do you think of our new friends?" I asked.

"They're really nice," Reginald said. "Why? What do you think of them?"

I shrugged one shoulder.

"I think they're a pair of earnest little twerps."

Reginald laughed.

"Can't they be nice *and* be earnest little twerps?"

The corner of my mouth twitched up as I remembered Elgar, the genius nincompoop.

"I guess they can."

Reginald grinned, and I felt a shock burn straight through me. Somewhere along the line, Reginald—pasty, clumsy Reginald, with his boring stories and unbearable moral fiber—had become my friend. But what was worse is that it felt okay.

Eager to recenter my emotions back to a more traditional demonic state, I cast my gaze around for anything that might make me mad. I noticed Gerard kept sneaking covert glances at us over his shoulder.

"Hey!" I called to him. "Mind your own business, or I'll unburden your body of the weight of your head. Are we clear?"

He yelped, pivoted, and took off at a run.

OUR GUIDE DEPOSITED us in Room Five, which had clearly been prepared for any guest hamsters the academy might need to entertain. Two cots stuffed with hay were shoved up against the walls, with a narrow aisle between them.

"It's nice how they've spared no expense for their guests," I frowned.

"Could be worse," said Reginald as he sat gingerly down on the right-hand cot. "One time I visited cousins, and the guest room was just a stall in the stable that had their dead prize horse's ashes in it."

Wrinkling my nose, I said, "That does sound worse. Although it smells a bit like a dead horse in here too."

At the end of the aisle between the cots was a wardrobe. I sidestepped Reginald's giant feet to get to it.

"Oh, good," I said, opening it up. "More robes." I tossed the bag inside and it made a dull *thunk*.

"I'm sure we'll get our clothes back soon," said Reginald, lying down on his cot.

I threw myself onto mine as well, although it wasn't as buoyant as I'd been expecting, and I came down hard.

"There's a wooden plank under the mattress," Reginald said.

"Yeah. Got that," I groaned, hugging my ribs.

I flipped over on to my back.

"What are we going to do about your brother?"

I felt a pang shoot through my body.

"I don't know. My current plan is to hope he doesn't make it here in time to stop us fixing the stone. And with Steadly's refusal, that seems more and more unlikely."

"Could you fight him if you needed to?"

I barked a laugh.

"Hardly. He could probably saw me in half with his fingernail."

"Oh. That's not good."

We lay in silence for a moment before I asked, "Do you think we'll really find anything at the library?"

Reginald yawned.

"I don't know. But if anyone can, I feel it's us."

I snorted.

"Because of our track record of successful missions?"

"No," he said, voice fading as he left consciousness behind. "Because even when we're failing, we make a good team."

CHAPTER 13
THE LIBRARY

The next morning, even Reginald was willing to rise and shine.

Well . . . he was willing to rise.

"That's it, Reg. Just a couple more steps. Then we'll dunk your head in the coffee cauldron and get straight to work." I had an arm around Reginald as I led him to the beverage station in the dining hall. I lifted the cover of the cauldron and was preparing to shove his face in it when the troll behind the counter slammed the cover down back down and handed me two mugs with a snarl. (I'm not being disparaging here. She was an actual troll.)

"I wasn't really going to do it!" I scoffed.

I mean, I was. But she didn't need to know that.

"Oh, good! You made it!" came a peppy voice from behind me. "We're ready when you are."

I looked over my shoulder and saw the beaming faces of Goodfallow and Saffron.

"I've got to get some coffee into this one," I said, tilting my head toward Reginald. "Do you want some?"

"Oh, no, thank you!" said Saffron with perverse cheeriness. "We don't drink coffee."

I removed my arm from Reginald's shoulders to pour the scorching liquid into the mugs and blinked at them.

"You mean . . . you're just naturally like this?"

Goodfallow grinned. "We sure are!" He even added a little fist pump into the air to emphasize this annoying trait. "Living and learning are a natural high!"

"Lucifer's irritable bowels," I muttered as I took a sip of coffee. "I'm going to need something stronger to deal with you two."

Reginald downed his cup in three gulps and started to show signs of life.

"Good morning, you two!" he said, his level of cheer now almost rivaling theirs. "Have you already eaten?"

"We have," said Saffron, "but we have some things to discuss, so why don't you grab some food and meet us over there?"

She pointed to an area by a window, which, judging by the angle of the sun, probably offered the pungent smell and scenic view of endless peat bogs.

We grabbed our food and ambled over to them. The table they'd chosen was covered in a colorful tablecloth with a haphazard pattern of numbers and letters. I pulled up a chair and was about to place my mug down when—

"What are you doing?" screeched Saffron.

I leaped away from the table as she threw her upper body on top of it.

"What? I was just going to put my cup down!"

Her eyes were incredulous and wild as she shouted, "Those are my research notes!"

I glanced down again and saw that, in fact, it was not a tablecloth covering the table. Over a dozen notebooks were laid out across the surface.

"Well, where am I supposed to put my coffee?" I asked.

Reginald had solved that problem already. He was sitting on

a chair near the table, shoveling food into his mouth with gusto. His coffee cup, which he must have refilled, rested between his knees.

"I don't know! But not on my notes!"

With the front of her body protecting the precious papers from potential coffee rings, she needed to arch her neck at an awkward angle to see me. It made the whole thing even more ridiculous.

"She's particular about her notebooks," said Goodfallow by way of explanation, and she shot him an angry glare. "Whiiiich, is not a bad thing!" he fumbled.

"Good save, Glasses," I said as I sat down next to Reginald. Goodfallow blushed and pushed his spectacles up his nose.

Finally, certain that no one was going to use the dining table for dining, she sat back and laid out her plan.

"Okay, so priority subjects are in red, see? Then sub-priority projects are in orange. Cross-referenced subjects in yellow, related subjects are in green, and specific books are in blue."

"Then what's with all the pink?" I asked, waving my mug over the notebooks.

She eyed the coffee as if it had dishonored her family and said, "I just like pink."

Reginald let out a burp that frightened the students at a nearby table.

"Well, I'm ready to go. And this all sounds great! Thanks for doing all of this, Saffron. We wouldn't have known where to start."

She smiled appreciatively.

"It's my pleasure. But I can't take all the credit. Goodfallow helped."

Goodfallow waved a few fingers in our direction.

"Thank you as well, then! Right, Mal?"

But my attention was on the time wheel on the wall.

"Yes, yes. Everybody's amazing. Is it time to go, then?"

Saffron gathered up her notebooks and began shoving them into her bag. When she'd clipped her bag shut, she looked up and said, "It is. And just so you know—this is no ordinary library."

"THE TWO SUBBASEMENT floors are mostly classrooms and offices for mages doing advanced study," said Goodfallow as we hiked up the interior spiral that led through the center of the tower. "But *this* is the library."

When Saffron had told us they had built the towers around twin fir trees, I sort of expected a cordoned-off courtyard with the rotting remains of the stumps somewhere near the center of each building. But I'd underestimated the scope of the *Prodigious* tree variety.

"Are we . . . inside the tree?" I breathed.

"Isn't it marvelous?" Saffron followed my gaze up the walls to the ceiling.

We'd exited the central column in which the stairs continued to spiral up above us and emerged into the library itself. The floor was the stump of the behemoth fir, and concentric rings rippled out, marking the many thousands of years the trees had stood in this spot. It was dotted with tables and the tables were dotted with students. Around us, pale wood stretched seven stories high and ended at a ceiling enchanted by thousands upon thousands of twinkling amber lights. The effect was a permanent golden hour, and it gave the space an otherworldly feel.

Curved staircases led up to platforms that ran the perimeter of every floor, each of which was lined with bookcases. The only exception was the librarian's desk, which was a rounded peninsula that jutted out from the east side of the third floor.

"I've never seen anything like it," Reginald breathed as he

craned his neck to see the constellation-like patterns the lights made on the ceiling. "You've probably seen a hundred places as amazing as this, though, haven't you, Mal?"

I made a noncommittal noise because I valued his awe of me, but also . . . I had not. This place was beyond anything I'd ever experienced. It was bewitching.

I bent down and rested my hand on the floor, feeling the slight ridges that marked each year of the tree's former life.

"I'll bet you have some stories to tell, don't you?" I murmured.

Saffron's face came into my peripheral vision with comic slowness.

"Would you like a tour?"

It was a tempting offer. But I was more tempted by the idea of regaining a life of independence unencumbered by the company of the most upstanding man in Widdershins—and, you know, keeping a horde of my dark brethren from enslaving the world.

I stood back up and Saffron followed suit.

"I think we should dive right in. Saffron. Glasses. You're up. What do we do next?"

Goodfallow opened his mouth, probably to protest the nickname, but Saffron spoke first.

"You two find a table down here. Goodfallow and I will go get all the books we need, and then the four of us will go through them."

"And you're sure this is the quickest way to get this done? There isn't just some spell you can do to summon the books to you?"

"Meaning no disrespect," said Goodfallow with an expression that signaled nothing *but* disrespect, "but summoning is fairytale magic, Lord Malgon."

I shrugged and turned to Reginald.

"It was worth a try, right?"

He nodded vigorously.

"It would have been very cool to see all the books flying around."

They left us at a table in the middle of the first floor, and we watched the lights blink out of time in the vaulted ceiling. That is, until I spotted something else to watch.

A stunning woman in long black robes seemed to glide into the room—a feat that became even more impressive when I noticed her patent leather stilettos. As she headed straight toward us, I noticed her lips were painted a lush, berry-red, and whereas every other person in the building was content to wear the shapeless, woolen wizard's robes as is, she had belted hers with a strip of thick, brown leather. The result was a kind of dark, sexy academic look, and I was digging it. I also cursed Reginald for ever letting me trade my morning coat for robes.

"Our famous hero and demon visitors, I presume?" She smiled and held her arms out wide. Then she slid into a chair opposite us. "I'm Professor Trenchant. I teach Physical Magic here at the academy."

Reginald looked at me.

"Are we famous?"

"Oh, quite!" she crooned, looking back and forth between us. "Everyone has heard of your journey to Seven—how you two rode a Grootslang and slayed a giant!"

"Well . . ." started Reginald, but I stomped on his foot under the table.

"Indeed, we are amazing. And now how can we help you?"

"Well, actually . . ." As she spoke, she traced a circle on the tabletop with a perfectly manicured fingernail. Beneath it I saw that someone had scratched "Cracking Rules" into the wood. "It's more how I can help you."

"What do you mean?" asked Reginald, frowning.

Her eyes got shiny, and her mouth pressed into a hard line.

"I heard that Steadly refused to help the two of you with

your . . . predicament. He said it was because of the Rogue magic, right?"

"That's right," I said.

She slammed a fist down on the table so hard that a few other students shushed us.

"Shush yourself," she yelled, throwing an arm in the air. Everyone turned back to their own business and buried their faces in the nearest book. "Anyway," she said. "That man is a bloody coward. The magic is absolutely possible—I've been studying it for years. He thinks because I'm a woman, I can't do magic properly, but I'm twice as good as any wizard here. Ask anyone! Everyone here is risk-averse, but to progress our art, we need to push the boundaries of known magic, right?"

"So . . . wait. Are you saying you'll do it? You'll help us?" asked Reginald.

She frowned.

"Well, no. I can't just do that kind of magic without the proper backing. The Council of Grand Wizards would need to approve it, and they absolutely won't with Grandfather Steadly at the helm. He's far too nervous about a mishap disrupting his long reign as headmaster. But if you help me, I can help you."

"What did you have in mind?" I asked.

"I want you to call a Quarrel."

She said it in a way that was clearly supposed to make us to throw a fit or gasp in surprise. But neither Reginald nor I knew what a Quarrel was, so the revelation was lost on us.

"What's a Quarrel?" asked Reg.

She sighed.

"Technically, any group comprising more than one wizard is a quarrel. But a capital-Q Quarrel is a meeting of the Grand Wizards. It's like a vote of no confidence in one of them. But it can only be called by someone outside the school. Wizards are so naturally argumentative that there would be endless Quarrels if we were allowed to call them on each other."

"That hasn't been our experience," Reg said. "Saffron and Goodfallow seem to like each other a lot."

"Ugh," scoffed Professor Trenchant. "Those two suck-ups? There's an anomaly I'd like to study sometime."

I laughed, and Reginald looked at me reproachfully.

"They're nice."

Her face softened slightly.

"Yes, yes, you're right," she said. "All I'm saying is that their friendship is not normal. Mostly we fight tooth and nail about the smallest things." She looked directly at me. "Look, I think you and I understand each other. I want to become one of the Grand Wizards, but I'm never going to get there the regular way. So I've made it my business to learn all of their vices and proclivities while I've been here. They'll support me in a vote—I've made sure of that. I just need someone to call it. Once I'm one of the Grand Wizards, I can do whatever magic I want. And my first order of business is going to be to help you."

At that moment, Saffron and Goodfallow returned with a pushcart piled high with research materials.

"Professor Trenchant!" said Saffron in surprise.

"Saffron. Glasses." She nodded at each of them, and my eyes went heart-shaped at our mutual lack of respect for Goodfallow. "I was just leaving. This," she said, pushing a folded piece of paper over to me, "is how to do it if you decide books aren't getting you anywhere."

"We'll think about it," I said, pulling the paper the rest of the way toward me and slipping it into my pocket.

"I've got a class to teach. If you want to get in touch with me, just send a crow my way."

I did not know what that meant, but I nodded anyway and watched her cross the floor and exit through the door.

"What was that about?" asked Saffron, thumping a pile of books down on the table in front of us.

"Professor . . . Trenchant, was it?" said Reginald. "She asked us to call a Quarrel."

Saffron and Goodfallow both froze.

"Why?" Saffron asked.

"Because she says she can do the magic that can help us," I said.

Saffron and Goodfallow exchange shocked glances.

"That is a terrible idea! You can't trust her," said Goodfallow. "She's unorthodox and the professors are terrified of her."

"Because she's a badass lady wizard and a visionary?" I retorted, leaning back in my chair and crossing my arms.

"Because on several occasions she's landed students in the infirmary after leading them in doing experimental Change magic."

"Oh no," said Reginald.

"I used to look up to her," said Saffron. "I mean—you're right. There aren't a lot of female wizards. And she's so confident and talented. But she has no limits, and that makes her dangerous."

"I still think we should do it," I said.

"For what reason?" asked Saffron.

I glared at her, but to her credit, she didn't shrink away.

"It's a calculated risk. Reg and I need to separate our lives, and we need to fix the stone before my brother makes the portal permanent. The Quarrel moves that goal from possible to probable."

Saffron frowned.

"I still think research is the path to pursue. The Quarrel is too risky. You'll make an enemy of Steadly—who is the most famous and powerful wizard alive today—and the procedure Trenchant mentioned still isn't guaranteed to work. You could risk it all for nothing and get kicked out of Seven in the same condition you're in now but with no leads. Or worse. Change magic takes an immense amount of power. It's certain to activate the Rogue magic. It could reassign you."

"Or kill you," said Goodfallow.

"I don't want to die," said Reginald. "Plus, I didn't trust her."

Saffron nodded. I threw my arms up in the air and let them fall to my sides.

"It's not about trust! Her interests and our interests align. That's bigger than trust."

"Still, though," Reginald said. "I know you're mad at Steadly, and I want to fix this as much as you do. Maybe even more. But I don't think the Quarrel is the solution."

The way he said 'maybe even more' made my stomach squirm the same way it had when I saw him laughing with Goodfallow and Saffron in the dining hall. I pushed the thought away.

"Let's take a vote then, shall we? All in favor of tabling the Quarrel option for now, raise your hand."

Goodfallow, Saffron, and Reginald put their hands in the air. I rolled my eyes at them, then reached for the book on the top of the pile: *15 Letters on the Language of Change.*

"Fine. You three win. We won't call one."

Not yet.

"Nothing," I said and slammed my book closed.

"Nothing here, either," said Reginald, following suit.

"That's all of them," said Goodfallow, eyeing the empty cart.

"That's all from the *green* category," said Saffron, clearly unaffected by our lack of progress. "We still have plenty more avenues to try."

For three straight days, we'd done nothing but eat, sleep, and visit the library. Actually, that's not entirely true. Goodfallow escorted us into town one afternoon to be interviewed by the editor of the town newspaper, a publication called *The Raven*. It's editor, Jane, had been eager to get our story, bubbling on about how there hadn't been a hero-demon duo in Seven for ages. But as we did most things, we'd botched it up, and she ran the article with the title "An Asshat and an Idiot Walk into an Interview." Every minute that ticked by, I knew my brother was coming closer and closer to Seven. We were running out of time.

Reginald's stomach gurgled.

"Fine. But can we do it after lunch? I'm starving."

"Lunch?" said Goodfallow. "It's almost eight in the evening!"

Reginald, who'd been balancing on the back two legs of his chair, toppled over and hit the ground.

"Eight o'clock? You mean we missed lunch?!"

"You two don't understand what a big deal this is," I explained to Saffron and Goodfallow. "Reginald never misses a meal—and if he must, he usually complains about it ad nauseam."

"No, I'm not nauseous. Just hungry," Reginald said, righting both himself and the chair.

"*Ad nauseam* doesn't mean 'nauseous.' It means 'a lot.'"

"Oh. Well, that's true, then."

"No problem. Let's return these books and get something to eat," said Saffron, already filling the shelves of the cart with our discards.

"You know, I didn't learn anything about the stone or connection magic today, but I learned other interesting things," said Reginald, passing books to her. "Did you know that there's a forest southeast of here called the Farrest that can supposedly transport you to other worlds?"

"That sounds unlikely," I said, examining my fingernails as the others cleaned up.

"Unlikely is not the same as impossible," said Goodfallow.

"And," continued Reginald, "there was another book by a

person named Mitchelry who discovered that certain types of stuff in nature can repel certain kinds of magic. Like sap and minerals and whatever."

Saffron stopped what she was doing and considered Reginald.

"Have you ever considered attending the academy? You really seem to enjoy research."

Reginald shrugged.

"Honestly, I didn't even know this place existed until after Mal and I got stuck together. My whole life, all I wanted to do was be a hero."

"Saff's right," said Goodfallow, his hands on the handle of the cart. "You should think about it."

I got that squirmy feeling again as I witnessed the interaction, and it made me vomit up some unkind words.

"Isn't he a bit too accident-prone for some place as dangerous as this? He'd probably trip over his own feet and accidentally light the place on fire. I'm not sure academia is the place for you, Reg."

Saffron and Goodfallow laughed and started pushing the cart toward the book return counter. A gold round fell out of Goodfallow's pocket onto the floor. I bent to grab it and went to give it back but then pocketed it instead. When I emerged from under the table, Reginald was there, sad eyes trained right on me.

"Why would you say that?"

The hurt in his tone shocked me. Either I'd been particularly callous or he was being too sensitive, because he usually let those comments roll off his back. Either way, I feigned nonchalance.

"What? You really think this is where you belong? That we're going to get detached and suddenly you'll be some academic scholar?"

"No. Of course I don't. But just because I'm not as old as you and haven't been as many places as you doesn't mean I'm not smart, Mal."

"Okay, okay," I said, holding my palms up in front of me. "It was a poor joke."

Reginald sighed.

"It's fine. I'm just hungry and tired."

———

ON THE WAY to the dining hall, a crow flew inside the building and landed on Goodfallow's shoulder. He didn't shriek or bat it away, which told me this was just a thing that happened here. I made a mental note to try not to murder any crows that flew into my airspace, and a memory flashed in my mind. *If you want to get in touch with me, just send a crow my way.* So that was what she meant.

"Oh, terrific! It looks like your clothes are ready! They've been delivered to your room."

I clapped my hands. It was the first bit of solid good news we'd had in days.

"Great! Let's go get changed."

"Mal," said Reginald. "We can do that later. Let's go get some food before the dining hall closes, and *then* we can go back to the dormitory."

I clenched my fists.

"But this," I said, holding out the billowing robes, "is not me. I can't think. I can't walk. I am not *myself* in this."

Reginald rolled his eyes.

"You're being dramatic, Mal. They're just clothes. We'll go back after dinner."

My eye twitched, and I visualized setting fire to his head with my mind.

"Fine. We'll do it your way, Sir Reginald," I said with a mock bow and stomped toward the exit, an annoyed Reginald and his two bemused co-conspirators following behind.

VEXED ABOUT MY CLOTHES, I decided to dampen the atmosphere for everyone.

"Why aren't we calling the Quarrel, again?" I asked as we rounded the corner and entered the dining room.

"Not this again," said Goodfallow under his breath.

"What? I thought Trenchant was delightful."

"Of course you did," said Reginald. Late as it was, only a few people were in the hall when we arrived.

"What do you mean, 'of course I did'?"

"She's powerful, beautiful, and conniving."

"I know," I sighed fondly.

"I told you, Mal. I don't trust her."

I narrowed my eyes at him.

"Well, you didn't trust me either, and look where it's ended us up."

Reginald waved away my comment and took a plate from the stack. Then he piled it high with a wide assortment of meats, fried breads, cheeses, and confectionaries.

"You ate earlier today, did you not?"

"Yeah, why?" he asked, spooning some gravy over the meat quadrant of the plate.

"No reason," I muttered, still staring.

Nobody spoke much at dinner. Saffron and Goodfallow made a little conversation, but Reginald and I didn't engage: he was busy eating, and I was busy fantasizing about slipping into my waistcoat for the first time since we'd left the mountains.

Finally, everyone finished eating. I stopped pushing the food around on my plate and stood up.

"Everyone's done? Great. Time to go!" I said and started out of the hall so quickly that Reginald couldn't move fast enough. I felt the familiar smash of his body against mine, and we fell in a tangled heap at the doors of the dining hall. Luckily, even the few students who'd been there when we sat down were gone. But Reginald was angrier than I'd ever seen him.

"What are you doing? You know we have to stay closer together!"

"I thought you were right behind me!"

Goodfallow looked like he was about to intervene, but Saffron put a hand on his shoulder and pulled him back.

"No, you didn't! You were only thinking about yourself. As usual!"

The speech knocked the air out of me. Reginald waited for a reply, but for once, I was speechless. So he scoffed, shook his head, and barged ahead out of the dining hall.

But I was still frozen to the spot. So the magic zinged us back together.

"By the Triplets, Mal!"

"Fucking hell, Asstradle!"

WHEN WE ARRIVED BACK at the dormitory, there was a crowd of people gathered around the staircase that led up to our quarters.

"What's going on?" I asked.

"There's been a fire!" exclaimed a round-faced boy with curly brown hair I vaguely recognized.

"Was it near our rooms, Chet?" asked Reginald. Of course he knew the kid's name.

Then I realized I did too. It was Chet, our next-door neighbor. The one that shared a bathroom with us and unknowingly let me clean my fingernails with his toothbrush.

"We don't know yet."

A broad-shouldered, soot-covered woman in light gray robes descended the stairs.

"Who lives in rooms three and five?"

Chet, Reginald, and a student whose name was either Margo or Janet—who can remember these things?—and I raised our hands.

"I'm sorry to say that the fire has consumed both rooms. We will set you up with temporary quarters. And the only things we could recover were these. Do they belong to any of you?" She held up the canvas bag with the pieces of the Stone of Eno inside and an armful of robes.

"Oh, thank goodness!" cried Reginald, pushing through the crowd toward her. "Yes! They're ours!"

He grabbed the lot and was making his way back to me when someone called, "Do you know what caused it?"

The woman nodded.

"We don't know for certain, but we believe it was a confluence of Rogue magic. Nothing anyone could have done to prevent it."

Reginald was back at my side, speaking to me as if he hadn't just chewed me out in the dining hall.

"Wow. That would have been awful. Good thing we had nothing else important in the room . . . hey. What's wrong? Is this about what I said? Look, I'm sorry. It's just that you . . ."

I held up a hand to stop him.

"There was something else important. My *coat* was in that room."

CHAPTER 14
SHORTCUT

To make an unpleasant situation worse, they bunked us with Saffron and Goodfallow. I was sitting on the lilac comforter on Saffron's immaculate bed while Reginald paced the floor in front of me.

"I'm just saying," he rambled. "We've just had our room burn down. We've gone through all of Saffron's lists. We're not sure what to do next, and on the way over here, we saw this poster." He produced a colorful sheaf of parchment that he'd snatched from a community bulletin board. "There's going to be a Yulesticetide festival in the city tonight. We've been so busy, I almost forgot that Yulesticetide was today. We should go!"

He was nearly jumping out of his skin with excitement.

"I don't know. Shouldn't we stay here and brainstorm some more ideas?" asked Saffron. She looked nervously at me. "I heard a rumor that a demon was seen terrorizing a town not far from here."

"What!" I exclaimed, jumping to my feet. "When did you hear that? How far was he, exactly?"

I started pacing back and forth.

"Northend. I heard it from someone while you were going back to change clothes."

Northend was the last town on the Inner Sea before the road that skirted the mountains to get to Seven. Depending on how old that rumor was, Tannith could be here by tomorrow.

"Fucking damnation!" I cried. "How can you be thinking of a Yulesticetide festival at a time like this, Reg?"

Reg frowned at me.

"He's not here yet. And we don't have any other options. Plus, my gran always says that sometimes you need an idle mind to come up with new ideas!"

"We have another option: the Quarrel. And by the way, do you know what we say an idle mind is in the Underworld? 'The Devil's playground.'"

"Not the Quarrel again," he said.

"Yes, the Quarrel again."

"We've just seen the effects of Rogue magic first hand. It's too dangerous. Plus, we can't trust her," said Reginald.

"You don't even know her!" I cried.

"But Saffron and Goodfallow do," he said, gesturing toward the pair. "And I *do* trust them."

And that was the crux of it. He trusted them more than he trusted me now.

"Look, there's going to be lights and street performances and tons of food. We have a festival in Beadledom too—it's my favorite time of year. Let's just go for an hour."

I didn't want to go. My lungs constricted at the thought of Tannith being so close and us being so far from a solution. I blamed myself, really. If I'd been a better demon, they'd understand the danger. They'd have seen what true evil was like. These kids weren't around at the end of the golden age. The darkness, the droughts, the pestilence—at the time I was mad at the humans for creating the Hero contract, but with five hundred years of hindsight, I didn't blame them. Plus, it was cold, my clothes had been burned, and no one wanted to take the one step that might help us achieve what we'd come here to do. But I was pretty sure I was about to be outvoted again.

"Well, I think it's a great idea," said Goodfallow, wrapping an arm around Reginald's shoulders. "Saff and I had a tough semester. You and Lord Malgon faced cartloads of peril. We should get to enjoy ourselves for one night."

Saffron smiled.

"I do love seeing the city all lit up."

"There you go!" said Goodfallow, thrusting a hand out toward her.

"So it's settled? Can we go, Mal? Just for an hour?"

I shoved my hands in my pockets and felt something hard and smooth. Goodfallow's gold round. A plan began to form in my mind.

"I think it's a great idea, Reg. When do we leave?"

"OH, MY GOSH, THIS IS DELICIOUS," said Reginald, his eyes closed in ecstasy. He'd gotten some kind of fried dough on a stick. It produced its own tiny cloud that hovered over the bread, precipitating powdered sugar. He was eating it as if it were his last meal. With my brother within rumor-mongering distance, maybe it was.

"Here—try this," said Goodfallow, pouring a few brown, button-sized morsels out of a painted silver cone into Reginald's hand. He popped them into his mouth and his eyes lit up.

"They're ping-ponging around in my mouth!" He paused. "And now they're fizzing." He paused again. "And now they're melting into chocolate!"

Goodfallow and Saffron laughed.

"They're called Valor Balls—after Quill Valor. The culinary wizards pull out all the stops for Yulesticetide."

It was true. We'd sampled a new flavor of the ever-popular coffee drink called the Yulesticetide Blend. The addition of vanilla, cinnamon, and cardamom brought to mind a roaring fire on a frigid night. Literally. It was a trippy kind of magic.

Light snow was falling—the kind that most would consider picturesque. But to me, it was a nuisance. The flakes stuck on my eyelashes and dampened both my robes and my mood. Sure, there was a sort of soothing wondrousness to it all, and the smell of cooking food almost drowned out the regular, less-palatable smells of the city. But it wasn't sinking in. In my mind I kept replaying the arguments Reg and I had been having lately. The ones in which he was wrong. The ones in which I was . . . not entirely right. The trip to Seven had been treacherous and terrifying, but it had also engendered a sense of camaraderie between us. But since we'd been in Seven, things had felt different. We hadn't been magically separated. But it still felt as though a wedge had been driven through whatever had built between us.

I watched Reginald, Saffron, and Goodfallow laughing and nudging each other a few feet ahead of me. Enjoying the festival and each other's company. I narrowed my eyes.

It wasn't one wedge driving us apart. It was two.

"Hey, can I see those brown things?"

Goodfallow looked over his shoulder at me and held up the packet.

"These?"

"Yeah, those."

"Sure! You can keep them!"

He tossed them back, and I fumbled the cone a few times before catching it. When I was sure their attention was elsewhere, I dumped the contents on the ground and pocketed the container.

"Oh look, Mal!" Reginald called over his shoulder. "Magic!"

Leave it to Reginald to get excited about magic in a city of magic, even after having lived at a magical academy for several days. The magician in question was juggling balls of light that changed in color depending on how high he got them to arc.

"That's easy magic," said Saffron. "Watch this."

She did something complicated with her hands—far too fast for me to see—and an illuminated swan burst from her palm and "swam" around us. She flicked her hand, and it turned into a phoenix, flew high into the night, then burst into sparks of every color.

Reginald and Goodfallow clapped, so I clapped along as well. It was spectacular, and if I'd been in a better mood, it might have even impressed me.

"That was so cool! Magic is amazing!" Reginald yelled.

Saffron made a quick curtsy.

"It was just a little illusion work."

She turned and walked away from the performance, and the three of us followed like dogs at her heels. Reginald stopped to throw away the wooden stick from his fried dough. I moved along with him, and just before it dropped into the trash pile, I snatched it up and broke off the tip. Then I pulled the piece of paper Trenchant had given me out of my pocket and consulted it.

Wood, gold, and silver you need
To ensure you will succeed
When you have them one and all
Stand upon our hallowed wall
Hold them up into the night
And know success by lightning strike

I'd give Reginald one more day to come to his senses. Then I was going to call the Quarrel whether he agreed or not.

THE FOUR OF us ambled back up the High Street, the sounds of the festival faint and dreamlike far below. Against their snow-whitened backdrop, the towers of the academy shone even brighter than the lights of the festival.

"That was better than anything we have in Beadledom. I'm glad we went."

"Me too," said Saffron. "I had a great time—and you were right! I even thought of a few more ideas for topics we can search in the library!"

"I guess an idle mind's not the Devil's playground after all," joked Goodfallow, shooting a smile in my direction.

"I guess we'll see," I muttered.

"Mal, why do you have to be so grim all the time? It's Yulesticetide! Can't you be cheerful for one night?"

"Let's see. Have my clothes become magically unburned? Have we found a solution to our entanglement problem? Have we fixed the Stone of Eno and returned it to the dryads? Has my brother returned to the Underworld? Did I want to help the ungrateful people of Widdershins instead of doing an evil deed of my choosing and returning home a demonic legend? Has any of that changed because it's Yulesticetide?"

"Has he been like this the whole time?" Goodfallow said it with such informality I wanted to scream. I was a fucking Lord of the Underworld. Show some damned respect!

Reginald looked at me.

"Pretty much."

I rolled my eyes.

"Yes, because Reginald's been the perfect travel companion as well."

"I don't know," said Goodfallow, wiping snow off his glasses with his overlarge sleeve. "Reginald seems pretty great to us."

I huffed a laugh.

"You only say that because you haven't needed to save him

from dryads, fairies, angry innkeepers, dwarves, spiders, and giants."

We'd just reached the threshold between the city and the academy, and Reginald stopped in his tracks.

"Seriously, Mal? You're unbelievable."

He spoke quietly, but there was a hint of fire behind his words that I wasn't used to. It roused something in me. I'd been sitting on my hands since we'd gotten here, swallowing everything down—the unbearable chumminess between the three of them, the devastating blow of the headmaster's refusal, the overwhelming panic about what Tannith had probably already done, what he could do with a demon horde at his back, Reg's diminishing respect for my authority—in an attempt to be the team player that Reginald had thought I'd become. But my frustration was bubbling to the surface now, and I was spoiling for a fight.

"Oh yeah? Well, you're a naïve weakling who throws up at the drop of a hat!"

He staggered back a step as if I'd punched him in the face. Then he widened his stance and stood his ground. It wasn't as threatening as he intended it to be. He was Reginald. He was a good kid with a kind heart, and he would never be terrifying. But he was mad.

"I haven't done that in like a week! And I may not be golden-age hero material, but I am a hero. I try to take care of others. You only think about yourself."

"Only think about myself? I've gotten you out of every crazy situation we've been in!"

"You've *caused* nearly every crazy situation we've been in! And everything you have ever done for me has helped you too!"

"Guys, please, I didn't mean—" said Goodfallow, trying to step between us, but Reginald held up a hand to keep him back. Saffron's dark eyes darted back and forth between us as if she was wondering whether she would need to provide magical intervention.

"Actually—no. You know what? I take that back. You did one thing for me. You taught me about anger. Before I met you, I didn't know what it was like to be angry. Not really. Not like I know now. It's so motivating—in fact, it's motivating this speech right now!"

"I can tell!"

"Good!"

"You know what I think?" he spat.

"What's that?"

"I think you lash out at me because you're afraid that when this whole thing is finally done, there won't be any place for you. You'll be alone. You embarrass your family. You've made enemies of the entire western half of Widdershins. If I stayed here with Saffron and Goodfallow, you'd be all by yourself. And rather than knowing it was because of some fatal flaw, you want it to be because of something you've done. You want it to be your fault."

"Afraid to be alone?" I scoffed. "Did you get that wisdom from your grandmother?"

"As a matter of fact, I did!"

"Well, both she and you are wrong. I am not afraid to be alone, Reginald. I'm the opposite of afraid. It is my favorite state of being! Why else did we take the shortcut across the mountains if not to get us here as quickly as possible? I cannot *wait* to figure this wretched magical connection out. In fact, I'm tired of sitting and reading and wearing these idiotic robes. Let's take another shortcut, shall we?"

I slammed Trenchant's instructions against his chest, then turned on my heel.

"What is this?" he asked, catching the paper and reading it.

By chance, Reginald had stopped right at the stone wall that surrounded the academy. It didn't take me long to shimmy up it. It was narrower on top than I'd realized from the ground, and I took a moment to catch my balance.

"Is this . . . wait, Mal! What are you doing?"

"Exactly what I said. I'm taking a shortcut!"

"No! Stop! I'm sorry for what I said. Come down and let's talk about this?"

"No, Reg. The time for talk is over. The time has come for action."

I thrust my hand into my pocket and pulled out the gold round, the silver cone, and the wooden stick I'd collected. I held them in my palms, arms outstretched. Tipping my head back, I shouted into the snow and wind, "I move to call a Quarrel of wizards!"

There was a moment of silence when I thought it hadn't worked. Then lightning forked across the sky. It struck the Wizard's Tower, and thunder boomed in its wake. The force of it threw me from the top of the wall. My back hit the ground first; then my head slammed onto the cobbles.

And I have no memory of what happened after that.

CHAPTER 15
A QUARREL OF WIZARDS

"Congratulations, Mal. You solved the mystery! Your death will not cause mine."

I blinked my eyes open. The light was too bright, and I was disoriented, but the room was vaguely familiar. Surrounding me were stacks of books and papers like towers about to topple to the ground, and the air held a faint scent of stale coffee. While most of my attention was on the spectacular headache blooming inside my skull, I thought I recognized it as the headmaster's office.

"Why am I here?" I asked.

"Because you've made a right mess of things," growled Headmaster Steadly.

"How's that now?" I asked, cradling my head in my hand and trying to sit up. That was a mistake, so I lay back down and pressed my hands over my eyes.

"For one, you nearly killed yourself falling off the wall," said Steadly. "In fact, you did kill yourself for a few seconds. If it weren't for the quick action of these two, the effects might have been permanent. Although," he said, facing Saffron and Goodfallow, "you should have used Merrowart instead of the slowing spell."

I peeked through my hands and saw Goodfallow and Saffron's affronted looks. Goodfallow was about to open his mouth to argue when Reginald said, "You weren't breathing." His voice sounded hoarse, as if he'd been shouting. "Goodfallow and Saffron did some kind of emergency magic thing. I don't really know. And then Headmaster Steadly came and . . . Well, you started breathing again."

I slid one hand to the side, testing my eyes again. I was on a cot, and Reginald was sitting on a chair next to me. Goodfallow and Saffron were standing behind him, still sulking. Steadly was standing right next to me, his massive frowning face like an angry dog's.

"Thank you, then, I suppose." At the moment, the headache felt like a worse option than permanent death. "How did you know to come?"

Steadly's anger flared.

"I know what it looks like when someone's called a Quarrel. I also know *how* it's done. So I just looked out my window for any unconscious idiots near the wall."

I sighed.

"For what it's worth, Trenchant didn't say remaining on the wall might kill me. But aside from that, I still don't understand why it's such a bad thing. Isn't the occasional turnover in management a good thing?"

"It's *bad* because as enigmatic as your new friend Trenchant is, she is equally as dangerous. Perhaps more so. Her methods are unorthodox, she values flash over substance, and she has absolutely no respect for the dangers Rogue magic pose. You're not the first that's been hurt on her watch, and you won't be the last. Plus, you know that her motives for convincing you to do this are entirely self-serving. And you're one to talk about overdue managerial changes. Lucifer's been the Archfiend since time immemorial."

Fair point.

"If she's so awful, then why do you let her stay?"

"I would have her out in an instant, but my colleagues have always voted in her favor, citing her brilliance and potential contributions to the craft. But your friends have informed me that their motives might also have been less than pure. She revealed to you that she's collected compromising information on some of the other Grand Wizards?"

I nodded my throbbing head.

"Yes."

"And you still thought it was a good idea to call the Quarrel?"

I removed my hands from my eyes and glared up at him.

"First of all, I don't see why that would be surprising to you. I am a demon, after all. We basically invented blackmail. Second, maybe none of this would have happened if you had *helped* us instead of sending us off to the library with a couple of toddlers." I acknowledged Saffron and Goodfallow. "No offense."

"Offense taken," said Goodfallow, frowning.

The headmaster sighed and lowered himself onto a stool that I hadn't seen behind his girth.

"Perhaps I could have done more. But why didn't you come to me first? I'm not going to be able to do anything now. Knowing what I know now about how she's been pulling the strings behind the scenes . . . Reasoning with them clearly will not work."

I made another attempt to sit up. My head felt as though my brain were attempting an escape from my skull, and it took a moment for the black spots to fade from my vision.

"Look, I'm not going to say I'm sorry." I shot a quick look at Reginald. His body was rigid, and his eyes were boring into his lap as if looking away would cause his legs to disappear. "I'm not. None of you know demons as I do. You're all in danger.

Plus, it's clearer than ever that Reg and I need to go our separate ways."

My eyes darted toward Reginald, but he stayed staring at his thighs.

Steadly sighed.

"Well, what's done is done. You can all stay here and get some rest. I'll send for some food and three more cots. The Quarrel starts at dawn."

Between the pounding in my head and the roiling in my gut, I wasn't sure I'd able to keep anything down. As Steady waddled away, I saw Reginald stand, and I stood as well. Wobbling, I steadied myself, then took a step in his direction.

"Reg—"

He put his hand up to cut me off.

"I can't talk to you right now, Mal. Okay? Not right now."

I felt a pang in my chest and opened my mouth to argue, but he walked to the other side of the room and sat down with Saffron and Goodfallow. They huddled together in a little circle until the food and cots came in.

A plate clattered at my feet. The contents shifted, and a handful of beans slid off onto the floor. When I looked up, Steadly was wheezing next to me.

"Eat up, demon. I made that plate myself and I assure you, I was furious."

"Grand Wizards. Thank you for coming," said Steadly, standing in front of one of seven throne-like chairs in front of me. I almost couldn't hear him over the clanging in my ears.

"Not like we had a choice," muttered a wizard in mustard-colored robes to his left.

We were on the top floor of the Wizard's Tower. A set of

grand oak double doors marked the entrance to the round block-stone room, which was laid out like an amphitheater. Its walls were set with windows long enough to let the light in but not wide enough for a body to fit through. Considering the high-stress nature of a magical education this was most likely an intentional design. Light poured in from the eastern side, slicing the room into ribbons of dark and light. Tiers of benches lined the perimeter of the room, surrounding the arena floor. But no mages were filing in and settling themselves down to work today. Today was just for us: the Quarrel, and the one who had called it.

And Reginald, of course, because everywhere I went, he had to go too.

Steadly shot the mustard mage a dark look, then continued.

"We are gathered today because Malgon Belroth Kirranith, Fifteenth of His Name, Giver of Papercuts, Collapser of Souf-flés, and Inventor of the Humblebrag, Lord of the Underworld Suburb of Artifice-on-Lethe, has called a Quarrel. Lord Malgon, if you please."

Steadly motioned for me to take my place in front of the Grand Wizards. Half his face was bathed in sunlight and the other cast in shadow. My shallow breaths sounded loud in my ears, and my palms were sweating.

Get a grip, Kirranith.

I moved into position and began.

"Your Grand Wizardnesses . . . or High . . ." Great. I hadn't even formed one sentence, and this was already going to shit. "Your Excellencies." I recovered with a deep bow. "I called the Quarrel because I wish . . ." I glanced at Steadly, who was grimacing.

"Finish what you started, demon," he said with a wave of his hand.

I looked at Reginald, but he was staring at the ground, still in the ridiculous, billowy black robes, his unkempt red hair nearly to his shoulders. He hadn't spoken to me since telling me he *couldn't* speak to me in the early hours of the morning. I was angry at him, but deep down I knew it was in the way you get angry when your hand hurts after you slam it in a door. It's your fucking fault, but you're mad about it, anyway. I called upon that anger now to steady myself and turned back to the Quarrel.

"I wish to report my lack of confidence in the ability of Master Steadly to continue on as headmaster."

"And what leads you to that grave accusation?" asked another member of the Quarrel. He was wearing maroon-and-gold robes, and his gnarled hands gripped the arms of his throne. Grand Master Pendergast, perhaps? Saffron had tried her best to educate me about the members of the group, but with them in front of me, I realized her descriptors of "gray hair, pasty," and "male" were not going to help me distinguish between them.

"When we first arrived at the academy, my partner and I," I motioned to Reginald, who was still fixated on the ground, "petitioned the headmaster for assistance because we find ourselves in a literal bind. A few weeks ago, Reginald accidentally summoned me through an error in his Hero contract paperwork, and we ended up on a quest to return the Stone of Eno to the dryads in the Forest of Arden."

Murmurs broke out amongst the group, but they were for show—I knew that Trenchant had prepared all of them for this assembly.

"When we tried to fix it, we ended up absorbing the magic. As it was a connection stone, Sir Reginald and I became magically entangled. We can't get more than a few yards away from each other without the magic throwing us back to each other's sides. It has been a trying ordeal. Plus, breaking the stone has apparently opened up an unsteady portal between the Underworld and Widdershins. Not long after we started our journey here, my brother escaped through the portal, and he's headed here as well. But he doesn't want to *fix* the stone. He wants to find out how to make the portal permanent—and he will use any means necessary to get that information. For all I know, he could be here right now. So we need someone on the Council of Grand Wizards who will do the necessary magic to repair the stone."

My eyes flicked to Steadly again, but he was examining a spot on the arm of his throne, so I continued.

"We asked Headmaster Steadly for help, but he refused, citing that Change magic was too dangerous to try. But the next day, in conversation with Professor Trenchant, I discovered that she felt confident doing the magic. She seemed to feel that the headmaster was being unnecessarily cautious so as not to disrupt his long reign."

The group shared uncomfortable looks.

"I say, Steadly," said Pendergast, the wizard in maroon and gold who'd initially posed the question. "Surely there's enough talent in this room that we can help these two?"

"Help them?" cried the wizard on the throne all the way to the left. He had a puffy white head of hair and wore powder-blue robes. He spoke in an almost singsong way. Scouring my brain, I remembered that this was Master Wisp. "If we separate these two, we'll have two demons running amuck!"

"That's your objection?" boomed a deep voice belonging to the man all the way to the right. Powerfully built, he looked more like a golden-age hero than a scholar. Possibly Master Black? "I'm sure we could manage two demons. And if we don't allow Trenchant to do the magic, we'll have a whole horde of demons at our doorstep!"

"We don't even know the nature of the stone itself. Without understanding that, it would be foolish to attempt the magic," said a fifth wizard. He was in green robes, and his white hair and beard reached down to his waist. I couldn't even guess his name.

"We don't need to know the nature of the stone, Hawksmoor."

So, Long Beard was Master Hawksmoor, then.

"What do you mean, we don't need to know the nature of the stone? Change magic is dangerous enough without cutting corners!"

Master Black covered his face with his hand.

"Because the stone is just a stone right now—the two of them have the magic!"

"You know what I meant."

"You should say what you mean."

"Why I ought to . . ."

This . . . went on . . . for hours. The arguments drifted in and out of relevance. The insults became more frequent as well: words like "scallywag," "dingbat," "laggard," and "blunderbuss" were used in heavy rotation. Light shifted through the windows as the day wore on. At noon, the entire room dimmed, giving everyone a gold-gray tinge as shadow mixed with the ever-present Rogue magic.

"It seems pretty clear who Trenchant has in her pocket," whispered Reginald. I jumped. He hadn't said a word until now. His face—always so open and earnest—was unreadable to me.

"You mean that the ones arguing in our favor are people she's blackmailed?"

He nodded.

"Couldn't it be that they want to help?"

He raised a shoulder and let it drop.

"Sure, Mal."

I rubbed my temples. Fatigue mixed with anxiety was doing strange things to my body. I felt as if I were being buffeted by the winds of a Centennial Storm and simultaneously so tired that I might drop straight to the floor.

"Do you think we're going to break for meals?" I whispered to Reg.

"Now look whose being guided by the whims of their stomach," he replied.

The sun was on a crash course with the horizon when the wizards finally stopped arguing. Steadly placed his hands on the arms of his throne and hefted himself to his feet. The light was at his back now, and it made it difficult to see his expression.

"The sun is about to set. It is time to call a vote. All in favor of removing me as headmaster of the academy, raise their hand."

Two hands went up right away: Master Black's, and a wizard whose name the proceedings had revealed to be "Master Dodge." Then Pendergast raised his hand as well.

Trenchant had said that she had enough of the Grand Wizards under her thumb to win the vote. So where was the vote to decide in her favor?

"All against?"

Four hands rose into the air, and Steadly bent forward slightly, light shining on his face again. He looked as if he'd fallen over in relief. He was going to remain headmaster.

I had lost.

"This is an outrage!" came a scream from the door as it burst open. The flawless face of Professor Trenchant, who must have been listening at the door, was contorted into a mask of fury as she strode down toward us. "He is a spineless, weak-minded, power-hungry fat cat!" She paused near Reginald, her entire focus on the seventh wizard. "Master Pratchett—how could you?"

The wizard drew himself up, smoothing his purple robes as he smiled calmly from his place next to Steadly.

"Steadly came to see me just before dawn. It turns out, my dear, that you had nothing on me that the headmaster couldn't set right."

Steadly turned his stern gaze in Trenchant's direction.

"And I believe we'll be discussing the end of your tenure here at our next regularly scheduled meeting."

"You useless, sexist, egomaniacal tyrant! I can do the magic! I can guarantee it!"

Trenchant's eyes bugged out of her head and spittle flew as she continued to fire off insults at Steadly. I didn't like that I'd lost, but I was kind of sort of maybe coming around to the fact that she was not the solid source of assistance I'd originally assessed her to be.

"Someone get her out of here," growled Steadly.

She continued to rage for a while, but Reginald—always the gentleman—placed a hand on her arm and whispered something to her. By the time someone arrived to escort her away, she seemed much more pleasant. Amiable, even. But I didn't have time to dwell on what Reg might have said to calm her because Steadly turned his ire on us. Well, on me.

"Reginald, I am sorry that this has been such a trying time for you, and I feel terrible sending you away still attached to *this*," he gestured at me. "But I'm afraid that my answer is the same as before. There's nothing we can do. And I want *you*," the full force of his gaze upon me now, "*out of my sight*."

———

STEADLY GAVE us until the next morning to pack and leave.

"At least we'll be on the move with the stone when Tannith arrives," said Reginald.

"At least there's that," I said.

"Where will you go?" asked Saffron, uncharacteristically biting her fingernails. Goodfallow gently captured her wrist, bringing her hand away from her mouth, and she gave him a wan smile. We'd picked up a couple of threadbare messenger bags from the lost and found and grabbed food from the dining hall before returning to Goodfallow and Saffron's room. My bag was laid out on her smooth bedspread, and I was tucking the sack of stone pieces inside.

"I don't know," said Reginald with a shrug. "Steadly said we should try talking to an actual magical creature. That maybe they'd be able to help."

Goodfallow nudged Saffron. They exchanged a look, and then he said, "Maybe this will help as well."

He handed Reginald two squashy brown packages. One said "Lord Malgon" and the other "Sir Reginald." Reg handed mine to me, and we exchanged quizzical looks.

"No sense wearing academic robes when you're traveling around the world. They can get a bit breezy underneath," said Goodfallow, blushing slightly.

I picked at the paper of the package and sucked in a breath when I finally pulled a corner back.

"Is this . . . are these my clothes?"

Saffron grimaced.

"Not exactly. You can't recover something that's been lost to Rogue magic. But I was able to do a memory recall spell on Reginald, and we had them remade as close as possible."

"And Reginald's clothes were . . . not that great. So we just chose something that we thought would look good on him," said Goodfallow.

Reginald ripped the paper off his package, and his eyes went wide. Beneath was a fresh white shirt, a white cravat, and a green velvet jacket.

"We thought the green would look good with your eyes," said Saffron, smiling.

I glanced at Reginald. Had I ever noticed that his eyes were green? Now that I really looked—his eyes were stunning. They were bright like a spring day, with long dark lashes. I'd always been so focused on his flaws that I'd never really *seen* him.

"I am nearly speechless. Thank you, both. Saffron, Goodfallow," I said, nodding at each of them. Three pairs of shocked eyes drilled into me.

"Did he just use my name?" Goodfallow whispered to Saffron.

"You're welcome," was all she said in reply to me.

Reginald took out his pocket time wheel and consulted it.

"Yes. Thank you both so much. But we should really finish packing," he said.

"Of course," said Saffron. "We'll go get something to eat— the dining hall is about to close. We'll see you again before you go." She squeezed his arm and Goodfallow waved. Then they were gone.

We dressed in silence, and once we were both done, we turned to examine one another. The transformation in Reginald was astounding. Saffron had even given him a haircut, and the style was now less "disheveled" and more "artfully mussed pompadour."

"You look perfect," he said, the corner of his mouth twitching up. "Just like yourself."

I hitched a smile onto my face.

"It feels good to be back." I tugged down the sleeves of my jacket, then held my arms out to inspect them. It was identical to the morning coat that had burned in the fire. Reginald, unlike me, had been paying attention.

He sighed.

"I'm really going to miss them."

A feeling that I strongly suspected was guilt ate at my gut. To make it go away, I did the only thing I could think of: I started yelling.

"I'm sorry, okay? I . . . I'm going to be a more considerate demon. I might have given you anger, but you gave me . . . well, it's either guilt or an ulcer. Hard to tell. But I'm sorry about my part in breaking the stone. I'm sorry about getting you into so much trouble on the way here. I'm sorry I got jealous of you being friends with Saffron and Goodfallow, and I'm sorry I didn't listen to you guys about the Quarrel. Trenchant is clearly unhinged!"

Reginald's face was pale and horrified.

"Ah. Well. Then I guess I'm sorry too."

"For what?" I asked.

Something thumped against the door, and then it slammed open.

"For this," he said.

Two giant men shouldered into the room, each with a sack in his hands.

"Reg—what's going on?"

Something knocked me upside the head, and everything went black. Again.

CHAPTER 16
TRENCHANT'S GUARANTEE

"What is going on?" I yelled, but I knew the bag was muffling my voice. I was being carried forcibly, and I tried to figure out where we were headed, but the night was dark, and the bag had no noticeable holes. A muffled whining sounded nearby, and I relaxed a fraction in realization that Reginald was still conscious.

My body was slammed down onto a chair, and I heard the thump of Reginald being flopped down next to me. Rope bit into the skin on my wrists and ankles as they—whoever *they* were—bound me to the chair. They whipped the bag from my head, and I saw we were back on the arena floor in the amphitheater where the Quarrel had taken place earlier that same day. In the intervening hours, it had been transformed. Clusters of pale crystals were placed at regular intervals along the top row of benches. The only light in the room came from about a thousand lit tapers lined up to form a pentagram hovering a few feet over our heads. The arena floor was chalk-marked with lines and symbols that formed a winding path from the perimeter to Reginald and me, who were sitting in creaking wooden chairs in the center. A magical labyrinth. What was going on?

"You should be ashamed of yourselves," spat Reginald. "That bag smelled disgusting."

"Sorry for the cloak and dagger," came the smooth voice of Professor Trenchant. She rounded my chair and stood before us, smiling madly. She wasn't just unhinged—she was fully unraveled now. When we'd first met, her lips had been meticulously colored. Now they were chapped and cracking. Her hair, which had been sleek and shiny when we met, was disheveled and strawlike. But the biggest difference was in her eyes. Once cool and calculating, they were now red-rimmed and manic. "I had to be stealthy if I was going to go ahead with this against the Quarrel's wishes, as Reginald suggested."

"So you kidnapped us? This is what—wait. *Reginald* suggested?"

One of her goons—both of whom I recognized as students from the dining hall—handed her the sack of stone pieces as her smile faltered.

"He didn't tell you?"

She shuffled away and busied herself with preparations as I turned to face him.

"What is she talking about?"

Reginald looked abashed.

"I talked to her before they escorted her out. She was so angry, and she kept insisting that she would succeed. That she had a guarantee. I also thought you were mad and—" he paused, searching for the right words. "Do you remember when Goodfallow was talking about poisons and he said that sometimes a little bad can do a lot of good?"

"Sort of," I said, not understanding where this was going.

"Well—that's you. For me, I mean. You're . . . not good. You cause trouble everywhere we go, you insult me, and you're the most self-centered creature I've met. But you've been good for me too. When you died, I—" His voice caught in his throat. "I know it was only for a few seconds. But it shook me. I saw so clearly that this didn't need to happen just for Widdershins. I needed to do this for you."

I gaped at him.

"Reg. That is extremely thoughtful and far more than I deserve from you—but it was also idiotic. I was the one who was wrong. That woman is certifiable!"

We stared at Trenchant. She was clutching a book to her chest and muttering to herself. She kept glancing at the door—probably afraid that the headmaster would come and shut her down. Reginald grimaced before he turned back to me, his features sculpted into a mask of bravery.

"Maybe. But the time we spent in the library gave us no answers. Now that you've called the Quarrel and Steadly has kicked us out—what else was I supposed to do? You were right, Mal. I should have taken the threat of Tannith more seriously."

A deep voice, smooth and saccharine as honey sounded from the door.

"Yes. You should have."

My breath caught in my throat. I reluctantly rotated my head toward the entryway.

Out of the shadows emerged a tall figure in a black waistcoat. From his head rose twisting, dark horns, and a scar ran from his forehead, across his eye, and down to his ear. A pointed tail flicked briefly into view. His yellow eyes found mine, a wicked smile playing on his face.

My brother had come to Seven.

"Little brother," he boomed in his rich baritone, extending his arms outward in greeting as he slowly descended the staircase down to our level. With each step the stone floor trembled ever so slightly, and I silently hoped that Steadly was in his office and could feel it. "How good it is to see you again." He paused on the last step before the arena. "I only wish it were under better circumstances." His mouth turned down into a mock frown. "Mother and father are going to be so disappointed that you forsook your own kind in favor of these topside dwellers."

I was tall, but Tannith was a mountain. His broad, muscular shoulders spanned four full feet, and at nearly eleven feet in height, he probably experienced entirely different weather systems. I couldn't take him in a contest of magic or strength, but I glared at him anyway.

"Professor Trenchant! Take the stone and run!" I shouted. "He's here for it!"

"What's that?" she said from the other side of the room, where she was removing the stone bits from a sack and placing them in a triangle on a silver platter. "Oh, Tannith. Good. You're here. I was beginning to think you weren't coming."

My eyes flicked from one to the other as Tannith stepped down onto the arena floor and strode over to where she was standing. Even being careful not to disturb her chalk work, he was there in an instant.

"Wait—you're working together?" I cried, horrified. This was so much worse than just Trenchant or just Tannith.

"I hope that coat of yours has you feeling more like yourself, Mal," murmured Reginald out of the corner of his mouth. "We could use one of your quick yet terrifying exits right now."

"I said I would be of assistance, Professor, and I would *never* go back on my word," Tannith said, ignoring Reginald and me. "I was just taking care of a soon-to-be-former headmaster for you."

Reginald paled and whispered, "Steadly is dead?"

I swallowed hard and tapped my foot nervously against the floor. It wasn't easy to do with my ankles tied to the chair legs, but I had to do something.

"I don't know. But Tannith wouldn't have any qualms about doing it, that's for sure."

Reginald squirmed in the chair, trying to free himself from the knots. When that didn't work, he started yelling.

"Don't believe him, Professor! Mal might not be very good at being a demon, but he's still almost always lying about stuff!"

"Way to throw me under the cart, Reg," I muttered under my breath. But then louder I said, "He's right! I do that. And Tannith is a hundred times more liar-y than I am."

Trenchant raised her deranged eyes to me.

"Oh, this is bigger than trust. Our interests are aligned. Tannith wants to see Change magic become viable as much as I do, don't you?"

"I most certainly do," he said. Then, when her back was turned, he shook his head and mouthed to us, "I absolutely do not."

"You know," I called, "I used the same logic about working with you, and all it's gotten me is certain death, so maybe just pause for a moment and think about this?"

She cast her eyes on me, and for a moment, they looked lucid once more.

"I've been thinking about this ever since I heard you two were in Seven. And if using a demon to get what I want is the way to do it, then that's what I'll do. It worked in the golden age. It's working for your pet over there. And now it's my turn."

At that last, her eyes took on their mad sheen again, and I could tell there'd be no reasoning with her.

That just left my brother.

I tried to shuffle my chair toward him, but I only moved a few inches.

"Tannith," I pleaded. "Can't you just . . ." I realized I was about to plead with him to let Reginald go—but it was impossible. I tried again. "Has she told you about Rogue magic? How very wrong spells can go here? Say you manage to open a portal —it could still potentially destroy the Underworld!"

I didn't know if that was true or not, but it seemed like a logical extension of everything Saffron and Steadly had been saying. And it had the intended effect. I saw a flash of doubt in my brother's eyes. She hadn't been truthful with him, either. Then he settled his face back into relaxed amusement and said, "Rogue magic may be trouble for a human. But you and I, brother, are creatures of magic. We do not need to fear it." Coming closer, he brought his face level with mine and whispered, "I tortured my fair share of village witches and wizards on my way here, you know. They all told me that the only magic that would get me what I wanted was Change magic— the forbidden magic. So imagine my delight when I ran into Professor Crazy Pants here right after you called a Quarrel. She was gushing about how she was going to use Change magic to fix the stone. All I had to do was convince her she could bypass the Rogue magic by helping me create a portal, and I had everything I needed. Plus," he said, his expression hardening into disgust. "It told me two things I needed to know. First—that you were a weak little traitor. That wasn't much of a surprise, if I'm honest. But second—that there was someone here willing to do what all those little souls along the way were warning me against. So say what you like to scare me. It won't work. I am going to open this portal, and demons will toast my name for eternity. We've been in each other's company for far too long. We could all use a little . . . change of scenery."

With that, he stood and walked back over to Trenchant. Their heads bent together over something in the book she'd been holding.

I screamed in frustration and pulled at my bindings. The chair wobbled and scraped across the floor, but it didn't topple.

"What are you doing?" hissed Reginald. "They're going to

knock you out again if you keep making a fuss, and I'm not sure three concussions in one day is good for you."

"I'm making use of my newly returned coat, Reg," I whispered, staring into his eyes and then looking pointedly at the floor. Reginald followed my gaze, and he inhaled a quick breath.

As I'd been tapping my foot in nervousness, shuffling my chair around to beg, and wobbling around in frustration, I'd also been systematically erasing the last symbol in the labyrinth—the last piece of magic that would fix the stone or stabilize the portal, depending on whose will won out.

"That could kill us."

"If Tannith opens that portal, we're dead anyway." I paused for a moment. "And I'm not sure Trenchant is in the right headspace for successful magic."

"Oi—you two!" called Professor Trenchant to her goons. "The prisoners should be back to back! And don't you dare touch that chalk line while you're down there."

"Please," said Reg to the goons when they reached us. "You don't have to do this."

They ignored us, rearranged our chairs, and tiptoed back out of the circle and off the floor.

"It is time," said Tannith, and the candlelight from the tapers dimmed as the crystals around the perimeter began to glow.

"Do you have any regrets, Reg?"

There was silence for a moment. Then, with a firm tone, he said, "No. How about you?"

I paused as well. My life had been turned upside down in the past two weeks, and I'd truly never met anyone who drove me to madness more than Reginald P. Asstradle did. But there was another side to that coin as well. Plus, I had my clothes back. What more could I want?

"No. Not one."

"If you're quite finished," growled Trenchant. "It's time to begin. No more talking." She held the platter with the pieces of the Stone of Eno in one hand, and her other hand was outstretched in welcome to . . . magic? Madness? We will never know. Beside her stood my brother, holding out the book so that she could read from it.

Light was creeping in from the eastern windows and hid the symbol I'd botched in shadow. We would soon see if it would be enough to collapse the whole spell.

Trenchant waved a hand, the tapers flared, and the rocks flew off the silver tray and were suspended above our heads, just below the pentagram. I had a brief, wild thought that I should throw the whole "summoning is fairytale magic" thing in Goodfallow's face later. Then I remembered that with a powerfully insane wizard and dishonorable demon about to do magic on me, there wasn't likely to be a later.

Trenchant and my brother started down the circular path she'd chalked. As they walked, she murmured the spells at each symbol

"Is it getting warm in here?" asked Reginald.

"Silence!" she hissed as she and Tannith continued through the labyrinth.

But he was right. It felt as if we'd been tossed into a fucking furnace. It was literally almost as hot as Hell.

"Halfway through a change begun / Halfway till the change is done."

Trenchant's voice got stronger the closer she got to us in the center. Soon it was like a drumbeat in my ears. The air shimmered all around us, though I didn't know if it was from heat or magic or both. A gust of wind tore in from one window and swirled around Reginald and me, pulling air from our lungs. The stone pieces above our heads spun, and Trenchant laughed hysterically. She raised her hands, and between them I could see a spinning sphere of darkness forming. It grew to the size of a melon, and she shouted, "Release these two from their bond / Let the magic go / Change thy will and set them free / Become the Stone of—what are you doing?!"

At that moment, Tannith picked her up with one hand and tossed her across the room. She slammed against the benches, and I heard a crack and a scream of pain. With the other hand, he'd grasped the darkness. Now, grasping the sphere with both hands, he spread his arms wide. As he did so, the darkness grew, and though I could barely breathe, I detected the slightest hint of brimstone. His fucking plan was working.

My brother took the irrevocable step forward onto the symbol I'd marred, and the darkness shifted in his grasp. I saw the shock on his face as he fought to keep it steady, but he was losing control. At the same moment, the doors to the room burst open, and I was shocked to see Steadly in the archway. His eye was black, his lip was torn, and fresh blood trickled out of his ear, but he was steady on his feet.

"Rezelda, no!" he shouted, looking from Professor Trenchant's prone form to Tannith struggling with the portal. He stretched out his hand, shouting words in a language I did not understand. But it was too late. The darkness exploded around us. I felt something hit my head, and for the third time in two days, everything went black.

CHAPTER 17
LASTING EFFECTS

I awoke splayed flat on the floor with broken chair legs still attached to my ankles.

I'm alive?

I blacked out again. When I came to, my head was pounding. But behind my closed eyelids, the answer to why I was in this state flashed in my mind. Bolting inadvisably upward, I swooned and crashed back down.

Several minutes later, I opened my eyes for a third time. Taking it slower, I stared up at the ceiling, which I had never noticed before. A dozen gray stone buttresses met in the center to hold up the peaked roof. It looked like a very fancy, very heavy spoked wheel.

"Reg?" I asked.

"Stay still if you can. He hasn't come around yet."

It was Steadly. He was kneeling next to me, looking like a white-robed bullfrog. Light filled the room now and illuminated his battered face. It looked so much worse close up.

"You look like hell," I said, closing my eyes again. My head still felt as if an anvil had landed on it.

"You're one to talk," he grunted. "You and Reginald look as though you've been overcooked."

My stomach went into free fall.

"Is he okay? Is he . . . dead?"

"No, he's not dead. But he's still unconscious."

"What happened?"

"I don't know exactly. I was hoping you could tell me. But Rezelda . . . Professor Trenchant . . . did not complete the labyrinth correctly. Her last symbol was a mess, and it made your brother's portal impossible to sustain. Funny—it wasn't the Rogue magic that tripped her up. It was first-year symbology. Anyway, when I arrived, your brother was attempting to regain control. With him distracted, I was able to cut off the spell, but not without consequences."

"Oh. Well, did the spell work on us?"

"I don't know," he said.

My eyes shot open.

"What happened to my brother?"

"I don't know. Maybe he escaped into the portal in time and he's in the Underworld. Maybe he's in another dimension. We may never know."

I growled in frustration.

"Do you know *anything*? Where is Professor Trenchant?" I twisted my head around and saw a gaping hole in the floor where Tannith had been standing. There was a scorched smell in the air—the spell had burned a hole in the floor. *Burned.* Through the stone. The edges of it still glowed and smoldered. A few feet closer, and that would have been Reg and me, presumably.

"The magic . . . reassigned her."

Reassigned?

"To desk duty?"

"Not quite," he said and cocked his head to the side. I sat up slowly this time and squinted where he'd indicated. A black chicken was strutting across a bench on the far side of the room. It turned an eye toward me and clucked.

"She's ... a chicken?"

As I watched her, a group of mages tasked with dealing with the damage hurried in.

"It's such a shame. She was a lot to take, and she did just try to get me fired, but she was exceedingly talented."

"Mm. You know what they say about karma. She's a little B," I said.

He frowned at me.

"If that were true, you should be maimed, dead, or at least humbled beyond recognition."

"There's still time for that," I said wryly.

I was about to ask him if he at least knew about the stone when I heard my name.

"I think your coat worked, Mal."

Sweet suffering.

"Reg?" I left Steadly and crawled to where he was lying. "I'm here. And you're alive. And, wow, Steadly wasn't kidding about you looking overcooked."

He was soot-stained from head to toe. His magnificent green jacket black as pitch. He sat up slowly and rubbed his cheek, his skin reappearing in all its pale glory.

"Did it work?"

"I don't know. All the headmaster could confirm is that Tannith is possibly back in the Underworld or possibly in another dimension and that Trenchant is a chicken now."

I pointed at her, and she let out a *bawk.*

"Oh. That's too bad," he said, as if I'd told him that the dining hall had run out of meatloaf. Like it was a pretty normal thing to say. Though, in our lives, maybe it was.

"Are you okay to stand?" I asked.

"Let's find out," he said, and the two of us leaned on one another as we rose to our feet. We could now see that the round room was in chaos. There were char marks on the walls, shattered pieces of broken crystal strewn across the floor, and merged pockets of Rogue magic floating in the air.

"Glad I'm not on cleanup duty," I said.

"Even if we hadn't just survived an attempt at creating a stable portal to the Underworld, I don't think they'd trust us with it."

I huffed a laugh, then asked the question I'd had since I first woke up.

"So . . . what do you say? Do you want to try? If you're not feeling up to it, I understand."

I didn't want to seem overeager, but I really wanted to know if the spell had worked. He didn't answer—he merely nodded —and so we stood back to back.

"Ready?" I said.

"I guess so."

We took off in different directions, each of us taking slow, cautious steps in anticipation of the magical tether snapping us back into place. Steadly and a handful of other mages who were there doing mitigation stopped to watch us. But it never pulled us back. I moved a little faster and was out the door. I started running as I hit the staircase. Hardly able to contain my elation, I leaped ten steps down.

"I'm freeeeeeeee!" I shouted, a manic grin plastered across my face. Student mages and professors dove out of my way as I careened down the stairs. "So long, you fuckers!"

I skidded to a halt.

"Wait, wait," I said aloud to myself. "Weren't you trying to be more considerate? Is running away without saying goodbye what a considerate demon would do?" Plus, the spell had disconnected Reg and me, but we still didn't know if it had it fixed the Stone of Eno. Grumbling, I turned around and stomped back up to the top of the tower. Everyone was still standing down on the arena floor; my eyes fixed on Reginald.

His arms were crossed and his face—still soot-caked—was unreadable.

"Wow," he said. "Not even a single backward glance, Mal?" His tone was accusing, but his eyes had that special Reginald twinkle to them that told me he wasn't really angry.

"Yes, all right." I said, holding my hands up in surrender. "It was poor form, I'll give you that. But in my defense, it's not like there's well-developed etiquette for how one reacts to being magically unhitched from someone."

Reginald's gaze rose to the ceiling, and I could see by the way he scrunched up his mouth and pointed at invisible things with one finger that he was puzzling out my sentence. Maybe the word "etiquette" threw him off. I turned to Steadly.

"So, what about the stone?"

"The two of you have been separated, obviously. Though we don't know what the lasting effects of that kind of connection might be. As far as I can tell, you'll be able to lead separate lives. The magic did not flow back into the Stone of Eno, however. Professor Trenchant never should have expected it to. I suspect that only a magical being can restore it. And it is quite clear to me now that the stone *must* be restored. If there is still a portal flickering at the edge of the Forest of Arden, then our problems are not over. I will do what I can from here, but your journey must go on."

"What kind of magical being?" asked Reginald.

Steadly considered.

"There are many kinds. Sprites, vimaways, witches, demons, dryads—though the dryads clearly do not know of how the stone was made. No, you'll need to consult a creature with deep knowledge accumulated over a thousand years. And there's only one of those alive today. You'll have to ask Fafnir."

I blanched, but Reginald asked, "Who is Fafnir?"

Steadly looked at Reginald as if he was an idiot. Which he kind of was sometimes.

"Who is . . . What kind of nonsense education did you receive not to know Fafnir, boy?"

"Hey—don't you talk to him like that!" I said. "Why would he know that?" I turned to Reginald. "Reg, you donkey's ass— didn't you ever learn about Fafnir? The enormous, nasty, fire-breathing dragon?"

Reginald's face turned the color of cottage cheese.

"You mean . . . to fix the stone . . . we'll have to talk to a dragon?"

I cocked an eyebrow at him.

"'We'?"

"Well, the dryads said we couldn't come back until the stone was fixed. Plus, there's the portal problem, so I figured . . ."

"No. No, no, no. No," I waved my hands back and forth in dismissal.

"Seriously, Mal?"

"No! I'm not doing it! I have free will again, and I am exercising that to say, 'Reginald. If you have a death wish and want to go talk to a dragon, be my guest.' But Fafnir's island is across the Outer Sea. And demons do not swim. I am not going."

"Okay, Mal. Good joke."

"Reg, I'm not joking. I'm not going. You said yourself that I'm the most self-centered creature you'd ever met. I'm going to use all this free will I now have to go drink my weight in fire-water and have sex till my dick falls off. But also—" I paused, my smile faltering. "You're better off without me. All I did was get you into trouble. It's time to go our separate ways. You go off and do your heroing. Maybe I'll go check out that spa on the Inner Sea from the pamphlet we found."

"Oh," said Reginald, blinking at me with glassy eyes. Did he really want to stay together after all of this? After all the trouble I'd caused him? There was the smallest tickle of regret somewhere near my gallbladder, but I ignored it. "Yeah. Right. That makes sense." He sniffed, then turned to Steadly.

"I, Sir Reginald P. Asstradle, will take the stone and go see the dragon Fafnir. Alone." Steadly nodded solemnly and handed him the bag of stone bits. "Uh, just one question—"

"What is that?"

"How do I find him?"

WE STAYED one more night at the Academy. It gave us time to get cleaned up, rest, and bid a tearful farewell to Saffron and Goodfallow. Well, Reg's farewell was tearful, anyway.

"I guess this is it, then," said Reginald. It was morning, and we were standing outside the mammoth ivory doors that marked the entry to the Wizard's Tower. The day was warm by winter's standards, but a light breeze blew chilly air down the back of my morning coat. I shivered. Reginald's face and jacket were clean once more—though in washing the soot from his face, he'd discovered an angry cut across his eyebrow that must have come from the exploding crystals. It would probably scar, and that, in combination with the leaner, stronger body he'd developed through our adventures, would erase some of his natural guilelessness.

"Where's your bag?" I asked.

"Master Pratchett gave me some kind of invisible, interdimensional pack. He said it could carry an infinite number of things with only a little weight gain, so I put the stone shards and all that in there. All I have to do is snap my fingers and it appears!"

"Handy."

"Yeah, it's pretty cool." Reginald looked at the ground and scuffed his toe in the dirt. "I'm going to miss you, Mal. I learned a lot these past weeks. And as glad as I am not to go winging into you every time we put an iota of space between us, I sort of got used to your company."

I rested my hands on his shoulders. I had an entire speech planned about how he'd changed my life and that he was a different person now and that every once in a while he showed flashes of golden-age heroism. But I chickened out and made a joke instead.

"I expect that not having to wonder if you're going to throw up every other day will take some getting used to." I winked at him and smoothed the velvet of his jacket before removing my hands. He produced a half-hearted smile.

"I bet." Looking up at my face, he said, "You're *sure* you won't come with me?"

I shook my head.

"No, Reg. But I hope you take care of yourself. And who knows? Maybe we'll see each other again sometime."

He shifted from foot to foot and nearly fell over when a cobble beneath his feet wobbled. I felt a surge of guilt for not going with him, but then I reminded myself he would never have been in as much trouble as he'd been in if I hadn't been around.

"Where are you going?" he asked.

"I was serious about that spa town. And then . . . who knows?" I shrugged. I really didn't know.

"Well, I hope you get a nice rest," he said. "You deserve it."

I tried to arrange my features into a smile.

"Thanks. And you know where you're going, then?"

Reginald nodded.

"I take the road out of Seven straight to the coastal town of Searfoss. There, I bribe a fisherman to sail me to Fafnir's island and convince the dragon to help me fix the stone."

My stomach dropped thinking about Reg surviving all of that, but I pushed the thought away. He was no longer my responsibility.

"Sounds simple enough."

Reginald smiled.

"I thought so too!"

"Well, then. Goodbye, Reg. I'm not entirely sure it was a pleasure getting to know you, but it certainly was an adventure."

"It sure was, Mal."

Then Reg turned and walked away. I took a deep breath to stifle the sob that almost escaped my lips. Then he whipped back around and I blinked furiously.

"What is it?" I asked, letting out a long, quick breath.

"I almost forgot! I got something for you."

He snapped his fingers, and out of nowhere a worn leather backpack appeared. Opening it, he rummaged inside for a moment, then pulled out a parcel the size of his palm. He handed it over, saying, "It's just a little parting gift to remember me by. Open it when I'm gone, yeah?"

I nodded, unable to speak.

"Okay—bye for real, then," he said with a wave and trudged off down the winding cobble road toward the arched gates out of Seven. I waited until he was out of sight and tore the paper open. Inside was a note and a pocket timewheel. I read the note first.

Dear Mal,

I know you think I'm better off without you, but I wanted to let you know I don't think that's true. You had the choice to get everything you'd ever wanted for the past five hundred years, and you gave it up to help me and my gran and everyone. You're cranky, you can be kind of mean, and you can't seem to help making trouble. But way down deep (very, very deep?), I think you're more than that.

I had this made at a stall at the Yulesticetide Festival. I can't give you your horns, so I hope you'll accept my gift as the next best thing.

Sincerely,

Sir Reginald P. Asstradle, Hero of Widdershins

I looked at the timewheel in my hand. It was made of black metal with a long graphite chain. In the center, etched in slightly lighter black, were two horns. Around the outside, stamped in the same gray, were the words "A little bad to do a lot of good."

"That fucking bastard." I grumbled as I wiped at my eyes. I was about to shove the piece back in the packaging, but instead I stamped my foot and squeezed my fists in frustration before relenting and hooking it to the pocket of my waistcoat. Then I walked in the opposite direction toward a grassy field within the city limits. Saffron and Goodfallow had told me there was a secret door out of the city in that direction, which would put me on course to the spa. I took the time to list all the reasons traveling without Reginald was going to be sublime.

"No more of his boring-ass stories. No more disappointment when he doesn't understand your jokes. No more wondering if he's going to throw up because he's stubbed his toe. This is better. Alone is better. Alone is perfect, actually. Who is better to keep you company than yourself?"

I had a flash of meeting Reginald for the first time in the park outside of Beadledom, where he fainted at the sight of his own blood.

"He'll be fine," I said aloud.

I could just see the swaying, golden field near the city walls and picked up my pace. As I ran, I thought of the time we sprinted away from the giant, of Reginald getting picked up and nearly eaten. Twice.

"But he escaped. He doesn't need you."

I ran faster, but the visions came more swiftly now. Reginald throwing up in the Marais. Reginald's face on stage at the inn. Reginald trying to assist ants across the road. Reginald and the doors to the dwarf warren.

"Dammit all straight to Hell!" I shouted as I stopped short at the edge of the field. My chest was heaving from the exertion of running and from the war raging within me. "You're a demon,

Mal. Maybe not as evil as Tannith—but still a demon. You look out for yourself."

But was I just a demon anymore? Steadly said he didn't know what the lasting effects of the connection would be. That we "should" be able to lead separate lives now. But what did that mean, exactly? I had a sinking feeling that no matter how far I ran, I would never stop wondering if Reg was okay.

"Hellfire and fucking damnation!" I cried as I turned and jogged back to the city to find the High Street. I had to catch Reginald before he left the city—but I needed to make two stops first.

THE LOWER TOWN was bustling as the arched gateway came into view. I passed a man fighting with his hat so it would stay on his head. A woman with four children crossed my path, each child holding a bubble wand that made bubbles shaped like unicorns and dragons. Maybe Reginald was right. Magic was kind of cool.

I spotted his back just as he reached the gate, and my chest constricted. His shoulders were slumped, and he was more shuffling than walking. I hurried forward, ignoring the smell of manure from the horses inside the city walls that mixed with the effluvium wafting in from the peat bogs beyond them. Maneuvering as close to him as I could, I stopped, then yelled, "I come bearing gifts."

Reginald froze in place. He turned around in slow motion and swiped at his swollen eyes when he saw me.

"Wha..."

"I couldn't let a Hero of Widdershins go without the proper accessories. And I certainly couldn't have a human outdo me in the gift-giving arena."

I held out a dark leather belt with a scabbard and a sword—

not, mind you, a broadsword to delight the likes of Quill Valor, but a small, ornamental sword I'd stolen off a days-of-yore exhibit during my detour back through the academy. The golden hilt was engraved with vines, and an emerald was set at the base of the pommel.

"Oh," said Reginald, reaching out to take it. "Thank you. It's lovely." His eyes shot up, then narrowed. "Did you pay for this?"

"I'd rather not lie to you, Reg. Just put it on."

He ran the belt around his waist and clipped it on.

"How do I look?"

I tilted my head this way and that, looking at him from multiple angles.

"Fancier."

He shrugged. "I'll take it."

"Also," I continued, "I brought us coffees for the road."

"Gosh that's a good idea—I hadn't thought of . . ." Reginald trailed off as he stared at me. He glanced from my face to the mugs balanced in my right hand and back again. "Do you mean . . . ?"

I handed him a coffee, then brushed at a speck of something on my sleeve.

"Clearly, Trenchant and Tannith were a couple of hacks who botched the separation job. I mean, the farther away I got, the more I felt compelled to come back. Honestly, those two were a menace. I don't know where Tannith ended up, but hopefully Trenchant, at least, won't be able to do any more harm as a chicken."

Reginald smirked.

"Hopefully not."

We walked through the gates in silence, sipping our coffees. A horse-drawn cart passed us going the opposite direction, and the driver gave us a double take before continuing on his way.

"Nice timewheel," said Reginald, looking sidelong at the

chain poking out from beneath my coat. "How long did it take you to open the package?"

"It was open and on within three minutes of your leaving."

He snorted.

A thought occurred to me, and I laughed.

"You know what Fafnir is probably going to say when we get there, right? 'A demon and a hero walk into a dragon's den.'"

Reginald grinned.

"'Sounds like the beginning of a joke, but how does it end?'" he said.

"Probably in a horrifying, fiery death. He is a dragon, after all."

"Way to make it morbid, Mal."

"You think I'm wrong? With our luck?"

"I'm just saying. It wouldn't hurt to be more positive."

"I am positive! Positive we're going to be eaten by a dragon."

"Mal—"

"Fine," I said and held up my hands, almost dropping my cup in the process. "But on the way, I'm going to compose an aria to sing when we're engulfed in flame. It's going to be called, 'I told you so.'"

Reginald chuckled and rolled his eyes.

"If you say so, Mal."

And with that, both our bodies and our positive attitudes left Seven behind in search of a dragon.

Like fucking idiots.

DID THIS BOOK MAKE YOU LAUGH?

See? I tricked you. I didn't ask if you enjoyed it. I asked if it made you laugh. And even if you found it laughably bad—you still laughed, right?

Seriously though, if you enjoyed this book, please help me get the word out by leaving a review. It helps more than you know.

And if you want to be the first to learn about new releases from A.E. Kincaid, you're in luck. Newsletter subscribers also get exclusive content, like sneak peeks, behind the scenes, and additional stories for free. You can join at my website.

www.aekincaid.com

ACKNOWLEDGMENTS

If you're reading this, you're probably on this list.

J.L. Vampa - If you had not said "yes" when I asked if we could start trading words each Wednesday, this book would not exist. You are my write-or-die and beautiful friend. Thank you.

Jaime Brockway - You have been with me from the beginning. I can't begin to tell you how grateful I am that you are the person who responded to my "will an editor edit a short story?" query on Reedsy. Your edits and suggestions have been invaluable and for that I owe you a t-shirt.

Alyse Bailey - The attention and enthusiasm you poured into this story at such a busy time in your life was incredible. I am forever grateful to that other client of yours whose word count allowed you to take on my project on such short notice. Maybe I'll see you on I-84 some day.

Sara Oliver - I knew from the moment I saw your work that you were my dream cover designer. Thank you for the thoughtful detail you wove into your art. It has made all the difference.

Olivia Nash - Thank you times 1000 for agreeing to Beta this book on such short notice. I felt better putting it out into the world having had your keen eyes on it first.

Writer's Group - JL, Katelyn, Autumn, Liz, Christiana, Michelle, and Michelle. The closet funny one thinks you all are the bee's knees.

Sacha Black - Hey, look! I wrote the fucking book! Thanks for your encouragement and friendship. Your periodic check-ins on my writing have always given me a boost—especially on the hard days. Thank you.

Mom, Dad, and Adrian - You've been with me on this journey the longest. I'm so happy to be able to share this long-awaited book with you. It wasn't the LOTR knock-off I always thought I'd write. But I think, in the end, this is more "me." Thank you for your loving support.

Justin - You have listened to every dream. You've been around for every false start and bump in the road. Thank you for championing me and this story. Your interest in this project and pride at its completion means more than you can possibly know. I love you.

Clark - You are already a brilliant, conscientious story teller with an eye for plot holes. Because of you, my four year old son, the Stone Rot Mountains will have a pre-rot name. I love you so much, bud. I can't wait till you're the one telling me the stories.

ABOUT THE AUTHOR

By day, A.E. Kincaid is the messaging director and COO at a creative studio in Iowa. By night, she is an award-winning fantasy author. She is best known for her Mal & Reg Novels of Widdershins in which a snarky demon and an inept human hero are bound together on an ill-conceived quest. Much like the titular characters of that series, Kincaid has a deep appreciation for coffee—which helps her keep up with her charming, active kiddo. Her fiction work appears in The Rebel Diaries Anthology and the Exquisite Poison Anthology, and her nonfiction work appears on websites, commercials, and blogs across the country.

www.aekincaid.com

instagram.com/aekincaidauthor
facebook.com/authoraekincaid
tiktok.com/aekstory

THE STORY CONTINUES

Drab peat bogs blurred past as we ran.

"Why didn't you put our stuff in the inter-dimensional backpack like I asked you to?" Reg yelled as we sprinted down the road between Seven and the coastal town of Searfoss.

"How was I supposed to know that there were horse-sized muskrats out here who enjoyed a good hard cheese?" I panted, holding a stitch in my side.

Our feet thunked against the packed dirt road—the only road between Seven and our destination—but not loud enough to cover the snarls of the mammoth muskrat in hot pursuit of our food.

"If you'd just done what I asked you wouldn't have needed to know!"

"Well if the story you were telling last night hadn't been so boring it put me to sleep, maybe I would have remembered!"

"Oh sure. Blame this on me. How typical!"

I rolled my eyes mid stride.

"Why aren't we just giving it the cheese again?" I asked.

"Because I don't know how far we are from Searfoss. I might want to eat again before we get there!"

"Well your need for food is going to get us eaten. Just open the fucking backpack."

The thing with an inter-dimensional backpack is that it's not always around. And because, at the end of our last adventure, I'd decided not to come on this one until the last possible second, the bag was only spelled to Reginald.

"Ugh. Fine!" He snapped his fingers and caught the pack as it appeared in the air next to him. Still running he thrust his arm inside, wriggled it around, then pulled it back out, cheese in hand. "I hope you're happy!" he yelled as he threw it back over his shoulder. We heard a squeal of delight as the muskrat chased the cheese that now bounced along the road behind us. We slowed to a stop, Reg snapped his fingers, and the backpack disappeared again.

"See?" I gasped, still winded. I gestured with one arm towards the turophilic varmint in our wake. "Isn't it better this way? You know. With less running?"

He threw his arms up with a grunt and started walking again. I jogged a few steps to catch up—forgetting that we were no longer proximally connected by magic and could walk wherever we pleased.

Reginald sighed. "I do prefer not running." He shot me a sidelong glance. "But what I *really* prefer is not running on a full stomach."

I waved a hand dismissively.

"I'm sure we'll be in Searfoss in no time. We've been walking for three days. How much—" I caught myself before I finished the sentence, "How much farther could it be?" Because uttering those words is the kiss of death for arriving at a destination in a timely fashion.

"I hope you're right. I don't want to have to camp out here for another night. This place gives me the creeps."

We'd been trudging down the only true "road" that ran

between Seven and Searfoss for three days now. Three days of cold swamp and three nights of spectral nightmare illusions and random explosions caused by gasses emitted from this particular variety of northern peat. On the first night out of Seven Reginald was so startled by a whiteish, humanoid form that he fell right into the bog behind him. Three days later, I still don't think he was entirely dry. Bog water was part glue, apparently.

"Why didn't we take horses?" I asked.

"Well, I don't know how to ride one. And you said you weren't coming. Plus, I doubt Steadly would have given them to us. I think he still hates us a little."

"Ah. Yes. Right."

We walked in silence for a few moments—the maximum Reginald can go without speaking—and then he said,

"I'd love to never smell another peat bog again in my life."

"I'd drink to that. If we had any water left, that is."

He sighed, the subtext of which was, "And whose fault is that?"

"Oh, sure. Blame that on me too. I—do you smell that?"

For the briefest moment the smell of brine cut through the gassy, rotting smell of the bog.

"The sea!" he cried.

And sure enough, as I squinted my eyes to peer into the distance the faint, boxy outlines of houses appeared.

"Searfoss?" he asked.

"It must be. We haven't deviated from the road. Unless the bog fumes have finally gotten to us and we're hallucinating."

"With our luck, it's not impossible, but I'm going to hope it's the town."

Reginald was right. As a general rule our luck was not terrific. In the past month we'd escaped angry dryads, fairies, and dwarves—not to mention an ogre, a Grootslang, an overlarge spider, and a giant. Plus there was the trouble with the wizards and my demonic older brother in the City of Seven that ended in someone being turned into a chicken.

Was most of the trouble my own doing? I will never admit to that.

"Assuming it's the town, I was right," I said.

"Right about what?"

"Giving up the cheese!"

"Ugh," said Reginald and strode ahead towards the town of Searfoss.

Want more Mal & Reg? The story continues in The Demon, the Hero, and the Secret of the Stones

Printed in Dunstable, United Kingdom